HOME SICK

Also by Rhiannon Grist

The Queen of the High Fields

HOME SICK

Rhiannon Grist

SOLARIS

First published 2026 by Solaris
an imprint of Rebellion Publishing Ltd,
Riverside House, Osney Mead,
Oxford, OX2 0ES, UK

www.solarisbooks.com

ISBN: 978-1-83786-763-9

10 9 8 7 6 5 4 3 2 1

A CIP catalogue record for this book is available from the British Library.

Designed by Rebellion Publishing

Printed in Denmark

Dedicated to my therapist.

INTO THE COUNTRY

CHAPTER 1

The symmetry should have tipped me off. Two sets of windows, two arched eaves like eyebrows raised in surprise, or in the voyeuristic glee of watching a couple fight in public.

And two front doors.

I sat in the driver's seat of my car staring up at the house, hoping some new detail might surface and prove me wrong. But the longer I looked the more I saw it: the subtle line between the two properties.

The small stone cottage was perched on a grassy mound. Its own private, tiny hill. Flat slabs of stone cut into the curve of the mound, providing steps up from the gravel driveway, where I was parked, to the gabled awning where the two front doors sat side by side, just over a foot apart. In the middle of the slate-tiled roof a single chimney stuck out against the sky.

I dug out my copy of the paperwork from the glove box. The photo in the listing could have folded in half perfectly, like a book, or two slices of sandwich bread, or two palms pressed together. Looking closely at the pixelated image now, I could just about make out the two doors, barely visible in the shade of the awning. When I saw the 1b on the form, I'd assumed it was a contract thing. Clause 1a, 1b, 2ai, 2aii. I just assumed. That's what I get for refusing a viewing. That's what I get for rushing things. But I had wanted the house. I'd needed the house. So, I signed without reading it properly. *Move in when you're ready*. Perfect. No wonder it was so cheap.

I thought it was because of the remote location, clearly a limiting factor for the more socially inclined. But I didn't mind. I was ready for a slower pace of life. The quiet. The trees. The copse of Douglas fir. The rounded peak of Ben Ledi. The forested Trossachs all around. The shade. The wind. The rain. The hour's drive from the nearest city. The scenic walk to the nearest village, a tiny tourist stop decked out in pretty flowers, no doubt. The short gravel driveway branching off a slim country road. The gate overgrown with grass until it was almost invisible. The peace.

I didn't realise 1b was the address.

I thought I'd bought Sgàthan Sìth, far-flung cottage with a proper Gaelic name, right on the boundary fault where the Lowlands met the Highlands. My retreat. My recuperation. My rebirth. A place to grow flowers, wear cotton aprons and let my hair hang loose. A chance for a new way of life.

No, I'd bought 1b Sgàthan Sìth. A semi-detached. The right half of a stone cottage in the middle of nowhere. To intimately share my rural dreams with a complete stranger.

At least it made sense now, the rhyme the estate agent had made when I'd asked how to pronounce the name of the place.

"One-two, buckle my shoe. One-bee, Skah-than Shee."

I got out of the car and looked again. No, still two properties.

I looked at the documents. There was no mention of it being semi-detached. I was sure that was something they were supposed to mention.

There were no other cars on the driveway when I arrived and the lawn on 1a's side of the mound was wildly overgrown. On 1b's side it had been cut, quickly and lazily, perhaps by an estate agent getting the place ready for photos for the listing. There had been a few weeks' growth on top, but nowhere near as overgrown as on 1a's side. Thistles towered through long, yellow tufts of grass and the odd patch of bramble. It was practically humming with insects at this time of year. I supposed they weren't selling 1a so why bother to mow it?

Or maybe 1a was empty.

My heart lifted. I'd have preferred the whole building, but living next to an empty one would do. I could possibly even put up with a holiday let, occasional tourists coming and going during the summer, keeping to themselves. They could be ignored, as long as their stay was short.

A flicker of movement drew my eyes up and to the left, to the top window of 1a. A pale, patterned curtain was suddenly pulled tight. It couldn't have been the wind. The movement; the shape of the pinch in the fabric. It could only have been a hand.

I froze with the feeling of being unexpectedly observed, like I'd been caught absentmindedly picking my nose. I watched the window for more movement.

The curtains in the upstairs room stayed still. Were they hiding from me? Maybe they were wondering if I'd seen them, feeling the same sense of awkwardness. *Oh no, now you know I exist.*

Or maybe they were just as put out by having a neighbour as I was.

A high-pitched note whined in my ears.

A sudden pain in my hand forced me to look away. I'd scrunched the listing into a tight ball, my knuckles white, and now the sharp folds were pressing into my palms.

I shook out my hand, took a deep breath and closed my eyes.

No, I told myself. *You're fine, Tamsin. This is fine. The house is fine.*

After the incident at work, the police contact had signed me up for a course of counselling. They'd made it very clear that it wasn't a suggestion. But I didn't need counselling. I wasn't crazy. I just needed some time and space to sort myself out. A fresh start. Not someone nosing into my business.

I trudged back down the gravel driveway to the back of the car and threw open the boot. I dragged out my single suitcase—everything I'd managed to pack in the time I'd given myself; the rest I'd left behind—and let it crunch down onto the ground. I slammed the boot shut loud enough to produce an echo on the walls of the house. My own frustration, magnified, projected back at me. Petulant and ugly. I cringed.

But the upstairs window showed no acknowledgement of my presence, my noise. The curtains remained pulled tight.

I frowned. They hadn't come out to meet me. I thought that was something that happened in places like this, coming out to meet your new neighbours. Lonely, rural places with no one else around.

Admittedly, the thought of it made my skin crawl. And I wasn't about to knock on their door to introduce myself either. I was tired and I couldn't think when I'd last showered. I probably smelled and couldn't tell.

That's something that happens to people, isn't it? You get used to your own stink and then you walk around subjecting everyone to the smell of your clammy, crusty body, wondering why people avoid you or make those pained faces when you draw near. But they're all too polite to tell you. People don't usually walk up to someone and say, "Hey, you need to go to a doctor about your BO. You reek!" No one wants to make that kind of social sacrifice. So, they just avoid you instead and you're left wondering, 'Do I smell or is it something else?'

I'd often wondered if that was why I never got invited out to lunch at work. It would have been the easier fix.

The elm tree at the base of the drive swayed in the wind, shaking loose a fluttering shower of papery seeds.

I shook my head, as if my brain was an eight-ball I could rattle to get a better prediction, and pulled my suitcase up the steps in the hill to the front door—my front door.

When I first saw the picture of the house, I'd expected to open it with an old iron key, or at least one of those intricate brass ones, slightly tarnished by hands and time. Getting a standard, square-head Yale lock key had been a surprise I couldn't verbalise to the estate agents. It had a metal ring attached, but no tag, not even one of those cheap plastic keyrings bearing the estate agent's branding like a modern shield of arms. Just a bare key on a ring. I'd stared at it a moment too long. The receptionist had shifted uncomfortably in his seat on the other side of the high pine desk. "Is everything okay?" he'd asked, then quickly clarified, "With the key?"

"Of course," I'd said. "Why wouldn't it be?"

It had been more to myself than him.

Why wouldn't it be?

I looked at the chrome lock protruding slightly from the pine-green, gloss-painted door, clumsy and anachronistic in its shine among the weathered beams and the old brickwork. Like white slimline headphones sticking out of a gramophone.

But it wasn't just new; it was brand new.

A new lock. Did estate agents usually change the locks when houses changed hands? It was my first home that wasn't a rental. There had been a lot about the buying process that had surprised me. The extra fees, the affordability checks—I'd applied off the back of my full-time position; I hadn't told them I'd recently gone freelance, and not exactly by choice. But it got me approved for the mortgage, and that was all that mattered.

I ran my hand over the surface of the door. They'd been careless placing the lock. Didn't matter how much gloss paint they'd used; they'd failed to hide the deep scratches in the woodwork all around the edge. Maybe they'd had to pry it open after the last inhabitant. I peered through the small, mottled window in the door, slightly worried I might see said inhabitant staring back out.

Well, who cared? It was mine now. My anachronistic lock. My scratched door. My new life. My new neighbour hiding behind their curtains.

I put the key in the lock.

Next door, a movement.

My eyes flicked to the left.

I waited a moment, watching 1a's downstairs window not more than a few yards away from me.

Nothing.

I swore I'd seen the ground floor curtain twitch, like the flickering of an eyelid about to wake.

I exhaled. Maybe the police were right. Maybe I was crazy.

I turned the key and headed inside.

CHAPTER 2

THE FRONT DOOR opened straight into the main living space, with nothing but a thick musty curtain and a sunken tiled entryway to usher me between outside and in. A practical choice for farmhands, but something I'd need to sort before winter hit.

The ground floor was a single, open-plan room with warped wooden floorboards, blackened with age, and an unpainted, beamed ceiling. There was no furniture. On the left-hand side was a fireplace with a thick wooden mantel and a stone-clad chimney breast reaching up into the ceiling; on the far edge, a bank of yellowing cabinets made up the kitchen, complete with a small fridge-freezer, an electric stove, and an enamel sink with a faded gingham curtain hiding the space underneath it; then on the right there was a staircase leading up to the first floor. Under the stairs was a door, cut at an angle to fit the incline. Probably a cupboard. Extra storage.

I took in the alien, lived-in air. It was like going over to a friend's house as a kid, and finding all the furniture smelled of unfamiliar cooking. It was small and wonky, and certainly nowhere near insulated enough, but it was a house. Not a flatshare, not a single-bed apartment close to a ring road. An actual house. With an upstairs and a downstairs and a garden.

And it was mine.

All the earlier exhaustion and disappointment melted away. I was here. I'd arrived. Home. My new home.

In the far corner I imagined a second-hand dining table. A round one. I'd put a vase on it and keep it filled with flowers. In the centre of the room, I saw a sofa, small but plush, covered with a handmade throw. I could get a TV. I could watch TV in a living room again, and not just on a laptop balanced on the end of my bed. I envisioned winter with a fire in the hearth and a Christmas tree by the window. I saw autumn with pinecones on the mantelpiece, a warm pot of tea on the table and golden foliage on the trees outside. Spring rain. Windows open in summer. The future felt inviting for once, and within my reach.

I left my suitcase in the tiled entrance, slipped off my boots and stepped up onto the floorboards.

And instantly onto something hard and sharp.

Some things in life are clear. Pain, I think, is the clearest. It's so easy to know you're in pain. The good kind of pain. The stubbed toe. The snapped bone. The pin or splinter through the arch of your foot.

I fell back into my suitcase, banging the small of my back into the handle and knocking my elbow against the front door. I lost my balance, put my hurt foot down to stop me from falling onto my side, only to spark another lightning bolt of pain. I fell anyway, into the entryway, scraping my arms on the edge of the floorboards.

"Fuck. Fucking bastard, fuck!"

Wonderful. First words for my new home. A smashed champagne bottle of curses.

Sat slumped on the edge of the entryway, I checked my foot. A circle of blood bloomed through the grey wool of my socks.

I'd bought these socks specially for the move. Something about escaping to the country gave me the idea that I should own more thick woollen socks. How do you get blood out of wool again? Was it cold water? Something about baking soda? Whatever had cut me had also torn a hole in the sock, so they were ruined anyway.

I pulled off my sock and took a look at the sole of my foot. It was a small, neat wound. Not as deep as I feared, but it would still need cleaning. Blood wept out of the small pink puncture mark. I made a mental note to google tetanus.

I searched the floorboards for the nail or splinter that had stabbed me. I found a small blotch of blood, but no nail. The blood seeped into a small hole in the wood. I carefully ran my fingertip round its edges. I must have pushed whatever it was under the floor—

A creaking sound broke the silence, as if someone hiding close by had adjusted their position.

I froze.

It came again. My head jerked to the fireplace on my left.

It was coming through the wall.

The neighbour.

Oh God, they must have heard me. Jesus, they probably think a madwoman has moved in next door!

I stood up and watched the wall, like my neighbour might step through the dark mouth of the fireplace at any moment.

The creaking stopped.

I turned back to the bloody hole in the floor. The blood was beginning to coagulate around the rim. I decided to leave it. An offering to whatever small gods ran the place. Let them get a taste of the new kid in town.

I hobbled into the kitchen and, balancing on one leg, angled my foot up and into the enamel sink to clean it under the tap. I checked the freezer for some ice for my foot. Inside it was dark and room temperature. The fridge, too. I looked for a switch on the wall, found one—tacky to the touch—and flicked it, but nothing happened. I probably had to notify the utility company first. But at least that meant the place had electricity. It had plug sockets and light switches. I checked the crumpled-up listing. Electricity, yes, but no gas. I eyed the fireplace. Perhaps there was a store of firewood somewhere. I hoped the shower was electric. Not that that would help much until I got the place hooked up. I leant against the kitchen cupboards. Were all house moves like this? I felt like I'd been sent back to the start of my adulthood, wondering how everything worked again.

I went up the stairs, angling my foot so as not to get blood on the threadbare runner. Every wooden step creaked as I climbed. At the top was a small landing with a sloping ceiling. The first floor was probably a later addition to the cottage, a conversion of some ancient loft or storage space once used to hold firewood, turnips and sacks of barley.

The doors on the first floor were more like the kind you'd see on a garden gate: panels of wood, heavily painted in white gloss and bound together with black iron braces and hinges. The handles were fist-sized black iron rings that I had to pull and twist to raise the latch on the other side. They shrieked like a banshee. No robber would be silently sneaking into my room late at night.

The door directly at the top of the stairs opened into a tiny bathroom tucked under the eaves with a single PVC skylight looking up at the powder-blue sky. I could probably see the fields behind the cottage if I went up on tiptoes, but from this angle it felt like the window of a space capsule, only instead of stars there was a great blue void, a bottomless ocean of clouds and sky. I half believed that if I jumped into it, I'd be falling upwards forever.

There was an avocado sink and a bath with a shower attachment. Due to the sloping ceilings, there was no way to turn it into a full stand-up shower. I would have to kneel or sit curled up inside the bath to use it.

More importantly, there was no electric shower.

I turned the hot water tap on at the sink and waited with my hand under it. It coughed a few remaining air bubbles from the long dormant pipes, sputtered, then ran a steady stream of clean but cold water. I waited, but it wouldn't heat up. I checked the listing again. Under "Bathroom" it just stated, "shower bath". No mention of any kind of water heating. I flicked to the back page with the list of stuff that made my eyes blur every time I'd tried to read it and searched for any mention of heating or boiler.

"Biomass heating system" it read.

What exactly did "Biomass heating system" mean? I'd assumed it was just gas or electricity that was generated through some fancy scientific means, like a car that ran on grubs or banana peels. I saw this special energy being pumped into the building, a green pipe filled with clean white light, untouched by any exploitation or pollution. I hadn't interrogated any of those thoughts, hadn't identified them as thoughts I was thinking, until just then. Now I noticed the euphemistic tone of it. "Biomass heating system". I think it was the word "system" that did it. I thought I'd seen a coal scuttle by the fireplace downstairs. I imagined myself heating water over a coal fire and carrying it upstairs. Where would I even buy coal from?

I looked in the small mirror over the sink, once again hoping a different view might change the facts. But in my reflection, all I saw was my tired face, my hair falling out of the hasty ponytail I'd thrown it into, and the sad cold water tumbling out of the tap. I turned it off and left the bathroom, firmly closing the door behind me.

I stood out on the landing and sighed.

Okay, bedroom, don't let me down.

The bedroom was everything my five-year-old self would have loved.

The sloping ceiling gave it the internal structure of a large tent, the kind I would have filled with books and cushions and blankets, hidden away from where anyone could find me. There was another skylight to the back of the house with views across the rolling fields behind, and a small window to the front, hooded by the gabled eave that had so reminded me of an eyebrow at first glance. Unlike in 1a, my upstairs window had no curtains. No blinds, no shutters, nothing. That was going to be a pain, what with the long summer nights. I added it to my mental checklist.

White painted cupboards promised storage under the eaves, which was good because I had no idea where I'd put a wardrobe. Anything taller than a chest of drawers would have to take up prime real estate in the middle of the room. I reached up a hand and touched the beams ribbing the space. That was alright. I'd never been good at fashion. A few jeans and jumpers, plus a nice shirt or two, would do me fine. It's not like I was expecting invitations to balls and fancy dinners.

The previous occupant had left a mattress behind, thank God. No bedframe, mind. Just a mattress on the floor. But at least I wouldn't have to sleep on the bare wooden boards. I hadn't budgeted much for furniture. Tables and sofas I could do without for now, but a missing bed would be a problem. The mattress didn't look too old, and there were no obviously dodgy stains. I bent down to give it a cautious sniff. Maybe I wouldn't have to replace it.

After a cursory bounce or two on the mattress, I nosed through the cupboards under the eaves, thinking about what I could fill them with. Linen, books, secret treasures. Inside one was a clotheshorse, lying on its side on the floor, spindly and at ease, completely unfolded. The last occupant must have stashed it here after putting away a load of dried washing. It was a weird choice to have it unfolded in the cupboard. God knows how they even got it inside. They would have had to fold it, then unfold it again.

Let's not look a gift clotheshorse in the mouth, har har.

I snorted at my own joke then reached in to pull the clotheshorse out.

As I folded the mechanism, images flashed before my eyes.

Fluorescent light. Laughter. Hot pink nail polish.

The muscles in my arms tensed.

Stop it now, I scolded myself. *It's just a clotheshorse.*

A normal thing. A boring thing. An inoffensive thing. A thing of chores and Sunday afternoons and ugh-I-can't-believe-I-forgot-to-put-a-wash-on. Something not to think about. A nothing kind of thing.

But the more I tried not to think about it, that motion of folding, the more it kept coming to me.

A startled gasp.

Silence.

Then that awful scream.

I slammed the cupboard shut. The clotheshorse clanged on the other side of the door.

Look, you can't even see it anymore, I thought. *It's just a shut door. Stop being stupid!*

But behind the door I knew it was there. Its folds neatly snapped shut.

I sat on the mattress and picked at my nails. My legs bounced, the movement building into some bodily action outside of my conscious control.

I got back up.

I pulled the clotheshorse out of the cupboard, trying my best not to look at it. Then I half-jogged, half-jumped back down the stairs, yanked the front door open like a screaming mouth and exited the house. I had to get it out of my home, out of my sight. I strode down the steps, looking for somewhere to dispose of the horrid thing. Next to the driveway was a patch of bramble just before the woods. There, that would do. I threw the clotheshorse toward the trees.

My aim was off.

It slipped out of my hands and into the windscreen of my car, instantly spiderwebbing the whole thing with cracks and shards. Then it bounced lightly away, spiralled like a gymnast, like a mischievous Norse god, and disappeared into the bright May foliage, swallowed up by the countryside and all that green.

My car's alarm broke the birdsong peace of the countryside around me.

I stared at the broken windscreen with dismay.

I checked back up at 1a. Nothing. Not even a curtain flicker.

I turned off the alarm, grabbed the rest of my bags and hurried back inside the house.

CHAPTER 3

Unfortunately, the hob was also electric. With no clue how to turn the electricity on, there was no way to cook anything. I popped the pasta and sauces, which I'd hurriedly bought at one of the big supermarkets on my escape, into the empty cupboards. Thankfully, though deeply outdated, the cupboards were clean and structurally sound. Then I sat in the middle of the living room floor and ate the crisps and grapes I'd bought as snacks for the road.

It was a poor first meal for a new home. I'd imagined a takeaway pizza and champagne in a mug. I hadn't brought any champagne with me. Probably couldn't have justified it, even if I had remembered to buy some. Instead, I cupped my hands under the kitchen tap and drank water from my palms.

I watched the sunlight shift around the space, a slow spotlight warming then cooling. As the room started to darken, I felt a stab of panic.

What had I done? I'd moved my entire life to a place I didn't know. To up sticks and move so far, alone, in my thirties was an insane thing to do.

Suddenly I missed my old room in Edinburgh. I missed the grey view from my small window. I missed the street outside, the near-constant sound of other people. I missed knowing which cafés were good and which were tourist traps. I missed the smell of the place, the malty toasted scent from the breweries, the odd sea-salt-tinged gust from Leith.

I stood up.

No, I was not going to think like that. That was my old life, the one I'd escaped. I would commit to this new life and forget what I'd left behind me.

Then, and only then, would I be happy.

I wiped my face and checked my phone. Thirty percent battery. It was getting late. What I needed was sleep. Yes, a good night's rest. I'd feel better in the morning.

I checked the front door. The shadowy silhouette of the elm tree outside shimmered through the mottled glass of the door's single small window. Soon it would be properly summer and the dusk would creep along the horizon until it became dawn again. True darkness was not a real thing in Scottish summers. Everything just turned a dull, dark grey. The door was locked, but I slipped the chain on as well. Then I climbed the stairs to my new bedroom.

I shut the garden gate door and covered the mattress with the single towel I'd brought with me. I couldn't remember where I'd packed my pyjamas, so I undressed down to my underwear and slipped into bed under the towel. I frowned at my sad makeshift sleeping arrangements. I should have bought bedding. After a thought, I got back up, grabbed my hoodie and bundled it into an improvised pillow.

I lay in the growing gloom.

God, it was going to need so much work. Furniture. Insulation. Possibly a new boiler. New wiring.

I kneaded my forehead with my knuckles.

It was probably unrealistic to think things would go smoothly. Moving house was stressful. One of the top three most stressful things, even. Up there with divorce and death.

Weren't there more stressful things though? Like escaping war. Or the death of someone you loved. Or serious illness. Now I thought of it, there seemed like a million and one things that should be more stressful than moving house.

I asked myself these things and realised, like I sometimes realise at the end of a long day, that I hadn't really spoken to another living person in a while. Sure, I'd spoken to the receptionist who handed over the anachronistic key to my anachronistic lock. But when had I last properly engaged another human being in conversation?

How many years had I spent just talking to myself?

I wished I could think of someone to call, to talk to about my day, to tell them that I'd arrived safe, but I couldn't think of a single person. I'd left everything and everyone behind. I thought of the miles and miles of countryside all around me. Instead of soothing, the silence felt claustrophobic. I wrapped my arms around my shoulders and—not for the first time in my life—pretended they belonged to someone else, someone giving me a hug and telling me I'd be okay.

A creak came through the wall behind me.

I tensed up in bed, ears pricking.

Calm down. It's just the neighbour.

By the sound of the creak, they were really close by. Literally inches from my head.

I sat up in the dim grey light and listened.

On the other side of the wall, there was a shuffling, like footsteps moving around the room next door.

Could they hear me as much as I could hear them?

Had they followed me upstairs?

I leant closer to the wall.

There was a sudden bang right by my ear.

I fell back, clapping a hand over my mouth.

A loud screech reverberated through the wall. What on earth were they doing? It sounded like they were moving heavy furniture around. It was hard to figure out the sounds through the old walls. Something about the stone warped the noise.

I scrabbled for my phone and checked the time. Who moves furniture around at eleven at night?

I watched the wall in the near darkness as the clunks and thuds continued. I didn't know anything about my neighbour. Their character. What they looked like. But I could hear every move they made in uncomfortable intimacy.

Maybe they worked nights. Maybe they were nocturnal.

I lay back down and pulled my hoodie-pillow over my head.

I heard 1a shuffling around for the rest of the night. Their muffled scrapes and knocks, the constant fiddling, pattering, shifting, came through the wall, the hoodie, the fingers in my ears until finally exhaustion took me and I slipped into sleep.

My mind swept through the hills and roads I'd covered on my travel north. Trees flashed green in my peripheral vision and the grey stream of tarmac felt unending before me. In my rear-view mirror a darkness followed. Not a cloud or a storm or a monster of any kind. Just darkness. And anything that fell within it vanished. If I could just get to the cottage, I knew I could escape it. But the road kept going and the darkness kept coming and frustration rose in me until I wanted to tear the steering wheel straight out of the car.

Then, miraculously, I arrived.

This time only one door greeted me. Just one house, all to myself. What a relief! Everything else that came before must have been a stress dream. I'd always been plagued by them. Dreams of my hands turning to lead right as an exam starts. Dreams of my university getting washed away before I was due to arrive. Dreams of my father unpackaging me from a parcel, the look of excited anticipation falling from his face as he set his eyes on me.

But not now, for here was the house, whole, as promised, as hoped.

I ran inside to get away from the gathering darkness, shutting the door just in time for it to fill the windows with an unending void. I turned and the inside of the house had become my old office, complete with glass dividing walls, funky furniture and vases of orange lilies. My reflection mirrored me as I traversed the glass corridors. My suitcase had become a rucksack. I hugged it close to me. Hadn't I just left this place or was that a stress dream too?

Knock-knock

I turned to the sound.

Someone was knocking on the other side of a wall. A wall close to my head. But there was nothing but a bank of desks. Only now every desk was a black standing desk: those cheaper weighted ones folk put on top of their normal desk, wobbling under the weight of computer monitors and books and mugs, their hinges and springs straining.

The darkness from outside started to leak in through the windows.

My old colleagues bustled around me under the fluorescent lights. They tutted and rolled their eyes at my disorientation. I went looking for my desk, but in its place was a meeting room. Oh, I must not work here yet.

Knock-knock

The noise was louder. Urgent. It came from inside the meeting room. I must be late. I straightened my purse strap across my chest—my rucksack was now a purse—and stepped inside.

The room was barely more than a cupboard. The interview table filled it save for space for one chair on my side and one chair on the other.

The director of my company sat on the other side of the table, her hair perfectly coiffed, eyeliner impeccably winged, fingers with their hot pink nails steepled in front of her face.

My heart immediately began to pound.

She regarded me with a cool glance. I sat in my chair. Perhaps it hadn't happened, I thought with relief. Maybe it had all been a bad dream.

"What do you consider to be your greatest weakness?" she asked.

Her eyes scanned me up and down as I recited my weaknesses.

Knock-knock-knock!

The knocking was now a constant banging on all the walls around me, which were now made of glass and perfectly black. The darkness from outside had eaten up the rest of the office and all I could see was my own haunted face reflected back at me. I held my hands over my ears to block out the sound.

"What's the biggest mistake you've ever made?" asked the director.

I gestured at the gathering dark.

"Something's wrong."

Without blinking or moving her eyes from me, she un-steepled her long elegant fingers and pinched her left pinkie between the thumb and forefinger of her right hand.

"Do you think you're a good person?" she asked.

Then with a flick she snapped her little finger in two.

CHAPTER 4

I JUMPED AWAKE, choking on a gasp that stuck in my dry throat. I pulled the hoodie off my head, coughed, rolled onto my side, leaned up on my elbow and tried to work up some spit in my cheeks.

It took me a moment to remember where I was.

The bedroom waited around me. Still bare. Grey light pooled in from the skylights.

I put a hand out behind me. There was the wall that split the cottage in two, quiet now after all the rustling and commotion from last night.

I flopped back down onto the naked mattress, towel twisted around my legs. The air was thick and the sky through the skylight was mottled with cloud. An old, unwashed duvet thrown over the world. I got up and looked out of my bedroom windows.

1a's side of the front lawn was now neatly mown.

I stood staring at it, brain breaking a little at the sight. It was now perfectly green with those alternating rows I'd sometimes see in pictures of stately homes. Each corner was a tight ninety degrees. Not a weed or a thistle or a bare patch in sight. I rubbed the top of my chest. It definitely wasn't mown yesterday. I remembered that. I remembered specifically thinking about how my side had been mown and 1a's had not. It was unnerving in a way I was convinced I'd never be able to relate to another human being.

What's wrong, Tamsin?

My neighbour's lawn has been mown.

Okay, what's strange about that?

It wasn't yesterday.

Isn't that a good thing?

I don't know. It doesn't feel like a good thing.

Girl, you need to get out more.

I checked my phone. Ten o'clock in the morning. Maybe that's what all the noise had been about last night. Maybe they'd felt embarrassed by the state of their lawn yesterday. Maybe they'd never been bothered by it before until I, another person, had arrived to pass judgement on their unruly yard. Maybe they'd been enjoying a quiet solitude in the country, uninterrupted for years and years, until I'd shown up.

I pressed my lips together. It was time I said hello.

I ate the last of my crisps and grapes, plaited my greasy hair as neatly as I could, then stepped out to make my first new acquaintance. Maybe they'd know how to turn on the electricity in the house. And perhaps I could convince them to keep it down after eight.

No, nine.

No, definitely eight.

The curtains were still drawn across 1a Sgàthan Sìth, despite the clean manicured lawn.

I knocked on the door and mentally prepared for what I would say.

Hello. Hi. *Too boring.* Hi there. Morning! *No, that sounds deranged.* Hey there? *No, hi. Hi will do. Boring is fine. After all, you are boring. Hi is fine.* Hi, I'm Tamsin. Hi,

I'm Tamsin, your new neighbour. *Of course, they'd know you're their neighbour, stupid. After all the noise you made yesterday. And that absolutely batshit thing of throwing the clotheshorse. Probably thinks you're a headcase, headcase.* Hi, I'm Tamsin, you probably saw me move in yesterday. *Why say that? You probably saw me. Is that implying something? Like, are you saying you know they saw you and they should have come out to meet you? They're not your maid. Do you hear how entitled you sound?* Hi, I'm Tamsin, you might have heard me move in yesterday. Sorry about all the noise. Sorry for the disruption. *Yeah, that's good.* Sorry about that. Anyway…

The door opened before I was ready, a dark crack into the house.

"Sorry," I blurted into it.

In the darkness inside, I could just make out half a face. It peered round the door at me, partly masked by lank shoulder-length hair. Faintly, I could see a single eye staring at me, round and watery, unblinking. And a slanted eyebrow, slightly pleading. I shuffled my feet uneasily, hoping my eyes would adjust or perhaps my neighbour would realise I couldn't see them properly. Even so, there was something about them that plucked a tripwire in my brain. Something about the shape of their face, the way they held themselves. Something oddly familiar. I waited but they did not move into the light. I recovered my senses and smiled gormlessly.

"Hi, I'm Tamsin. I'm your new neighbour."

"Oh." Her voice, I assumed 'her' by the pitch, was small and muffled by the door. "Um. Hello."

She reached out a limp hand. From the look of it I guessed she must be about my age. I hesitated shaking it. It hung there, stuck out in the light, waiting for me.

Just a hand.

Feeling rude, I took it, tucking away that odd thought about her face.

It was a normal handshake. A little damp, maybe. A little cold. But no sudden yank into the dark. No teeth collapsing like a mousetrap around my wrist.

Paranoid. You have to stop being so paranoid.

Maybe it wouldn't be too bad to have a neighbour. Maybe it would teach me to relax. Maybe we would become best friends. Two gals living their best lives together out in the country. Perhaps I would be the outgoing, bubbly yang to her quiet, thoughtful yin. It would be nice to be the loud one for once. Perhaps we'd have picnics in the trees or share a cup of tea on the front porch on sunny mornings. Maybe the local children would think we were witches. We'd hand out toffee apples on Halloween grown from our orchard. Inside the apples, we'd sneak funny little fortunes and wise sayings, and the locals would wonder aloud down the pub how we did it. Perhaps we'd even become lovers—I'm not closed to the idea, opposites attract. And when we married, we'd knock down the walls between our two homes and Sgàthan Sìth would be one again.

"Ah," she said, watery eye looking at our still shaking hands.

"Sorry!" I said, letting her go as if she was electrified.

I hadn't even finished shaking her hand and we'd been married.

I hooked a thumb in the direction of my half of the cottage.

"Um, I don't know if you could hear me through the wall at all last night."

The face in the dark briefly looked to the wall in question, as if being aware of it for the first time. She shook her head.

"Oh, that's good."

I nodded my head. We were silent for a moment.

"I'm driving into the village. Do you need anything?"

What the hell? I'd just met her. Why did I say that?

"No, thank you," she said, then added, "Thanks for asking. You're very generous."

"Oh." I felt my shoulders lift. "No problem."

"Would you like to come in?"

She pulled the door further open, which oddly did nothing to illuminate the inside. It did nothing to illuminate my neighbour either. She tucked herself behind the door, so only that corner of her face—that eye, that hair, that limp hand—could be seen.

I eyed the dark expanse within.

I should go in. I should stop prejudging people. Go in, get acquainted, and make friends like I'd imagined just moments ago.

Just around the edge of the door I caught the corner of her mouth. She was smiling.

"That's okay." I stepped back. "Just wanted to say hello."

"Oh, alright. Hello," she said.

Then she smoothly and quickly closed the door.

I stood at her doorstop for a moment, feeling a little lost, then walked away down the stone steps.

That went okay, right? I hoped I hadn't come across too rude. I'd definitely go in next time. There would be a next time, surely. What had she said about me? Generous. That's good. I supposed I would have picked up something for her in town if she'd asked. As long as it wasn't too expensive. Or too out of my way.

I found myself thinking about her face again, what I'd been able to see of it in the dark. There had been nothing unusual I could see, save the weird smile, and the fact that she could probably do with a shower, and to open her curtains once in a while. But the sight of her had struck me so strangely. Something about the mix of that pleading eyebrow and that smile. My mind couldn't stop clawing away at it.

I'd pulled open the car door before I remembered the windscreen was smashed to smithereens. Then I realised I'd forgotten to ask my neighbour how to turn on the electricity, and if she'd mind keeping things down after eight.

Fuck's sake. Hopeless!

I went back inside 1b, grabbed my backpack, emptied it straight out onto the floor, packed my laptop and my charger cables, then headed back down the gravel drive. It would be a forty-minute walk to the nearest village.

The air was both soupy and breezy, so I was both too hot and too cold at once. It felt to me that life was full of these extremes. My porridge was always either too hot or too cold. My bed too hard or too soft. My neighbours too loud or too quiet.

I looked back at the house. All that noise last night didn't match up with the odd quiet person I'd met at the door. I felt embarrassed for my earlier imaginings. My father always said I expected too much from people. It was probably better to expect nothing of anyone and be pleasantly surprised. But how to become like that? How do you change who you are to accept 'the chance to be pleasantly surprised' as enough?

The leaves on the elm tree hushed in the wind, like a small audience clapping me off stage.

INTO THE COMMUNITY

CHAPTER 5

THERE WAS NO footpath along the road, but it was straight and quiet enough in places that I'd hopefully get a heads up if a car or a lorry came careening through.

Past the stretch of road that came closest to Sgàthan Sìth 1a and 1b, there was a fork in the road. I checked my phone with what was left of my dying battery. The closest village was a place called Carlinsrest. VisitScotland called it "a friendly stop for tourists on their way up to the Highlands." TripAdvisor called it "a rambler's delight." I'd never heard of it before my moonlight flit.

Was it Cahr-lins-rest or Care-lin-srest? It felt rude to ask. What if everyone thought I was just another ignorant southerner come to buy property out from under the noses of locals? It was probably better to keep my mouth shut. Don't bother anyone. Just—

"Morning!"

I came up from my thoughts so fast I swear it gave me the bends. A grey moustached man in an anorak was stood on a stile. He smiled and waved. A group of similarly anoraked people smiled behind him. A hill rose above them, like a great green wave coming to crash down on us all.

"I said, morning!"

I froze, mouth gulping air.

"Thought the countryside was supposed to be friendly," one of the man's companions muttered.

The man laughed. I walked away, taking the left road to the village, flustered but determined not to look back.

The man had a point. I was a countryside person now. I should probably make the effort to be more friendly. Did that mean waving to every hiker, dogwalker and weekender I saw? I wasn't sure I'd ever feel comfortable doing that. *Hello! Morning!* It felt so weird. But that's what I was here for—to do better, to become better—so I had to try. Fake it till I make it!

Then keep faking it and faking it and faking it and—

No, this time will be different.

In the past, I know I've come across as a bit of a cold fish. I'd say I'm guarded, but some mistake it for snobbishness, I think. What happened my first day at the office is a prime example.

I don't come from office workers. My dad was a postman, my mother a nurse. Everything I knew about working a desk job I'd learned from TV and films. When I got the job, I bought myself a whole wardrobe based on those assumptions. I imagined a confident modern career woman, thought about what she'd wear, and bought that: a white blouse and some waxed black trousers, the closest I could get to leather without having cloying dead animal hide on top of my skin all day. It was an outfit that was soft and hard at once. Do no harm, take no shit.

As I was walked around the office, I made sure to smile and shake hands with everyone, trying my best to memorise the dozens of names. Then I was shown to my desk. It was on the edge of a bank of other desks, sticking out into one of the main walkways through the office. There was no computer.

Just a branded notebook and a desk phone. When I pointed this out, I was given an iPad to look over the company website and 'familiarize myself with their brand'.

That's okay, I thought. *They're probably too busy to onboard you just now.*

I looked around at my new colleagues, wondering if I should ask what they were working on and if I could help. Bounce some ideas. Make a round of tea. Everyone had their heads down, focused on their screens, headphones firmly set in place. I noticed that everyone wore hoodies and t-shirts, not the blouses and tailored trousers I'd been led to expect.

The desk to my left had one of those weighted, standing desk add-ons; the kind that could be placed on top of a normal desk instead of replacing it with an actual and expensive standing desk with motorised pistons and extending legs. It belonged to a taciturn man called Alan who was big into body-building and unseasoned, microwaved chicken. The standing desk's sprung crossbeams shook under the weight of design books, a treasure trove of dirty mugs, and the force of his typing. I half-expected a note to be taped to the edge saying KEEP OUT or NO GIRLS ALLOWED.

The phone on my desk rang. I'd looked around at the rest of the team. No one looked up. I reached for the phone and hesitated. I wondered why someone would be calling me already. I looked at the others again. No reaction. I picked up the phone.

"Hello?"

"Who's this?" A voice, clipped, terse.

"Uh, hi, I'm Tamsin. I'm the new email writer."

"Oh."

Silence.

"This used to be Issy's phone."

I looked around the bank of desks. There was a white-blonde woman on my right. She had her headphones on, eyes glued to her screen. The mug on her desk said ISOLDE'S PATIENCE. I think the person who'd shown me around had called her Issy.

"Maybe they moved the desks around? I don't know. It's literally my first day."

"Can you get Issy to call me?"

"Um, yeah?"

And the voice hung up. I looked at Issy. Her eyes were still on her screen. I tried to lean into her field of vision without disturbing anyone else. I waved at her. She glanced at me, a flicker of annoyance crossing her face, then looked back at the screen. A few seconds later she licked her lips and took off her headphones.

"What do you need?" Her tone had that forced friendliness to it like you get at the end of the night at a bar.

"Sorry, are you Issy?"

She took a deep breath and nodded.

"Yep, and I'm chasing a deadline."

"Uh, someone called asking for you." I pointed at the phone, as if that might clear things up. "Sorry, I didn't get their name."

"Probably Mel."

"They wanted you to give them a call."

"Okay." She moved to put her headphones back on.

I looked at the phone then back at Issy.

"It seemed pretty urgent."

Issy looked at me for a moment.

"Yeah, I'll give her a call in a second." Friendliness even more forced now. She put her headphones back on and got back to work. I pretended to look busy on the iPad for the rest of the day.

By the time it came to six o'clock all I wanted to do was go home and recuperate. I'd done nothing, but I felt exhausted. I hurried down the stairs toward the foyer. Before I could leave, Issy tapped my shoulder.

"Some of us are heading out for a drink. Want to come with?"

I couldn't read her expression. She had that cool impassive look that could be boredom or disinterest or nerves. I was so tired I couldn't figure out which. That's when I made my fatal mistake.

"Sorry, I've got a thing."

Her eyebrows raised and she huffed a little out of her nose.

"Oh, sure. A 'thing'."

Standoffish. Snobbish. A cold fish.

"No, I really—" God, what was I doing? "Next time, yeah?"

"Sure," she said and left through the door without looking at me. I already knew there wouldn't be a next time.

I saw my outfit reflected in the glass doors as she left. The shirt was wrinkled in several places, and the waistband of the trousers had slid down my hips a little so they sagged around the crotch. It looked like I had deflated. The overhead lighting caught my hangdog expression perfectly.

I'd like to think if Issy and the others had ever stuck around, waited for me to warm up a little, they'd find me worth the wait. But very few did. Stick around, I mean. Not at the office. Not anywhere in the city, really. I tried the usual antidotes: going to bars, signing up to gym classes, joining a book club. But none of it worked. There seemed to be this need to be instantly knowable, constantly reachable, but always at a polite distance. Everything was organised through convoluted apps and always-on instant messaging that left me feeling both dizzy and violated.

That's why it was so important now to be different here, where life was slower, more intimate. This was my chance at a fresh start. A friendlier, warmer, more open me. I would not make the same mistake again.

I followed the river toward Carlinsrest, until eventually I reached the bridge into the village. It was an ancient-looking thing, made with rounded stones dotted with lichen and moss. A less-ancient-but-still-visibly-old sign had been fastened to one of its pillars, reading BODACHS BRIG. Coming over the other side was an elderly gentleman, wearing a tan sweater vest and a flat cap tucked between what looked like two antlers atop his head. I squinted. As he got closer, I saw the antlers were two tufts of wiry white hair. He was pushing a wheelchair bearing an equally ancient lady, wrapped up in an old wax jacket, two sizes too big for her, hood up, head back, mouth open and snoring. Next to the two of them trotted a lively collie, tongue flapping out the side of its mouth.

Perfect. Here was my chance. Time to be a countryside person.

I put on my best most happy-normal-person smile.

"Morning!"

The old man shuffled past with barely a glance in my direction. Not even the dog paid me any attention.

I felt the smile turn to a rictus on my face. Had I got it the wrong way round? Was it only tourists that said hello to strangers on rural roads?

The old man shunted the woman's wheelchair over a cobblestone and a folded bit-of-something fluttered out of his pocket. A dying pink butterfly. No. Two fifty-pound notes. They scuttled across the floor, caught on some breeze, and came to a rest at my feet. I caught them with my boot before they could get blown off the bridge and into the river.

I looked up and down the road. There was no one else to notice. I briefly considered my rapidly disappearing savings and the price of replacing my broken windscreen. Then I quietly gathered the notes off the floor, dusted them against my sleeve, and jogged after the old man.

"Excuse me," I said. "You dropped this."

The old man looked at me, looked at the notes, then took them slowly out of my hands with a curt nod. Then he turned, farted—a low, singular parp—and went on his way.

I blinked in surprise. I didn't know why I had even bothered.

My reflection gazed up at me from the river below, expression veiled in shadow.

Well, what did you expect? A fucking parade for not being a thief?

Okay. Maybe the next interaction would be the one. Then I would be better.

CHAPTER 6

ON THE OTHER side of the bridge, the village of Carlinsrest congregated along the bank of the river and the road that ran alongside it. There were three cafés, which were hard to tell apart, one post office, three restaurants—one tapas, one earthy organic-looking place and a squeaky-clean steak restaurant promising one hundred per cent Aberdeen Angus beef—a tartan shop, one large pub and a green-painted butcher's. A war monument stood next to the village-end of the bridge accompanied by three gloss-painted benches. Past the few main streets of the village, a handful of cottages and small hotels branched off into the forest and the hills beyond. There was a hardy practicality to the place, all rough-hewn stone and cattle grids. I pursed my lips. From the descriptions online, I'd expected more bunting and hanging baskets and cheery community centres and jam jars. It was still early in the season though. Maybe they'd decorate the place properly later in the summer.

I stopped at the corner shop by the bridge to pick up some supplies. Milk, cereal, bread, cheese, some crackers, a couple tins of beans, soup and chili, and a tin opener. Things I could eat without gas or electricity if needed. I'd found a saucepan in one of the kitchen cupboards back at the cottage, and a set of two forks and a spoon in a drawer. I promised myself I'd do a proper shop later. For now, this would do.

Okay, I thought. *Time to go say hello.*

I wandered down the road along the river and ducked into one of the cafés.

Maggie's Café was clean and cheery. It had white painted wood panelling halfway up the wall and everything above that was a pale duck-egg blue. A chalk board listed the various tea and coffee options, and cakes were proudly displayed on ceramic stands with glass covers. I took a deep breath and strode up to the counter.

"Morning," I said.

An older woman with a plastered-on smile and unsmiling eyes looked up at me from the till.

"Morning," she said. "What can I get you?"

"What do you recommend?" I'd read that was a good question to ask in new places. Shows curiosity, interest. Starts a conversation.

The plastered-on smile faltered for a moment.

"What kind of thing are you looking for?"

Oh shit. I hadn't thought of a thing to ask after.

Quick, think of a thing.

"Food," I blurted, my shopping still clearly on my mind.

The woman with the now-decidedly-unsmiling eyes glanced over at the wide selection of cakes on their stands, the traybakes and scones in the glass-fronted cabinet, and the menu full of hot food up behind her.

'*Food.' Way to narrow it down, genius.*

The woman sighed. "Well, if it were up to me, I'd go for the macaroni pie. It's not the fanciest, but it's the best I've seen around."

Thank God! Macaroni pie!

"Yes," I said.

"Yes to the macaroni pie?"

"Sorry. Yes," I said. "Oh, and a latte. Please."

The woman nodded. "I'll bring it to your table."

I paid and escaped the rest of the interaction unscathed. Avoiding the round painted tables, I made for the bar at the window with its single stools and—more importantly—plug sockets. I tucked myself into the corner of the window, plugging in my laptop and my phone, hoping no one would question me taking up both sockets.

The bright familiar screen of my laptop immediately anchored me. There were a few freelance opportunities I'd hoped had got back to me by now—old clients I'd contacted before I'd left Edinburgh. I'd never had the entrepreneurial spirit of my colleagues when it came to side gigs. Technically, it went against our contracts, but everyone did it, from the designers to the developers. Everyone except me, that was. I was always convinced I'd be caught the first time I took work on the side. I'd have to catch up quick, though I'd never been comfortable selling myself, which was ironic given my line of work.

Back at the office I'd been a writer for their eCRM Services. CRM meant Customer Relationship Management. The 'e' bit meant electronic. In reality, this all just meant email marketing. My job was to create emails that no one really wants to read, only I'm not supposed to say that. A brand needs just zero point zero five per cent of recipients to click through to their website to consider the email a success, so I spent my career writing to the five in one thousand. It had often felt like screaming into the void.

I flinched at a sudden noise outside. A gaggle of teenagers walked past the window, excitedly gathered around one of their phones. Probably some prank video or whatever the kids were into these days. Definitely not one of my promotional emails.

Still, I happened to be pretty good at it. I could mimic brand voices with ease. I just had to pretend to be them. Holidays, clothing, banks, nappies, I'd written emails for them all, shifting between serious conversations about insurance to quirky puff-pieces about fruit-flavoured yoghurts. It was a lucky line of work to fall into in my twenties. The job market had been poor at the time, and I couldn't go home, so I'd held on to the position as if it were a life raft.

A group of young women wearing rucksacks came into the café and grabbed a table behind me. Their happy conversation, along with the general bustle of the other customers, disrupted my thoughts more than I'd like to admit.

I'd struggled with the office environment too, with its constant chatter and coded culture that I could never get my head around. That and the expectation that a single email might perform some black art of persuasion. And the impression that most of my clients didn't seem to care about their customers or their products even, just some min-max calculation to increase their shares by a point.

And the audacity of trying to get strangers to like the brand you're writing for when you can't even get anyone to like you.

But now I was out of the office and away from all those problems. I'd be able to work in an environment that suited me, pick my clients, do work that mattered.

Do what you have to do to survive.

The group of women behind me laughed.

So what if sometimes I hated it? So what if there were mornings where I'd sit on the end of my bed just willing myself to get up and go to the office? Everyone hates their job. There's nothing unusual about that. We all just have to pretend we don't.

And I'm very good at pretending.

The same woman who'd taken my order delivered my pie and coffee. The pie was huge; golden crispy cheese and pasta spilled over the top of the high shortcrust sides. I was suddenly aware of how little I'd eaten lately.

The woman wiped her hands on her apron and left before I could say thanks. Probably too busy to start a conversation.

See, everyone's just pretending. That's what work is. Pretence.

I logged into the café internet and checked through my emails. My heart sank. No one had got back to me. I quickly calculated my finances in my head and eyed the gently steaming pie on the bench in front of me. I would be eating out a lot less over the coming weeks.

Maybe, now I was here, I could pretend myself into another job. New life, new job. Why not? Long before this move, I'd had the fantasy of disappearing to a rural town, where folk did honest land-based work and didn't care for cities and CVs. I'd imagined the kind of person I'd be if I could just escape and start over.

Perhaps I would be a stoic gardener of a great house now fallen into dilapidation. That woman in the flannel shirt, wellies, and waxed coat that's never been washed, hair pulled back in a sensible bun, flyaway hairs catching the autumn light and ringing my head with a fuzzy halo, carting barrow-loads of fallen leaves and dead wood to a fluttering bonfire, flames barely visible in the daylight, white smoke flying over the dew-laden grass. I'd wipe my forehead with the back of my arm, stand and stretch out my lower back, carry a rake over my shoulder, nod tersely to friendly greetings. That's just how she is, they'd say—whoever they were—grounded, a mystery, full of hidden depths, trust her to the moon and back. Sure, invite her to the dance; if you're lucky maybe she'll come. She's quiet at first, but stick with her; she's worth it in the end.

Or maybe I would be the plucky fidget who resurrects the neglected community library being kept on life support by a small group of older folks who are running out of steam. That girl who brings new energy to old ideas, perhaps with a well-meaning folksy handmade decorating scheme to brighten up the shelves, or a scrappy marketing idea that draws new users—parents looking for children's groups, teens looking for a place to study, older folks wanting to get online. That girl whose mix of boundless enthusiasm and verbal diarrhoea—off-putting and a little intense at first—casts a spell on those who meet her. She's charming really. Humour her oddness; she's worth it in the end.

Or maybe I'd be that enigmatic woman with the knowing smile who takes over an empty shop on the main street. I'd paper up the windows while I did up the store, setting all the neighbourhood gossips' tongues wagging. Locals would try to peer between the sheets to see what I was up to, claiming glimpses of hand painted murals and incense smoke. Eventually I'd open my shop selling… handmade soaps? Handspun wool? No, flowers. Healing flowers. A magical florist. There'd be some disappointment at first amidst the curiosity—perhaps hoping for a phone shop or something. Get their laptops fixed without having to trek to Stirling or Glasgow. But over time I'd win them over with carefully selected blooms that make them feel inspired again, fall in love again, feel safe again, help them reach out to lost loved ones and find them again in the weeds of some old long blown over argument, the treasure lost now found. And I'd be skittish and damaged and react to loud noises in a way that seems unhinged at times but echoes some hidden trauma no one can see. But they'll get the idea. Be gentle with her, they'll say, she seems flighty but hold your nerve; she's worth it in the end.

Choices ahead of me, I picked up my pie and went to bite.

There was a ding.

My eyes flicked back to the screen. I put down my lunch and searched through my tabs looking for the notification, before settling on a social media site I'd left open.

Floating up on a little friendly tile was a comment from an old school friend I hadn't spoken to in years.

"Congrats on the move!" it said.

My blood chilled. How did she know I'd moved?

The comment was on a post from the estate agents who sold me the house. They'd tagged me in a cheery smiling house photo with the message:

We hope you love your new home!

I probably missed the box to opt out when I skimmed the contract. I quickly untagged myself and hoped the damage was limited.

I watched the road outside the window, suddenly feeling eyes on me.

This was the worst thing about the internet. No matter how far you travelled, no matter how quiet you stayed, you couldn't get lost anymore. I'd read about missing persons groups on Facebook. About how they're causing problems for people genuinely trying to disappear. Adult children. Abused partners. Special witnesses. Folk just trying to start over where no one knows who they are or where they've been or what they've done. My fresh start, my transformation, would be in jeopardy if I was found out as the person I am—*was*. If I wasn't careful, that would be the 'me' here too.

My reflection in the window stared back at me.

There's the person you think you're going to be. And then, poof, there you are. Undeniably you, for better or worse.

No. I couldn't let that happen.

I deleted my old friend's comment, blocked her, then slammed my laptop shut.

The noise echoed around me. The slam had been a bit more forceful than I'd intended. It took a moment for the high-pitched tone in my ears to settle long enough for me to notice the rest of the café had gone silent. I looked around. The young women behind me turned away suddenly, eyes averted to their coffees and cakes, mouths curling up a little at the corners, eyebrows raised. The woman who'd taken my order huffed and went back to her work. I saw myself as they must see me, hands shaking, muttering at my laptop, body practically humming with residual frustration.

Uh-oh, watch out for the crazy lady.

My cheeks felt hot. Oh God, I was going to cry.

Before embarrassment could completely take me over, I quickly packed up my things, keeping my head ducked down.

I ripped my phone from its charger on the third try. Only thirty-seven per cent charged. That wasn't going to last me a day. I left with my inadequately charged phone before I caused another scene.

I was out on the street before I realised I'd left my macaroni pie.

CHAPTER 7

I STOOD ON the pavement and gave myself a moment to breathe.

That could have gone better.

Maybe it was a little soon to be diving into the community. Maybe a walk along the riverbank would help. Yes, calm down, get my bearings first.

I wandered back up toward the war monument next to the river. It was made of worn stone in the shape of a Celtic Cross. Two scuffed plastic planters sat at its base, holding half a dozen battered pansies. The flowers' pathetic, wilting petals looked how I felt. I frowned at the sorry display. I'd assumed a nice village like this would put a bit more effort into their flowers. It was nothing like the cheery hanging baskets and window boxes I'd imagined. Perhaps I could volunteer to help out with flowers around the town. Maybe I could even—

"BRAH!"

The noise knocked me sideways. Nerves jangled, I stumbled into the road. A mud-splattered jeep swerved around me, horn blaring. I leapt back onto the pavement, very nearly falling over my own feet. My hands flapped uselessly in front of my face.

Laughter erupted from the monument.

Adrenaline abating, I turned to the sound. The gaggle of teenagers I'd seen go by the café were gripping their sides, teeth flashing, mouths wide and red. One held up her phone, filming me, her other hand hidden inside her sleeve, stifling the laughter that escaped the sides of her mouth like air from a balloon. The owner of the bark that had sent me careening into the road—a boy, barely out of his rompers—watched me with his hands in his pockets and a self-satisfied grin plastered on his smug face.

"Sorry," he said, barely hiding a smirk. "Didn't see you there."

I stared at them, dumbfounded.

The boy frowned, all faux-concerned.

"You didn't wet yourself, did you, pal?"

The high-pitched tone filled my head as a heat filled my belly and creeped up my chest and into my arms and throat.

"Oi!" A hoarse, angry voice called out from the doorway of the large pub.

The teens quickly scarpered up the road. A burly man thundered past me, jumper sleeves rolled up, face red and sweating.

"What have I told you?" he roared after them, but they were already long gone, laughter trailing behind them.

I rubbed my head as the ringing in my ears cooled and the heat left my trembling arms.

The red-faced man turned to me, swayed slightly, alcohol on his breath.

"Kids, eh?" he said. "Spoiled rotten these days. You understand, eh? No need to get anyone else involved, eh?"

Something about the man's face looked very similar to the boy. I nodded and hurried away from him.

"No need, eh?" he called after me.

I stopped on the other side of the street and rubbed my chest. Why did I nod?

In my head I imagined the scene again. The boy jumping out at me. The girl filming with her phone. But this time, I saw myself take off one of my boots and approach the boy. Suddenly, I started to beat him about his sniggering face, my arm flying, smacking him repeatedly with the hardest part of the sole.

Is this funny? I imagined myself screaming at him. *Is this funny now?*

The image of me beating him with my boot kept repeating over and over in my mind. The violence of it. The look of fear I imagined on the boy's face. His mouth pulled wide in horror.

The satisfying thrill it gave me.

There's the person you think you're going to be. And then, poof, there you are.

I swallowed down the dull ache rising in my chest and took a sharp turn up one of the side streets.

CHAPTER 8

I'D BEEN IN Carlinsrest for barely an hour and I was probably already a source of gossip.

Fuck's sake. Get it together, Tamsin.

I didn't care where I was going. Just as long as it was away from the river.

Up the side streets and into the back alleys, Carlinsrest shucked off its tweed jacket and rolled up its sleeves. Garages, work yards and storage units lined the narrow road. At the end, a long, squat stone building hunkered against the back of the main street. Two small, dark windows were crowded with a display of practical odds and ends: hacksaws, shears, citronella candles, midge nets, fluorescent work vests, bags of tinder, seeds. A long blue sign ran the length of the building, reading in blocky white letters: CARLINSREST HARDWARE & SUPPLIES.

I stopped in front of it.

It was the sort of place that promised practical solutions to life's problems. *Life isn't miserable*, it seemed to say. *You just need to replace your terrible washing machine, fix the kettle that scalds your hand with steam, or brighten your front step with flowers.* Yes, this was what I needed. Maybe they had someone I could ask about whatever the hell was supposed to be heating my house. And I did need a replacement for the clotheshorse.

I stepped inside.

An electronic chime announced my arrival, a two-tone beep which probably cost more than the real bell it mimicked. Strip lights hung over a long, wide space filled with white metal shelves carrying everything from chainsaws to camping stoves. There was a smell of petrol, wood shavings and that outdoors-scent people bring in with them on their skin after they've been in the cold. It was cluttered, but clean and warm. All practicality and no style.

See, here people are comfortable. They don't need to blind you with flashy point-of-sale and froofy window dressing.

But would the sales staff be as equally fluff-less? Would they roll their eyes and tut when I didn't know what to ask for? I imagined them taking one look at my face and then fleecing me as the clueless tourist I was.

As if on cue, a man straightened up from behind a counter plastered with business cards and small notices. He was tall and broad, towering over the shelves. I imagined meeting him on a dark road and crossing to the other side. He lifted a large cardboard box up and placed it next to the till.

Then he saw me and smiled.

"Hello, shout if you need anything."

It wasn't the over-friendliness of city shop staff, who I always felt suspected me of shoplifting, but not the long-suffering sneer I'd half-expected of a tourist-tired local.

"Will do," I said.

His hair was dark, thinning at the front into a widow's peak and flopping over his tanned, lined forehead. His beard had a few sprinklings of grey, and he wore a checked blue shirt, rolled up at the sleeves, tucked into his jeans but undone round the neck. Neat enough to be 'at work' but without trying too hard about it. Everything about him said 'lived in'. Worn. Like he'd been through the wars, once upon a time, and had come out the other side. He returned his gaze to the contents of the cardboard box. Pocket-sized torches. He gently lifted one out of the box, softly pinched between large fingertips. He double-checked the computer screen then raised a pricing gun.

Suddenly, there was a cheery bleeping. Not the door this time. The man stopped what he was doing and reached into his jeans pocket. It was his phone. He rolled his eyes, swiped the phone then came round the other side of the counter and got onto the floor in a plank position.

He looked up at me and smiled self-consciously.

"Sorry, my other half has a habit of putting reminders in my phone," he said, gritting his teeth with the exertion. "Planks. Stretches. Drinking water. He thinks everything can be solved with an alert on your phone."

I stifled a laugh at the oddness of it all. The way he grunted as he got into position. The frown of concentration. All earlier intimidation suddenly felt silly.

"Uh." I cleared my throat and tried again a little louder. "Actually, once you're done, I was wondering…"

He let down his knees with a grunt.

"Yep?"

I froze for a moment, then stretched a smile onto my face.

"Do you have something for drying clothes?"

"Sure, there are wire dryers in the corner there."

I thought of the clotheshorse dancing off my windscreen.

"Do you have any washing line?"

"Washing lines are a bit fiddly. You sure you don't want a—?"

"Yes," I said, a little too loud. "A washing line is fine. Thanks."

"Alright. Um, I have some over here, I think."

He stood up and walked to a shelf loaded up with spools of wire, string and rope.

Come on, Tamsin. Be brave.

"Thanks. Um. I'm new around here and…" I waved my hands helplessly. "I'm a bit lost about some stuff. And you seem like someone who is capable and local and…" I sighed, genuinely, to my surprise. "I could do with some help."

He gave me a look for a moment, like he was weighing something up. Then his warm face slowly split into a smile.

"What do you need?" He reached out a hand. "Rowan."

Rowan, I thought, a tree. This is the place where people are named after the land. Cliff. Glen. Ivy. Rose. I wondered if his parents were thinking of a particular rowan tree when they named him. The thin green leaves. The red berries promising autumn while the world was still in the height of summer. Witchwood. They used to plant it in graveyards. Either the bane or the blessing of witches. I couldn't remember which.

How much better would you be at everything if you didn't have all this useless knowledge bobbing about your head?

I took his hand and shook it. Good business-level firm, like I'd practiced before every interview of my life. His hand was dry and warm.

"Tamsin." I shrugged. "Mum's choice. I'd change it if I could think of a name I like."

"Is that what you need help with? Picking a new name?"

I took a moment. Then laughed. Then snorted. Then, horrified at the snort, threw a hand up over my face. I checked his face for disgust, but no, he was smiling. He wasn't put off by the snort. In fact, he seemed to be smiling wider. Amused. Delighted by it. Perhaps he thought I was adorable.

"Sorry." I dropped my hands. "I've just moved into this place, and I have a biomass heating system."

He waited for me to elaborate.

"And I don't know what that is. And my house is cold."

Rowan nodded ruefully. "Ah, you've got a wood-fuelled boiler. They're just being fancy about it to appeal to the Greens in the cities."

"I couldn't see a boiler in the house."

"It's probably down in the basement. Maybe close to your fuse box, mains switch, that sort of thing."

The mains switch. Electricity!

"I don't think I have a basement."

"Do you have a set of doors outside by the wall? Or a door under the stairs?"

The door under the stairs, cut at a slant.

"I thought that was a cupboard."

"It's probably the way down to your basement."

I breathed a sigh of relief. Finally, things were starting to look up.

"Okay, so what do I do with a—a wood-fuelled boiler?"

"You put wood in it." He grinned at me.

I mock-smacked my forehead. *Idiot.*

"Of course. Sorry."

"That's alright. Can't blame yourself for not knowing if you've not used one before." Rowan wiped his forehead with the back of his arm. "If your seller was any good, they should have left you some firewood in the house somewhere. If not, you'll need to buy some. At least until you've figured out where you can cut your own and dry it out. As you're new here, I can throw in a bundle of wood and kindling with your axe."

"An axe?"

"You'll need an axe. For the wood. You're not going to want to keep buying it at"—he put a hand up over his mouth—"tourist prices."

"Oh, oh yes. Of course."

"See, a local already."

He's just being kind.

"Thank you," I said. "I didn't think… what with… never mind. Just thank you."

"No problem. You're not the only transplant up here."

He led the way to a range of axes. I never realised there were so many options. In my head I'd always imagined the red-headed, pale-handled type I'd seen in cartoons. Rowan had all sorts. Short, stubby handles. Black rubber handles. Square heads. Arched heads.

"Which one should I get?" I asked.

"Well, it depends. What are you doing? Splitting or chopping?"

"I don't understand."

"Different heads do different jobs—" He stopped himself, thought for a second, then said, "You're probably going to want a bit of both. These ones are good all-rounders. Which one do you like?"

I didn't know how to answer that.

"Um, which one should I like?"

He frowned, then laughed. Then the smile faded. A flash of something I didn't recognise flickered across his face. He licked his lips, customer service manners coming back into play, and considered the range in front of him. He picked out an axe with a pale handle, brand burned into the wood, and a bright steel head, black leather cover buttoned over the edge.

"I think you'll like this one," he said. "But I'll write you up a receipt in case you later realise you don't."

He rang me up. I paid for the axe and the washing line.

"So, whereabouts is your place?" he asked. "Are you up or down the valley?"

"I don't know. I'm in one of the Sgàthan Sìth cottages."

"Sgàthan Sìth?" He stopped writing up the receipt. "You're in Sgàthan Sìth?"

"Um, yes, 1b," I replied.

He sucked in his lips and raised his eyebrows.

"What?" I asked.

"Nothing." He handed over the receipt. "Well… okay, before someone else gets in and spooks you or something. It's had a couple of owners, but no one ever seems to—"

A clang interrupted him. His head flicked to the back of the store where a young man in a denim jacket had dropped a chainsaw display model onto the ground.

"Aw shit, sorry, I have to—"

I packed firewood, kindling and washing line into my backpack. There was no room for the axe so I just held it and turned to leave.

"Wait, before you go"—he turned back to me—"you should come to the Curtyard tomorrow."

"The Cut Yard?"

"Head up the alley between Maggie's Café and the tapas place then take a left. That's where the locals hang out in the evenings. As you're a local now, you should come say hi."

Then he half-jogged to catch the heavy chainsaw just before it slipped again out of the young man's hands.

CHAPTER 9

I WALKED BACK from town with the axe over my shoulder. I liked the weight of it. It made me feel capable. Strong. Like I belonged out here.

Look at this woman, I imagined passers-by thinking, *casually carrying her axe. She looks like she knows what she's doing. She looks like she can handle herself.*

It would be nice to be able to handle myself. And an axe.

After a mile down the road, and a few odd stares from passing car windows, I became convinced that I actually looked more like an axe murderer and I lowered it off my shoulder.

Back at Sgàthan Sìth, I set down my bag and listened for my neighbour. I tilted my head in the direction of the adjoining wall. Silence. I drifted closer toward the fireplace, ears straining, trying to hear something. Nothing. Such a difference to all the bumping about last night. Maybe she slept during the day.

I stretched my tired limbs.

A wave of body odour escaped from my T-shirt. I recoiled from myself. Ooft! I hoped that was from the walk back and I hadn't been subjecting everyone in Carlinsrest to this.

I needed a bath.

And for that, I needed heat.

I turned to the door under the stairs. It was much like the garden gate style doors upstairs. It was easy to see why I might have confused it for a cupboard. A basement wasn't a bad thing. I could store garden equipment in there, Christmas lights, suitcases. Maybe convert it into a gym.

The door opened with a squeak.

A slim set of stone stairs sank away into the dark of the hill below.

I felt for a light switch, found it on the wall to my right, and flicked it once, twice, thrice before remembering. The mains switch was down in the basement.

I stood at the top. Dread, like the words *oh no* rattling along my arms and legs, kept me frozen to the spot. I squinted as if that might help me pick out any glimmer of light down in the dark. It didn't look like there were any windows down there. I got out my phone and switched on the flashlight app.

I gave the lower stairs a brief sweep of cold blue light.

I took a step down.

Changed my mind.

Came back up.

I switched my phone to my left hand and picked up the new axe in my right. Then I slowly descended.

This is my basement, I told myself. *My basement. My house.*

There could be nothing in there that I didn't put in myself.

Unless the previous owner is hiding down there, dead, rotting, or waiting, with a knife. Or left bear traps all over the floor ready to shatter your shins. Or put up piano wire stretching across the stairway to take off your head.

"Stop it," I scolded myself aloud.

I checked the stairs ahead again with the light from my

phone. No piano wire. The only person down there in the dark with an axe would be me.

I descended.

My phone light bounced off white walls, grey in the dark. It was hard to get an idea of the size of the space. The sound of my footsteps came back to me in ringing echoes. The white-blue square of light shook and danced where I directed it. The air smelled of fresh paint and cold stone and old earth. I followed my phone light along the walls until I found a grey box with a big black switch on it and that tell-tale electric yellow triangle with the lightning bolt. I tucked the axe under my arm and reached for the switch.

Before I could flip it, I was plunged into darkness.

My phone bleeped pathetically. Not enough battery for the torch app. In my panic I slapped the electrical box, desperately trying to find the mains switch.

"Come on, come on!"

I found and flicked the switch.

The basement lit up immediately. I screamed.

After a few seconds, I remembered I'd left the light switch at the top of the stairs in the on position. At least that meant the electricity worked. Finally, I could charge my phone. I rubbed my chest with my free hand and looked around.

It was an austere, white-painted stone room, bare and empty, lit by a single bulb hanging from a naked ceiling. The floorboards from the living room above stretched overhead. That nail or splinter that caught my foot yesterday must have fallen down here. I tracked back to where the floorboards ended and the stone entrance began. There was a small pinprick of light coming through a hole around about where I'd been stabbed. I searched along the floor, but I couldn't see whatever had punctured me. I'd have to remember to wear shoes down here until I found it.

The boiler was right next to the electrical box, a thick grey metal column with a hatch for wood and a hatch for ash. At its base was an orange net bag of wood and kindling.

Oh well, at least it would be a while before I needed to chop down any trees.

I tore open the bag and tried to push a log into the boiler. Too big. I'd need to—what did Rowan say?—split it. I balanced the log on the concrete floor, raised my axe and hoped for the best. After a few tries—missed the first, only took a splinter off the second, only got halfway down the third—I managed to split a few logs. That would do. I set the kindling going with a match and the end page of the house's listing.

The flame took the kindling, enveloping it in flickering tongues. Carefully, I angled two split bits of wood over the growing fire. I watched, waiting for the fire to die or for the wood to collapse and snuff it out. But after a few seconds, the dry split edge took and flame crept along it like a bright orange caterpillar, sooty feet leaching the colour from the wood and staining it black.

My heart swelled. I'd done it. I had built a fire.

I stood up straight, hands on my hips, gazing with pride at my work. This was the most practical thing I'd ever done. *Here stands a capable woman*, I thought. *Look, she can make a fire, work out a boiler, use an axe*. I considered again my earlier daydreams. The stoic gardener, the plucky librarian, the enigmatic florist. Maybe I could do this. Maybe I could be the heroine of my own story.

I gathered up more wood to feed the fire.

But as I loaded up the burner, a thought niggled away at me. Why hadn't the estate agent warned me about the boiler? They must have known about it. This hadn't been the only rural property on their site. It would be a damn foolish thing to sell homes with boilers you don't understand. And I couldn't be the first person to ask. They must have known! Then why hadn't they told me? I had been in a hurry, yes, but this seemed like something important. Like the 1a/1b situation. Did they treat everyone this badly?

Or was it just me?

I rubbed my arms in the growing warmth of the boiler.

Maybe they had smelt it on me. That thing that made my colleagues not want to stick around and wait for me. Maybe they took one look at me and thought, 'oh, I see what you are.' The squinted eyes, the unsure smile. The expression Rowan made when he weighed me up at the store.

The question came again, like a body rising from still water.

Do you think you're a good pers—

A sound.

A soft, skittering sound.

My head jerked in the direction of it so hard my neck hurt.

Was it a rat? I scanned the room. It had sounded muted. Like it had come from within the walls. I peered at the wall opposite the stairs and the boiler. The paint in the basement smelt fresh. The floor was clean, like new. I looked closer.

As my eyes adjusted to the low light outside of the bulb's immediate radius, I started to make out a set of faint lines in the wall. I followed them, tracking them to points and corners. My eyebrows raised as I realised what the shape was.

I put a hand over my mouth and stepped back.

A door.

A distinct plastered-over door shape in the wall.

A shiver ran up my back.

Why the hell was there a door in my basement?

I held the axe clenched in my fists, ears ringing with that high-pitched tone, glaring at the door like I was staring down a mountain lion.

The door shape was in the joining wall between 1a and 1b. Perhaps the Sgàthan Sìth cottages had been one house until some property developer had split it into two to double their profit. But then why no connecting doors elsewhere? I hadn't seen anything like this in the living room or the bedroom. Only here in the basement.

I took a deep breath. There was no telling what had once been there. It could be a fireplace or a cupboard. And even if it was a door to 1a, it was clearly sealed up. No one could get in. I was fine. It was safe.

No monsters. Just neighbours.

I shuddered.

A bath! A bath would calm me. That's what women like me did in films and TV. A bath. Something in the hot water settled our… waters? Whatever those were. Probably a uterus thing.

Uterus thing or not, a bath would fix everything.

I set the water tank of the boiler heating using the instructions on the side. Then I headed back up the stairs and turned off the light. But after closing the door at the top of the stairs, I wedged my axe under the handle to hold it shut.

Just in case.

CHAPTER 10

As I LAY in the bath, I allowed myself another moment of pride. Hot steaming water, courtesy of my hands.

I hadn't brought any bubble bath with me, so I could see my whole body under the surface, bloated by the hot water. I tried not to think about my body most of the time, or even about being in a body. I'd often thought I would have preferred not to have one at all if I'd had the choice. To be able to just exist, floating about the world, quietly observing, never being perceived.

But this was now a body that could chop wood and build fires.

A capable body. A strong body.

A sore body.

With a splash, I pulled up my foot and inspected the puncture wound. It had long since sealed itself. Now there was just a dark brown mark, a perfect circle, where the hole had been. The thick skin around the edge had turned white and puffy in the water. I pulled at the wound slightly to check nothing had got underneath. The little hole of puffy white skin elongated and pinched together under the strain, like a tiny sulking mouth. It didn't look infected, thank God.

I'd have to check the basement again. I didn't want loose splinters or nails lying about. Something about the discovery of the door made me feel even more uneasy about not knowing what had pricked me. I wanted to find it, not just to pick it up and throw it away, but to be sure it was a nail or a splinter and not something else.

I listened to the quiet of the house. I hadn't heard anything from 1a since I'd got back. Even while I made dinner, thankful for the pasta and sauces I'd picked up on my way, I'd heard nothing. No cooking sounds of her own. No muffled footsteps like the day before. Not a peep. I started to wonder if maybe last night had been a one-off. I hoped so. It was probably a happy accident I hadn't mentioned the noise when I'd spoken to— I still didn't know her name.

I sank further into the bath, letting the water creep over my lips.

She seemed quiet, my neighbour. A shut-in, perhaps. I wondered what the inside of 1a was like. Maybe it was a hoarder's paradise: newspapers stacked to the ceiling, takeaway boxes piled up around the sink, collected bits and bobs lining a narrow walkway through the house. Or maybe she was fastidiously neat: furniture placed precisely throughout with not a speck of dust to be spied, sofas and chairs at right angles to each other, doily at the exact centre of each side table, pictures in a level line on the walls, bed made and properly tucked in and everything. I sat up and vigorously rubbed a bar of soap in my hands, trying to work up a tight enough foam to wash myself with. I imagined her soaps neatly paraded across the back of the sink, probably still in their paper packaging.

I rubbed the soap foam under my armpits and listened again. Nothing.

I caught my face reflected in the taps, warped and elongated beyond recognition. My shadow shattered to pieces across the ripples on the water's surface. I came to from my daydreaming and found the bath had grown noticeably cold around me. My fingertips had wrinkled to hard ridges.

There I go again, I thought. *Always losing myself.*

I rinsed off the soap and got out.

CHAPTER 11

I LOOKED AT the sad mattress and regretted not doing more to sort out my sleeping arrangements. My towel was now damp, of course, and I had nothing to sleep under unless I wanted to catch a cold. At least the house was warmer now I'd figured out how to use the boiler. I went digging through my suitcase to find something else I could use as a blanket. I'd left so quickly, I could barely remember what I'd brought with me. The whole process had been a blur, as if I'd watched someone else packing in a dream. I flipped the light switch to help me look. Pale yellow light from the single naked bulb painted a golden circle in the centre of the bedroom.

At the bottom of the case I found my terrycloth dressing gown. An old Christmas gift from my mother. One of those things that seemed indispensable to older generations yet completely forgettable to mine. I rarely, if ever, wore it back in Edinburgh. It had hung on the back of my bedroom door, a spectre in the night. Well, I was certainly glad of it now.

I'd never look down on gifts of slippers, socks and dressing gowns ever again.

I draped the dressing gown over the bed and took a moment to appreciate my ingenuity. It wasn't much, but it was starting to feel a bit better. Light, something cozy to snuggle up under, a charged phone, a full belly—even if it was just tinned chilli and a few slices of sandwich bread. It was almost bearable now. I could do this. I could make a life out here.

I eyed the joining wall between 1b and 1a. My neighbour was still behaving herself. Maybe I didn't have to ask for her to keep it down. Maybe she'd figured that out for herself from my wee introduction this morning—another good idea, looking back on it. That had been a slightly nervy thing to do, and I had done it. Go me.

I dried off, changed into my pyjamas and settled into bed. The internet hadn't been set up yet—I hadn't been able to find a router—so I couldn't spare the data for a podcast. Instead, I played puzzles on my phone—one of my tactics to keep my many, many thoughts at bay—until my eyelids started to droop.

I had almost fallen asleep, when a scream pierced the twilight. I kicked the dressing gown off me in fright. It had come from outside. The periwinkle blue of the dusk outside felt like it was peering in on me. I gripped the mattress beneath me, eyes not daring to leave the window. I spied a face floating in the gloom. It was mine, mirrored back to me in the glass.

The scream came again.

A fox. A fucking fox.

I collapsed back into the mattress. So much for my relaxing bedtime. I thought the countryside was supposed to be tranquil, calming. But you forget, don't you? All of the wilderness, the life out there, animals going about their business without a care for bedtimes, or mental health breaks, or any human ideas of calm and order.

If the fox wants to scream, she just screams.

Lucky fox.

Well, time for bed anyway. I looked about for a light switch, then realised the only one in the room was the one right next to the bedroom door. *Oh no.* My toes curled instinctively. I would have to turn off the light then run back to my bed in the dark. Even if I hadn't just been scared out of my skin by a fox, the prospect would have filled me with dread.

Oh God, don't be so immature, I thought. *You're too old to be imagining boogie men.*

I took a deep breath, got up and walked to the bedroom door.

My finger hovered over the light switch.

Did I remember to lock the front door? What about the windows? What if someone snuck in in the night and—

I reached for the door latch and stopped.

I swallowed. My palms went cold.

Are you too scared to look? Do you need Daddy to come check under the bed for you, too? Grow up!

I forced open the bedroom door and peered out onto the landing. The tap in the bathroom dripped. The stairs lay silently under the light of the pale night sky. I could just about see the front door from where I leant out over the first step. It was closed. And there was the chain, just where I knew it would be.

See. I exhaled. *This is your house. Nothing in it but you.*

I shut the bedroom door. Then, in quick succession, I turned off the light, ran to the bed and threw the dressing gown over myself.

I lay in the dark, waiting for my pulse to calm down, feeling more than a little silly.

Everything was fine. Just a bedroom at night.

I watched the sky darken to indigo and thought of the fox outside with her solitary life. As I drifted into sleep, the fox came with me. At first, she just followed me as I made the walk into the village, matching my steps, hiding in my shadow. Then she appeared in front of me on the road. I tried to pass by, but every step I took, she took too, mirroring my movements, blocking my way. Before I could shoo her away, she leapt up on me, covering me head to toe with her fur. She was surprisingly heavy. I struggled to walk upright, so I wobbled into Carlinsrest, gripping onto the fences with my front paws, opening doors by gripping the handles with my sharp teeth. But no one I met could see the fox I was covered with. The woman at the café, the ramblers from the road, the teenagers by the monument. They all welcomed me with "Morning's" and polite waves, then flinched as I struggled to wave back, my black claws striking at the air in front of their faces. The woman from the café asked me if I was alright. I tried to answer back, "No, there's a fox on my back. Or I think I'm turning into a fox. Or maybe I've always been a fox and now I'm only just realising." But every time I opened my mouth, all I could do was scream. I went all around Carlinsrest, screaming at people, until everyone started to avoid me, crossing the street, turning away from my desperate gaze. Rowan, the man from the hardware store, he was the only one who tried to help me. But the moment he got close, I clamped my jaw around his wrist, so he couldn't leave. And I knew I was hurting him—I could see the skin tearing around my teeth—but I couldn't let go. I was so afraid he'd run away and then no one would look at me and I'd be alone and…

The old man was watching me from the bridge. Him and his dog. His wiry grey hair reached up into the sky like branching horns. He clutched the handles of the wheelchair carrying the sleeping old woman, and grinned.

There was a drumming sound.

The old woman in the chair stirred in her sleep.

The drumming grew louder.

No, not drumming. Footsteps.

Someone was in my bedroom.

I jerked awake.

Footsteps skittered across the bedroom floor. The mattress juddered with the force of them. It stopped. I forced myself up through the antechamber of sleep, my limbs still heavy and ignoring my pleas to get up get up get up. My eyes adjusted to the dark just in time to catch a shadow dart across the open bedroom door.

Thud-thud-thud-thud-thud

They thundered down the stairs. Adrenaline flooded through my veins. Half-asleep, my scream turned into a whistle in my throat. I leapt up out of bed and threw myself toward the light switch.

The light from the bare bulb banished the shadows, stinging my eyes. I wished I'd grabbed my phone instead. I should call for help! There's an intruder in my home! But the house was quiet. Maybe I should check first. I leant back out onto the landing again, looking for who had invaded my home.

Downstairs was dark and silent. I found the light switch at the top of the stairs. Nothing scampered away from the light. Slowly, muscles tense, I made my way downstairs. My axe lay on the floor by the basement door. I quietly picked it up then checked the front door. Still locked. No sign of any tampering. With a squeeze of courage, I poked my head down into the basement. That plastered outline was still sealed over. Not a crack. I had to squint to even see it.

I furrowed my brow. I'd definitely heard footsteps. Felt them, even! They'd practically run down the stairs. But how could that—?

Thud-thud-thud-thud-thud

My head jerked toward the fireplace. It sounded like my neighbour just ran up her stairs. I sank to my knees and wiped my face with my hand. I'd probably just heard her next door and in my half-asleep state filled the darkness with monsters. The dull screech of furniture on wood reverberated through the wall. Well, so much for my quiet night.

I stood up and gripped the axe handle. Even with an explanation, I still felt deeply unsettled. Having a weapon nearby wouldn't be a bad thing.

I climbed back up the stairs, turned off the landing light and shut the bedroom door, flinching at the sound of its hinges.

Then I stopped.

I looked at the bedroom door again.

When I'd bolted awake just now, I could have sworn I'd seen a shadow through the open door.

But I'd closed the door before going to bed, hadn't I?

CHAPTER 12

I WAS STILL feeling unsettled the following morning when I woke tangled in my dressing gown-come-bedsheet, cuddling the axe. I considered knocking on my neighbour's door again to ask her to keep it down—for real this time—but after last night I found my courage waning. Nevertheless, I was warm and I was clean, so that was something.

The first thing I did when I got up was test the door to the bedroom. Its hinges shrieked and squealed. I must have left it ajar when I went to bed. There was no way it could have opened in the night without waking me. That settled it. Last night must have been one of those waking nightmares, a hallucination on the edge of sleep. That was all.

However, even with that matter sorted, the house felt alien to me that morning. Every room was both too small and too large. The doors were at wrong angles. The windows were in the wrong spots for light. Doorknobs just too low. Counters just too high. Lightbulbs in just the right place to leave shadows in every corner. It was as if someone had built this place to repel people. Like every detail was subconsciously making me dizzy and sick, broadcasting to my hindbrain, *Danger! Leave! This place might look like a home but it's not. It's a praying mantis camouflaged as an orchid. It's a grave in disguise!*

I frowned at the joining wall. It was my neighbour's fault. If she'd just keep things down, I wouldn't have scared myself in the night. Is it any wonder I felt uncomfortable in my own home? I'd barely managed to get a proper night's sleep in two days!

I decided that the last thing I wanted to do today was stay inside.

I left for Carlinsrest after a quick breakfast of cereal.

As I walked along the road, I puzzled away at how to make myself feel more 'at home.' I needed something cosy. Something inviting. Something practical. What I needed—what would cure the foreboding un-homeliness of the cottage—was a rug.

A rug to insulate my home and protect my feet. Okay, so I couldn't afford to fix my windscreen just yet. Or replace the mattress. But I could shell out a little for a cheap rug. No more errant splinters or whatever stabbing my soles. That's the kind of thing people bought to feel more at home. Throw cushions, blankets, rugs. Soft tactile things to wrap around the hard edges of the walls we build around ourselves. A rug for the fragile softness of myself.

Not that I like to think of myself as fragile. Not that I avoided giving away any hint of fragility, like a cat hiding an injury.

I shook the thought from my head.

No, I thought. Let's go back to dreaming of rugs and making 1b Sgàthan Sìth as cosy as can be.

Back in Carlinsrest, I crossed Bodach's Brig—no sign of the old man and his sleeping wife—and passed by the Celtic cross memorial. The handful of pansies had been joined by a few buckets of hyacinth and tulips. I cringed a little at my earlier judgement. Maybe the other flowers hadn't been set out yet and that's why there'd been so few.

I followed along the river, past the pub and the tapas place, looking for some kind of homewares shop. I'd considered Rowan's hardware and supplies shop, but from what I could remember it was mostly tools and sundries. I needed somewhere that sold fripperies. Like a gift shop, or one of those posh interior design boutiques I saw around Edinburgh. Further along the main street I found what I was looking for.

A squat stone building stood at the end of the row with sash windows complete with muntins and sage-green sills. The gilded sign above declared in a decorative, vintage font:

The Auld Antiques Shoppe

Bingo. Antique was just a fancy way of saying second-hand. And second-hand meant cheaper and better quality, right?

I went inside.

A real bell announced my arrival with a gentle tinkling.

The sunny front room was filled with beautiful items. Glass lamps. Small drinks tables. Embroidered footstools. Tea sets. Leather wingback chairs. An umbrella stand, full of walking sticks with various handles, some metal, some wood, some in the shape of animal heads. Mounted antlers and stag heads lined the upper parts of the walls. A lit scented candle beside the till perfumed the air with woody notes and toasted vanilla. It smelled as if I'd fallen into the pages of an old book. It was like someone had taken my every imagining of a cute antiques shop and made it real. The only detail that stood out was a line of cactuses and succulents in the window. Their spikes and spines felt oddly modern surrounded by all the soft curves and muted browns.

By the till, a sandy-haired man with a straw-coloured beard and a tanned forehead either ignored my presence or was so consumed by the book he was reading he hadn't had chance to notice me.

My initial instinct was to leave him alone. But no, I was determined to be better, to be more outgoing and sociable. My memory of that first day at the agency, the fumbled invitation, haunted me. I wouldn't make that mistake again.

I cleared my throat.

"Hi, morning, uh, do you have any—"

"Scottish books to the left," said the man, not even looking up from his novel.

I turned, struck dumb, to look at the shelves to the left of the front room. Green, tan and maroon cloth-bound books lined the shelves on the other side of the shop. I could make out multiple copies of *Peter Pan* and *The Private Memoirs and Confessions of a Justified Sinner*.

"Uh, actually I was looking for a rug," I said.

The man sighed, his face suddenly sullen. He put away his novel and got up. I could practically see the irritation coming off him in waves.

"Sorry, I'm new around here," I explained. "I'm trying to decorate and—"

"More homewares in the back." He opened a heavy curtain in a doorway, revealing a cluttered back room full of dining tables, linens and orphaned drawers of cutlery.

"Oh, thank you—"

He returned to his book at the till. As I passed by, I peeked at the cover. Something with spaceships. It felt as mismatched to the surroundings as the cactuses on the sill.

The back room was difficult to navigate. Pale light filtered in through a frosted window on the back wall, illuminating dancing motes of dust but barely lighting my way through the clutter. I squeezed past a wardrobe, turned a corner between warring chests of drawers and walked straight into another person, their surprised face just inches away from me. I put up my hands to apologise before realizing the face was mine. My reflection stared back at me from a tall gilt mirror leant against the wall. God, that had been close! I breathed a sigh of relief, chuckled at myself, and then backed into a vase on a pedestal. It made a horrible ringing sound as I managed to catch it just in time and slam it back onto its wooden perch. My eyes darted to the curtained gap, waiting for the sullen-faced man to come and give me a scolding. He must have been absorbed in his novel still, because no one came.

I found the rugs at the back of the room, rolled up and leant against the wall lengthwise like mummies, or victims of the mob. There was a stuffed fox on a high shelf next to them, all glassy-eyed and snarling mouth. I turned my face away so I couldn't look at it.

I ran my hand down a large, classic Persian-style rug. The pattern was a little busy for what I was imagining, but it would be warm, and it would protect my feet from splinters. And there had to be a way to style it right. I'd seen plenty of women on Instagram style their homes with an effortless manner that looked like witchcraft to me.

I checked the price.

I had to check it again.

There were four figures on that tag! And that was before the decimal point as well. My hand retracted as if the price had physically burned me. I don't know what the going price for rugs was, but that seemed excessive. Especially for second-hand. Maybe it was a size thing. I looked at the price of the next rug down. My eyes felt like they popped out of my skull. How was this one more expensive? It was smaller.

I eyed the rest of the rugs lined up against the wall. With growing dread, I began to suspect that they were all out of my price range. I also began to realise that I might have mixed up the rules of antiques shops with those for charity shops. Or 'shoppes' for that matter. Maybe these were those tourist prices Rowan had talked about. Though I couldn't imagine many tourists buying a rug on their way through to the Highlands.

There had to be a cheaper option.

I doublechecked the curtained doorway—still no sign of the sullen-faced-man—then I got out my phone.

I typed the name of the most memorable home décor site I could think of into my browser. I checked 'products.' No rugs section. I sighed. 'Decorative items?' No, just umpteen candles in jars. 'Textiles' then. Cushions. Curtains. Tablecloths. Rugs! Two thousand results. The first page alone had twenty more or less identical looking ivory-coloured mid-pile rugs. Inoffensive. Would go with anything. I felt my mouth pull to the side. I checked the 'style' filter. My choices were Traditional, Geometric and Abstract. What the hell was a 'traditional' rug? One that goes on the floor, I hoped. Would an abstract rug be a metaphysical rug, then? Here, let us sell you the concept of a rug. Geometric, well, I supposed that would be square or rectangle or circle. I'd never seen a triangle rug before. Suddenly I wanted one. I searched for a triangle rug and found five hundred options with tessellated triangles over them in sad shades of white and grey.

"Do you need a hand or something?"

I nearly threw my phone into the air.

The sullen-faced man was at my shoulder, looking at my screen. My cheeks throbbed with embarrassment. Oh no, he'd seen me browsing online for cheaper versions of his stock. Oh shit. Oh fuck. I thrust my phone into my pocket.

"No. No, no, no," I said. "I'm alright, thanks. Just browsing."

A cruel little smirk hitched up the side of his mouth. "You should check one of the bigger supermarkets just outside Glasgow. I'm sure you'll find what you're looking for there."

My pulse suddenly thrummed in my ears. All embarrassment leaving me on a hot wave of indignation.

Did this fucker just call me cheap?

Arse. Face like a slapped arse. Should slap his slapped-arse face. Slap his slapped-arse face!

I bit back the insults boiling up my throat and plucked up the closest—and smallest—rug within reach.

"Actually, I'd like to buy *this* rug. Please."

He rolled his eyes.

"You don't have to—"

"No. Please. I wish to buy this rug."

He furrowed his brows at me a moment. There was that

evaluating look again. Just like the one Rowan had given me. Then he shrugged and said, "Alright, fine."

I followed him back to the front room where he rung it up, jabbing each key on the ancient till like it had personally wronged him. I hid my flinch at the total and handed over my bank card.

He paused a moment, shook his head then put the payment through.

"I'll write you a receipt," he said.

"No-thank-you-don't-need-one." It slipped out of my mouth quicker than my good sense could tell me, *steady on!* Normally I would have chickened out by now. Well, that was the old me.

I snatched my bank card from his fingers and left the 'shoppe', rug clutched under my arm.

Once I'd walked a few feet away, I checked what exactly I'd bought. It was fluffy and cream. A sheepskin. Not terrible. Though I was doubly sure I could have bought it cheaper from the big supermarket the sullen-faced man had suggested.

I then realised I hadn't asked about delivery. Tonight was the meet-up at the pub. I could hardly walk around town with a rug under my arm all day, let alone take it out for drinks with me. I looked at Bodach's Brig and the road back out of town. My shoulders drooped. I would have to walk all the way home to drop off the rug and then walk all the way back.

Good work, genius! You chose the most inconvenient moment to have a backbone.

I shifted the rug under my arm and started the long walk home.

CHAPTER 13

The walk back took longer than the walk in. I had to keep stopping every few feet to readjust my grip on the rug. Despite being the smallest one, it was still that awkward size that was just too big to be carried under one arm. It always needed an extra hand to keep it from slipping down. I had to keep switching positions—over my shoulder, under my armpit, pressed against my hip—all the way back to the cottage.

By the time I got in I was a sweating mess.

At least I'd figured out the hot water so I could wash my pits.

I sank onto my living room floor and listened out for my neighbour. Back to silence again. Good. I wiped the sweat off my face. I should probably stop thinking about her. Maybe that would make the noises, when they occurred, less annoying.

I stood up and pondered the fireplace between the two houses. I wondered again if she was nocturnal. Maybe that explained why she was always so noisy during the night and never in the day. I remembered how she hung back in the doorway to her home. Maybe she was sensitive to daylight.

You were going to stop thinking about her.

Ugh. I shook out my hands. I needed to focus on making this house my home. I returned to the rolled-up rug I'd dumped by the entrance. I wrestled with the plastic ties for a few minutes before I admitted defeat. I needed a pair of scissors or a knife. Neither of which I'd thought to bring with me. I rummaged again through the drawers in the kitchen finding only musty liners and dried-out woodlouse carcasses. All the cutlery I'd found so far—both forks and the spoon—lay in the sink. How was I going to open up the rug?

I looked to the ceiling.

Of course. The axe.

I recovered the axe from the bed, still tangled up in my dressing gown, and brought it downstairs. Carefully, I nicked the plastic ties with its shining, still-new edge. The ties popped off one by one, and the rug sluggishly relaxed out of its tight curl. Okay, maybe this would be good. Maybe this would be cozy and cute and everything I'd been dreaming of for my cottage. With growing excitement, I took a hold of the fluffy edges and flicked the rug all the way open.

It flopped onto the floor with an anti-climactic *fwap*.

I leant back on my heels. The rug wasn't just small, it was tiny! Barely a metre long. It looked ludicrous in the middle of the living room. Like a doormat. A coaster. A postage stamp. I didn't know a rug could make a room look simultaneously too big and too small. I tried stretching it a little, but there was next to no give. That was as big as the rug was going to get.

I sat back down, defeated.

I should have taken the receipt.

Stupid, stubborn…

Maybe it would look better if I moved it in front of the fireplace. I wished I could ask someone for a second opinion. Now would be a great time to have some girlfriends over to share a bottle of wine and laugh at my stupidity.

You'd need to make some friends first.

I lay my head down on the rug. The cottage felt so still and empty. I turned my head to the fireplace. I wondered if my neighbour was lonely, living out here on her own like this. Or did she prefer life this way?

Maybe I should invite her out tonight, I thought. *Learn her name. Make up for the awkwardness of yesterday.*

Yes, that was a good idea. Perhaps I could help her out of her shell. Perhaps she'd be grateful someone finally saw her. Perhaps, thanks to me, she'd make friends, start dating, find her future partner. I imagined myself sat at the top table on her wedding day, all of her smiling friends around her as she gave a speech. 'Of course,' she'd say, 'none of this would have happened if my good friend Tamsin hadn't managed to drag me out of the house!' We'd laugh. We'd toast each other. We'd dance to some cheesy pop songs, coloured disco lights catching in our hair.

By the time I was imagining myself keeping an eye on her children in the back garden, I was running late.

I checked my phone, swore, pulled myself up off the floor and quickly made some pasta. I ran up to the bedroom to change, saucepan in hand, picking at penne with my fingers.

I spent longer than I should have selecting an outfit. I'd donated most of my nicer clothes in my rush to be gone, the waxed black trousers and the white blouse among them. I'd figured I wouldn't need them where I was going. I'd prioritized practicality and warmth, but I was missing my impractical dresses now. I picked out a clean pair of jeans and one of my less creased tops: a pine green long-sleeve made of lighter fabric. I hated being stuck with 'jeans and a nice top', but it was the only good option I had. Then I thought, if I was just going with jeans and a nice top, I might as well crack out the Aran jumper. I fished it out of my suitcase. It was a lovely cream woollen jumper, beautifully made with intricate cabling. I'd been saving it for a 'nice' occasion, but all of my occasions back in Edinburgh had either been too posh for just a jumper or not quite 'nice' enough to warrant it. So, it had lived on a shelf, untouched for years. It even still had its tags. Not anymore. I bit the tags off and pulled the jumper on over my head. There, now I looked the part. A proper countryside person.

Once dressed, I rushed out of 1b and hopped over to the door of 1a. On her doorstep, I raised my fist to knock and… were those hanging baskets trailing pretty little flowers? I was sure they hadn't been there earlier. I stalled for a moment, arrested by the sudden appearance of those flowers. Then I remembered the dark expanse inside, the barely seen face, the lank hair, the single watery eye. I started to reconsider the idea I'd spent so much time congratulating myself for.

What if she was left alone out here for a reason?

I retracted my fist and backed away from the door, hoping she couldn't see me from her living room window.

Then I left for the village on my own.

CHAPTER 14

I MARCHED BACK into town in the cooling air, arms tightly crossed over my body. Only Scotland could feel both muggy and cold at once. The mid-May sky didn't darken. It just became paler. A cornflower twilight hung overhead as the trees became silhouettes. Burnt-out matchsticks.

I rubbed my thumbs along my shoulders.

The brighter nights of the year had always held such a pervasive sense of 'ending' to me. *This is it*, they seem to say. *There will be nothing more. It's over.* I remembered lying alone in my bed as a child, watching the sunlight fade, suddenly terrified that I would never see it again. A windy cliffside in the setting sun. A yellow kite high in the sky. Two golden-haired girls laughing. The whole world drawing further and further away until it was just me, alone in the dark, forever.

I shook my head and uncrossed my arms.

No. I wasn't going to do that anymore. No more ruminating. No more worrying over every tiny detail looking for the one that's wrong. I was going to focus on the now. I was going to be friendly and sociable. I was going to be happy.

I was going to be better.

When I got back into Carlinsrest, I followed the directions Rowan had given me. I walked past Maggie's Café twice before finding the right small alley. It was a thin path that ran a shortcut between the main street and the street that held the hardware and supplies store. It definitely looked like the kind of place locals went to hide.

I turned left and found a courtyard, half paved and half cobbled, bordered with pots and trellises holding a smattering of hardy flowers and creepers. At the opposite end of the courtyard was a set of lead-lined windows. They had panes of that old-fashioned glass with a ripple effect, as if someone had dropped a pebble in a square pond. The kind that made everything seen through them look all wibbly-wobbly. The light from the windows warmly lit a couple of smokers chatting in the paling evening outside, their pints—in those old-style glasses with the handles—perched atop an upturned barrel. A few kegs lined the wall and a scraggly bay tree stood guard by a green wooden door with a small stained-glass window. Above the door, two light fittings illuminated a line of tarnished-brass-effect plastic letters reading "The C_ urtyard". The small metal studs where the "o" had once sat were still embedded in the grey stone wall.

So that's what Rowan had said: 'Curtyard'.

An inside joke. An inside joke of which I was now a part. This was definitely the place. I hope I'd dressed right. The smokers silently nodded to me—as if I were a local already!— as I made my way inside. I had the distinct feeling that I wasn't just stepping into a pub. I was stepping into my new life.

The Curtyard was warm and loud, a haven from the clinging damp and the gloom outside. People drank and gossiped in clusters around the small bar. Rows of spirits and optics lined the mirrored wall behind it. On the top shelf, a variety of china zebras looked down at the drinkers. Kissing zebras, drunk zebras, zebras doing ballet, zebras wearing sunglasses. Beneath this stripy zoo, hung up on a hook next to the bell that I assumed called time, was the Curtyard's missing 'o': a circle of brass-coloured plastic, chipped at the edges, with a small handwritten note beneath reading: *£10 for 3 tosses.*

I watched as someone handed over a note and tried to throw the 'o' over the rows of whisky bottles. After failing to land on any of the flashier malts, he was slapped on the back and given a double of a cheap blend.

To the right, tables clustered around a darts board and booths lined the wall. All the furniture was made of old dark wood, and the walls were decorated with green wallpaper reminiscent of the pine forests on the hills outside. A wagon wheel had been repurposed into a low chandelier with a rim of large, dusty bulbs—the ones with the wire filaments that hipsters loved so much these days.

To the left a long seating area led to a rustic stone fireplace. Sat by the hearth was a scuffed wing chair and a power-assisted wheelchair. Inhabiting these chairs were the elderly couple I'd met yesterday on the bridge. I blinked in surprise. It was definitely them. The lady was still conked out, a line of spit glinting on her chin in the wagon wheel light. The old man bent over to pour some of his beer in the collie's water bowl, then leant back in his chair and brought the same glass up to his lips in a slow, careful movement. I thought of the two fifty-pound notes I'd rescued for him earlier, and wondered if they were now being used to get a dog drunk.

A voice called from one of the booths behind me.

"Hey, Tamsin! Over here."

Rowan was sat at a table by the window.

Next to him was the sullen-faced man from the antiques shop.

I stopped in my tracks. No. It couldn't be. He wasn't Rowan's phone-alert-obsessed other half, was he? He glanced up at me coolly, did a doubletake then mouthed a swearword. Oh God. I couldn't back out now. Rowan had already waved me over. I forced a smile to my face and walked to the booth, praying they hadn't just been discussing me. The sullen-faced man took a sip of his beer and looked out the window. Rowan got up from his seat, only to awkwardly sit back down again as I arrived.

"You found the place alright then."

"Yeah, thanks." Rowan's manner toward me seemed unchanged. Maybe his boyfriend hadn't shared my faux pas from the antiques shop yet. There was only one thing for it. I had to make a good *second* impression. I turned to the sullen-faced man. "Hi, I'm Tamsin. I'm new here."

"I can see that," said the man.

Rowan gave him a nudge. "This is my partner, Fergus. He works at the—"

"The antiques place," I said.

"Oh." Rowan looked between us. "You've already met. Amazing."

Fergus nodded tersely.

"Hi, Gus." I put out a hand.

"Fergus," he corrected sternly and looked away.

I retracted my hand. "Sorry. Fergus."

"Tamsin," Rowan continued, "has just moved into the Sgàthan Sìth cottage."

Fergus turned back to me, suddenly interested.

"Sgàthan Sìth?"

My hopes raised.

"Yeah. I'm in 1b. There's… someone else in 1a."

"I didn't realise it was two houses." Rowan looked at Fergus. "Was it always split like that?"

Fergus shrugged. I thought of the sealed door in the basement.

"Looks like," I said. "We share a chimney, I think, but we have separate front doors. I've not been inside 1a, but I'm guessing it looks like mine, but backwards. Mirrored."

"They used to have long terraces like that all over," said Fergus. "For farmhands, then for seasonal workers." He glanced down into his pint glass. "Now they put all the workers in caravans and sell the buildings to rich English cunts for second homes."

Rowan cleared his throat in Fergus' direction. Fergus rolled his eyes. I smiled, determined to be undeterred.

"Well, not this one," I said. "I'm here to stay."

Fergus cast a cold look at me.

"Aye, course you are."

"Fergus is right," said Rowan quickly and a little too brightly. "They're probably farmhand cottages."

"I didn't see any farm buildings close by," I said.

"Probably an old farm then." Rowan turned again to Fergus. "Do you know whose farm they used to belong to?"

Fergus lowered his voice, "Well, it's a bit of an old story."

Ok, this felt a bit more promising. Sharing stories. I leaned forward.

"Yeah, Rowan was saying something about that—"

"It's just had few people live there over the years," Rowan leapt in. "No one ever seems to stay but—"

"You know the mound it's set on?" said Fergus.

I nodded.

"That's a hollow hill."

"What's a hollow hill?"

"It's one of the ancestral homes of the Fair Folk. A fairy hill. Story goes the man who built those cottages wasn't from around here, so he didn't know he should leave the hill be. He was starting a goat farm to make his own leather. He was an excellent leatherworker, but he wanted to control the entire process from start to finish. Herding, culling, tanning, the lot. One day, the man's youngest son disappeared right out of his bed. They looked all over for him and eventually found the boy in a small clearing in the woods. But something was wrong with him. He couldn't sleep, couldn't laugh, couldn't talk. Just stared. There was talk that the Fair Folk had stolen the boy away and replaced him with a soulless double. Just as the man was deciding what to do with the boy, he disappeared.

The whole family died of cholera the next summer. The man's final words were, *I never should have built those damned cottages*. Now whoever lives there has terrible luck."

I gripped the table.

"Really?"

"Nope." Fergus's face split into a grin. "I had you there, didn't I?"

"What?"

Rowan rolled his eyes. "'Sake, Ferg. He's telling you stories. Even had me with that one for a moment there."

My face felt hot. Fergus shrugged.

"Your house probably belonged to a smaller farm, back before they all got bought up by the larger ones," said Fergus. "Gobbled up to make them bigger and bigger. Digging up the hedges and turning the patchwork into one big boring blanket of rapeseed or potato."

The table went quiet.

I thought of the Sgàthan Sìth cottages. Just the two little houses left, holding hands together on the hill, like abandoned conjoined twins, forever reflecting each other until the hotel chain and the digger comes to mow them down.

"Well, I hope you feel at home soon," said Rowan. "I know what it's like to move to a small village. Especially one filled with grumpy locals like Fergus, here."

Fergus huffed. I forced a smile for all Rowan's trying. I hated that he had to try.

Perhaps you shouldn't have come.

As the thought entered my head, *she* walked in the door.

I looked up and saw a face in the crowd, smiling in my direction. I recognised the lank hair and the round watery eye. I quickly turned away and tried not to make eye contact.

It was the woman from next door. My neighbour. She was here.

And she was coming this way.

I snuck a second glance as she filtered between people. Her hair looked half wet. She'd probably only just stepped out of the shower before heading out. She wore a white blouse that fit her like a potato sack, and weird, tacky black trousers. Not that it mattered with the way she hugged her arms around her chest. So defensive. As if she were trying to hide inside herself, tucked away in her own ribcage, peeking out between the bones.

But her eyes were bright and wide and trained on me. Unblinking, open, hopeful. And her smile. The smile was new. A weird, wide, toothy smile.

I slid down into my seat.

I remembered offering to pick her something up from the village yesterday morning.

You're very generous.

Guilt gripped me. I wondered if she knew I'd ditched her.

Out the corner of my eye I saw her hover over Rowan's shoulder.

Oh no, I knew that hover. I'd used that hover while waiting to be noticed by chatting colleagues. I knew the dilemma: you need to talk to someone, but you don't want to be rude. So, you decide to wait until they're done talking. But they're never done talking. They keep going. And you're just standing there attentively, like a lemon, a big stupid grin on your face, waiting, and they won't stop. And it's slowly becoming more awkward, the longer you stand there, far too close to them now, and clearly listening but not saying anything. You know you should have just made yourself known from the start. Said, 'Sorry to interrupt, but…' Said something, anything. Not just stand there, smiling, like a massive creep. Like she was doing now, my neighbour, the wide smile straining on her face, clearly not reaching her wide eyes. God, I could see the whites all around her irises. She was terrified. She was terrifying. Had I looked like that? I'd always wondered if the folks I'd hovered next to, waiting for a good time to speak, had noticed me hovering there. I'd hoped they'd been unaware, but now I saw how stupid that was. The people they were speaking with were able to see me. I was standing right in front of them. They were probably very aware. As they continued on with their talk, they were probably thinking:

Oh dear God, she's behind me, isn't she? What does she want? Why does she have to be so bloody weird? Does she need something? Or—please no—does she want to be involved in the conversation and is doing it in the most uncomfortable way possible? Is she hoping we'll all feel too awkward and include her? I knew she was odd, but that's just manipulative. At first, I pitied her, but now I fucking hate her. Maybe if I just keep ignoring her, she'll get the message and fuck off.

Rowan stopped mid-sentence.

"Are you alright?" he asked.

"Fine," I said, too fast, too loud, too direct.

He flinched, blinking.

Fergus raised his eyebrows.

I looked at my lap.

"Sorry." I shrugged, laughed at myself. "I was a little distracted by—"

I looked up and my neighbour had disappeared. I scanned the pub for her, but The Curtyard was getting busier. People crowded the bar and voices bubbled around me. I craned my neck to see around all the many bodies, thinking I'd caught sight of her limp hair or her baggy blouse, but I'd lost her. It was like losing track of a spider.

Underneath the unease, there was that strange sense of familiarity again, that thing I couldn't quite put my finger on. That nagging sense that I had seen her before.

The table went very quiet.

Fergus drummed his fingers on the wood. He gave Rowan a pointed look then got up from the table.

"Shall we get some more drinks, then?"

"Oh, um, yeah. I'll help you with them," said Rowan.

He followed Fergus to the bar before I could protest.

I smiled politely, but if anyone had bothered to look closely, they would have seen my eyes blaring, 'please don't leave me alone'.

Then, as if right in my ear, real enough to feel cold breath on my cheek, the question again:

Do you think you're a good person?

CHAPTER 15

THANKFULLY THE PUB was too loud and crowded for anyone to notice me jumping at shadows.

I rubbed where my heart felt like it was pounding out of my chest. I forcefully slowed my breathing. It had to be the stress of the move, the lack of proper sleep, the lack of proper food. I patted my sweating forehead with the backs of my hands.

Calm down, Tamsin. I scowled at myself. *You'll cause a scene.*

I managed a few seconds pretending to look around with curiosity at the bar, before getting out my phone and pretending I'd got a notification. I looked up again to check for my neighbour. No sign. I scrolled through my socials. Nothing new. I looked up again. Still no sign of my neighbour. Where had she gone? Maybe she was meeting friends. Maybe she worked here. Maybe she was just giving me a friendly smile, a hello, a welcome to the community and I'd just read it unkindly.

A group of older men laughed by the bar.

My dad said I had a habit of thinking the worst of people. He said it was hard to talk to me sometimes. I always looked like I was cringing before a slap. It made people feel bad.

I switched between different apps on my phone, not really looking at any of them.

I couldn't help it though. Some people just felt… dangerous somehow. Like Marsha in accounts who everyone liked except me. Until it was found out she'd been spiking people's drinks at work events.

I didn't always get it right, like the time I'd slapped the hand of a man on the bus. He'd just been reaching for the stop bell, not my chest.

I wanted to be better, to relax, to be easy-going. But it was hard to relax when sometimes your worst suspicious are correct.

I spotted Rowan and Fergus, talking close together at the bar, lips to ears back and forth. Rowan was rubbing Fergus's shoulder. The touch was tender and encouraging. Fergus was shrugging and avoiding eye contact. Were they talking about what happened with me and the rug?

Fergus shot a look my way.

I quickly looked back at my phone. Yep, totally talking about me.

Shit. Shit fucking shit.

I looked at the bare table in front of me. That was the problem. I hadn't had a drink yet. That would loosen me up. Oh, but Fergus and Rowan had already got up to get drinks. They didn't say they were getting me one, though. I chewed my lip. It was probably presumptuous to assume they'd were getting a drink for me, too. And they hadn't asked me what I wanted. And if I went to the bar then I wouldn't be a sitting duck for my weird neighbour. That settled it. I got up, briefly worried about losing the table, then took off my jumper and lay it across the tabletop. I hoped that would do—and that my Aran jumper wouldn't get nicked—and headed for the other end of the bar to Rowan and Fergus.

Happy, warm bodies crowded around me. Hands patted backs. Red cheeks creased with laughter. Fingers pinched the fabric of a new coat or jumper or scarf, prompting communal nodding about how nice it was. I shrank myself around them, squeezing past the shoulders of the regulars, to get to the bar and see what beers were on offer. Each brass tap wore a colourful shield illustrating the ale they promised.

The barmaid turned to me next.

"What'll it be, hen?" she asked.

She was sporting a jumper featuring a fuzzy, sparkly zebra wearing a colourful garland of flowers. The stripy audience up in the balcony section suddenly made a lot more sense.

I pointed to a cardboard shield with a thick-lined illustration of two figures embracing. One figure was a cool and serene blue, with a calm and steadfast expression. The other was bright red and seemed to be screaming in rage or pain.

A nod. A clean glass procured. Interaction successful.

See, I thought to myself, *just don't overthink things*.

"Fantastic illustration, eh?" The barmaid smiled. "It's a guest ale from the borders."

I looked again at that screaming enraged face.

"What's it referencing?"

"Tam Lin." The barmaid noticed my nonplussed expression. "You've not heard the story of Tam Lin?"

I shook my head.

The barmaid pushed a wave of greying blonde hair behind her ear. "It's this folktale about two lovers. The man gets stolen away by the faerie queen, and the woman who loved him goes looking for him. She wins him back by holding onto him while the faerie queen changes him into wild animals and heavy stones and flaming fireballs."

"How did she manage that?"

"Love, of course," said the barmaid, like I was stupid.

My face flushed and the barmaid turned away to pump the pint.

To be loved that much. It seemed unreasonable. Something you only hear of in fairy tales.

"Careful with that shadow, young lady."

I looked over my shoulder. The old man who'd farted at me on the bridge yesterday morning was waiting in the queue behind me.

"I'm sorry?" I said.

His hunched back meant he had to peer up at me at an angle, eyes glinting over the top of his thick glasses. Those two wisps of white hair escaped the sides of his flat cap and arched up toward the ceiling.

"You'll have to have Wendy look at it. It's running ragged at the seams." He wagged a finger at the air around me. "If it splits then, oh ho, there'll be tears at bedtime!"

What the hell was he on about? I carefully controlled my expression.

"Thanks for the heads up," I said, turning to check on the progress of my drink, telepathically urging the barmaid to hurry it up.

"You're at Sgàthan Sìth, aren't you?"

Now he had my attention. His eyes twinkled at the mention of my cottage.

"Uh, one of them," I said. "How did you know?"

He laughed. "There's not much that escapes my attention, m'dear."

I had a thought.

"Do you happen to know my neighbour?"

He raised his wild, white eyebrows. I elaborated.

"The woman in 1a? Fine, longish hair. Seems quiet. I saw her here earlier, but—" I looked around again just in case. "I think she left."

At that the old man's shoulders sank dramatically, as if clowning disappointment for a hidden audience.

"Oh dear. Hanging by a thread then, I see." Then he suddenly brightened and jovially slapped my shoulder. "Good luck!"

There was a hard clunk on the bar.

"Here you go, hen."

The barmaid delivered my pint, the overflow gently running down the side of the glass. The colour of it really was something, a deep russet against the dark lacquered wood of the bar and the brass drip trays. I turned back to the old man, only to find he'd already returned to the fireplace. I blinked in surprise. I'd never thought a man like him could be so... sprightly.

You in the habit of patronising older folks, are you?

I quickly gathered my drink and retreated to the booth where Rowan and Fergus were waiting. With three pints.

"Oh," said Rowan, noting my drink.

Oh shit. So, they were getting drinks for all of us. *Stupid stupid stupid.*

"Sorry, I didn't realise."

"Told you we shouldn't have just assumed," said Fergus.

"It's okay. Our fault." Rowan waved a hand. "We didn't ask what you wanted—"

Fergus rolled his eyes and reached over. "It's fine. I'll have it."

I quickly pulled the second pint to me and took a sip of it. Caramel and citrus, pretty standard. Then I took a sip of the Tam Lin beer. It was sweeter and maltier than I was expecting. Something about the rusty red colour had made me expect an iron tang to it.

Fergus stared at me. Rowan leaned back in the booth.

Oh God, why did I do that? It was the rug all over again. What had got me feeling so territorial lately?

"Just saved me from having to get up for a while," I said.

Fergus shook his head. I straightened up.

"Besides, I think I need it after my run-in with that old guy by the fire."

Both Rowan and Fergus's eyebrows raised.

"He spoke to you?" they said in unison.

I looked between the two of them. "Yes?"

"He's, ah…" Rowan looked at Fergus, wordlessly checking something with him.

Fergus leaned forward.

"He's mad. Him and his wife. Can't make hide nor hair of anything that comes out of their mouths. He was convinced one year I was hiding some sort of pirate treasure or something. He'd chase me round the village, badgering me to share. Nutter." Fergus nodded his head toward the snoring woman. "She's not too bad, but only because she's asleep most of the time."

"They only come here during the summer when I'm busy with the forestry," said Rowan. "Apparently, the lady wilts a bit during the warmer months."

I turned to look at the two of them sitting by the fire. The old man was tenderly adjusting the hood over the woman's snoring face.

Fergus continued. "You know, he worked on Dolly. Some sort of consultant."

It took me a moment to realise what he was referring to.

"The sheep? The cloned sheep?" I asked.

"If you can call that monstrosity a sheep."

Rowan rolled his eyes.

"It's just a sheep, pal. No different from a twin."

"It is different," he stabbed the table with his finger. "It doesn't have a soul."

Rowan tucked his chin down and looked up at Fergus through his eyebrows, as if trying to peer under the blanket of madness he was hiding under.

"You saying sheep have souls now?"

Fergus hissed through his teeth. "You know what I mean. It's not right. And think what they've opened up now. A whole Pandora's box. They could clone anything. Anyone. All they'd need is a drop of your blood."

A shiver raced up my spine.

"He's still at it! They say he goes around in tunnels under Carlinsrest, pricking people with pins and collecting their blood, to make his own version of the village, a little toy town under the ground."

I became very aware of the pinprick in my heel.

Rowan shook his head. "He's pulling your leg again."

Fergus broke out into a wide grin. He nodded at me.

"Got ya, again!"

I made the face of a laugh, but no sound came out of it. I sipped one of my pints to hide it.

"He did work on the whole Dolly thing though. That bit's true. Point is, he's mad. As for the lady." Fergus sniffed. "She's a witch."

CHAPTER 16

FERGUS WENT ON with his stories, though I didn't remember much of what he said because at some point I finished the two pints in front of me. I felt good—well, at least not totally and completely inhuman—so I ordered two more pints, to keep the joke going. I was doing it! I was becoming someone better! Someone easy-going, outgoing, warm. And then I had a few drinks more, though I couldn't say what they were. I vaguely remembered Rowan getting another alert on his phone, then bringing a jug of water to the table. Around midnight, my inebriation reached its peak and my happy buzz quickly turned to dizzying nausea. Time to leave. I hadn't seen my neighbour since her entrance, so I snuck out of The Curtyard before she could catch me for an awkward walk back to the Sgàthan Sìth cottages. With any luck I'd be back and asleep before she started up her nightly racket. I'm not even sure if I said goodbye to Rowan.

I staggered home, walking alone in the dark, something I

would never do sober. But the alcohol had made me bolder, braver, stupider.

This is going to be my home, I thought. *I'm not going to be afraid of my own home.*

How I must have looked to someone—or something—watching, unseen. Drunk woman weaving in and out of the road, swerving into the hedgerow more than once. No streetlights. No moon. Only the navy sky overhead, dotted with faraway stars, and the shadow of the woods beyond the quiet fields. In the still air, my shambling footsteps echoed for miles.

I sifted through the conversations from the pub in the filter of my growing post-drink paranoia.

God, why had I claimed that second pint so quickly? And taken a sip of both! Like I was licking it to claim it was mine. It was Fergus's fault. What the fuck was his problem? Why had I let him rattle me so much? Ugh, I need to ignore arseholes. That's what you're supposed to do with arseholes, ignore them. Because they feed off… they feed off… Shit. What did I just step in? Shit? Cow shit? Horse shit? Sheep shit? Some kind of shit. That's the countryside though. Full of shit. Just like me, har har! What was that about the old guy? Dolly the Sheep. I saw Dolly at the museum. Dead. Stuffed and dead. Spinning on a little turntable, round and round and round and…

I vomited, bracing myself against the hedgerow. Only the hedge had turned hard and smooth. The back end of a car. Oh no, I'd thrown up right under the back wheel. That would be gross for someone in the morning. I wiped my sleeve across my mouth and looked around. I hoped no one saw. There was no one. Just a tree full of fluttering paper seeds. I edged my way up the side of the car, trying not to alert the car's owner.

Ugh. Why do my sleeves feel damp?

I wiped my hands down my jumper. I saw the car's windscreen. Totally smashed in.

Probably abandoned. What a relief!

I shuffled away, fell up a hill twice, and found myself at my front step.

I wrestled my key out of my jeans pocket. On the third try I got it into the keyhole, but it wouldn't turn.

"The fuck?"

I tried a few more times, rattling the door handle violently, before realising the handle felt different to before. I looked up. The door said '1a'. I almost fell back down the step.

"Sorry," I said, "wrong house."

The dark windows stared down blankly at me.

A laugh burst from my mouth.

Wrong house!

I creased over, laughing into my sleeves. Ugh, they were sticky. I clapped a hand over my mouth to make myself quiet. A laugh escaped around the seal of my hands, making a delicious fart noise. Just like the one the old man had done yesterday. I laughed harder and collapsed to my knees. I shhh-ed myself. I got up, one finger on my lips, the other hand waving an apology to my neighbour, unseen. I stumbled up to the right door and got the key in first time.

I flicked on the lights and flinched at their brightness. At least the electricity worked now. Still, all this light after so much darkness made me feel vulnerable somehow. My windows were a beacon. My location was lit up on the map.

I looked for curtains to pull closed over the living room window, but there were none.

Fuck's sake.

Another thing to sort. Another thing to buy. I made a note in my phone.

CUYRTASIN

God, it was cold. Goosebumps stood to attention over my arms. It was colder inside than out. Old stone buildings. No cloud cover above. I touched the iron radiator. Cold. I hadn't added more wood to the boiler today. With a sigh, I snatched my axe from the sheepskin rug and headed into the basement.

The stairs down swayed around me as I descended. I groped about for the railing, clinging on once I'd found it. I tripped and flung my arm out with the axe to steady myself. The blade sank into the stair next to my foot. I froze, then I laughed and yanked it back out of the wood.

It took me a moment to realise why it was so dark. I'd forgotten to turn on the light. I groaned and looked back up the stairs. Well, I was down here now. And I could see—sort of—from the light coming in from the stairs. Besides, I'd just walked home in the dark and nothing happened. It couldn't possibly be worse inside my own home.

I swung open the door of the boiler, banging it against the metal body of the water tank. I scooped the old ash out onto the floor with my hands, then mashed in a handful of tinder. At some point the tinder was alight, though I couldn't remember reaching for a match. I stared at it for a while. The flame dancing in its little cradle of paper and chipped wood. It was bright. I was still cold. I needed more wood. I reached inside the bag of firewood for a log. I jammed it a few times against the too small opening before remembering I had to cut it. That's okay. I had the right tool for this job.

If I was sober, I would have known what a terrible idea this was. But I wasn't sober. I was deliciously uninhibited. I was a 'Woman Who Could Take Care Of Herself.' I was a 'Woman Who Could Chop Wood.'

Are you chopping or splitting? Rowan had said.

Splitting, please.

I balanced the log on the concrete floor and raised my axe. I split the log in two on the first try. I whooped. Why wasn't I able to show this side of me to the people I met? I set another log on the floor. It was hard to be my best self when people like Fergus were smirking at me.

Or when people like my neighbour were hovering close by.

I split the log.

What did she have to hover for? What the fuck was with that creepy smile?

I set up another log.

Maybe she was just a bit odd. I'm a bit odd. I'd still want someone to be kind and include me.

I split the log.

But still, it was her that had made me act weird. I'd been fine until she showed up.

I set up another log.

What if she did that at every community event? I regretted introducing myself. A hot feeling rose into my cheeks.

I split the log.

The room turned slowly around my woozy head. I was starting to feel sick again from swinging the axe. But I kept splitting logs. More than I needed. That high tone rose in my ears. I split the logs more and more violently. I thought about how my neighbour had dressed. How she'd looked. How she'd behaved. I thought of all the times I'd hovered at people's desks. I thought of all the parties I'd found out about after the fact. I thought of a yellow kite above a cliff. I thought of slender fingers, nails painted hot pink. The light in the boiler had burnt out. I thrust the axe over and over into the already chopped wood, smashing it to splinters.

"Fuck you fuck you fuck you!"

Then, amidst the noise and violence, I was filled with the sudden awareness of something behind me.

The hairs on the back of my neck stood to attention. My brain flooded my body with adrenaline. My sobriety returned to me suddenly. Everything became very sharp and clear. Something was here. Something was behind me. Any other time I would have startled or frozen or screamed or ran.

This time, I turned on my heel and swung the axe.

My body moved, quick and lithe, my arms so suddenly taut, so suddenly animal. Muscle swept the axe head through the air, an elegant silver arrow, a shooting star.

A wet *shunk-crack!*

My axe found its home wedged into the left-hand curve of my neighbour's forehead.

I stopped still. Her wide, watery eyes stared at me, white, so white, in the gloom of the basement. Her lank hair was plastered to her face. Her hand was still reaching out toward me, fingers scant millimetres from my back.

Behind her, the door in the wall was open.

I froze, breath caught.

It was so dark, the blood pouring down her cheek didn't look like blood. She stumbled back. The axe, still gripped in my hands, slid out of her face with a sucking sound. The black blood glistened along the blade like a lumpy oil slick.

She fell back through the open door in the basement, disappearing into the darkness of 1a Sgàthan Sìth beyond. Then the door swung shut.

INTO
THE FIRE

CHAPTER 17

I DIDN'T REMEMBER much after my neighbour fell through the door.

I remembered throwing myself up the stairs. I remembered piling what belongings I had up against the bedroom door. I remembered the night sky through the window, swaying in my inebriation, and then darkness.

When I woke, I was gifted a few seconds of grace, of just lying in my bed in the soft light of morning, of feeling my way back into the world, toes and fingertips first.

Then I remembered what I had done.

I sat up suddenly and immediately regretted it. A stab of pain shot through my skull. God, after everything last night I'd almost forgotten about the pub. And all that beer.

Groaning, I tucked myself into the far corner of the mattress and hugged my knees to my chest. I was still wearing last night's clothes. My beautiful Aran jumper, lying limply beside the mattress, stank of vomit. My head swam. My body convulsed with my heaving breaths, fast, faster still, heart a pounding drum. Oh God, oh God, what had I done now?

It's not my fault, I told myself. *I couldn't be responsible. I wasn't with it. I was drunk. It was dark. She snuck up behind me. What was she even doing in my basement?*

I could see my defence. I was home, chopping wood, someone surprised me in the dark. I startled. I swung. I didn't expect there to be anyone in my house. It was self-defence. It was a horrible accident. I could see the police officer nod sympathetically, the jury look at me with understanding. A horrible tragedy. No one at fault.

I rubbed my chest.

They wouldn't see my thoughts. The thoughts I was having just before it happened. How wound up I'd been. How angry I was. Angry at the smirking faces behind computers. Angry at Fergus's sneer. Angry at how my neighbour had hovered and grinned. Angry at how I'd let her get to me. Angry at how I'd probably frightened off Rowan and all my chances at settling in here and leaving my past behind.

I shook my head, wishing I could just refuse it all away.

I could still feel how the handle of the axe juddered up my arm with the force of my blows as I split wood.

Was it really an accident? Or did you just snap?

I held myself tighter, feeling profoundly sick.

No one would have to wonder anything, I realised. They'd only have to ask why I hadn't checked to see if she was alright.

I threw on last night's jeans and the hoodie I'd been using as a pillow and staggered downstairs.

I'd just left her. She'd fallen through the door and I'd left her. How could I do that? I paced at the top of the stairs to the basement. I'd assumed no one could open that door down there. Could I have opened it last night and checked? Even if I couldn't, I could have gone round to see if she was alright. I hadn't raised the alarm. Hadn't called an ambulance.

I'd run and left her.

My hands shook in front of me. I had to go down and try to

get in. At least to say I did. At least to be a person I could live with being. I flipped the light switch, forced myself forward, and headed down into the basement.

I prepared myself for horror, for blood and viscera.

There was nothing.

I stopped at the bottom of the stairs, convinced I was seeing wrong. Haphazardly chopped wood and jagged splinters littered the concrete floor where I'd scattered them in my frustration last night. My axe lay where I'd dropped it. The door in the wall was still sealed over. And there wasn't a drop of blood to be found.

No destruction. No gore. Just a basement, dusty and dim and cold.

I picked up the axe. No blood on the blade. I ran my fingers gently across it. A black sticky soot smeared across my fingertips, but that could easily have come from some residue on the wood or grease from the boiler.

I pressed a palm to my chest. No, I had to be sure before I gave in to relief.

I padded across the basement and felt for the edges of the door in the wall. The plaster looked and felt as sealed as ever. I pushed at the centre of the doorway, but it didn't give. It was as if it had been cemented shut, almost part of the brickwork. Aside from the fact that it clearly looked like a door, there was no indication it had ever been openable, let alone opened last night.

I scanned the floor again for any sign, a spot, a spray, of the violence I was convinced I'd committed.

A bright glint of something metallic at the centre of the concrete floor caught my eye. I knelt down to look closer.

A thick, curved needle.

I carefully picked it up with my thumb and forefinger. It was a hefty thing. Thicker than the delicate tinsel-like sewing needles in my grandmother's sewing box, it had a weight to it, a robustness. It could probably be used to sew leather. Maybe it had belonged to the leatherworker Fergus talked about. I'd assumed he'd just made the whole thing up, but clearly there was some truth to his story. I rolled the needle between my fingers and looked up at the floorboards above. That was the spot where I'd been pricked when I first arrived. No wonder it hurt so much. But this didn't explain what happened—or what I thought had happened—last night. Tucking the needle into my pocket, I went back upstairs.

I looked about the quiet house. Maybe it hadn't happened at all.

I slumped down onto the floor in the middle of the living room, not stopping until I was fully laid out across the floorboards, head finding its way to the sheepskin rug. Relief flooded my body alongside the rising nausea and growing headache.

Of course I wouldn't do something like that. It wasn't too crazy to think that I'd imagined her there. Swung at nothing in the dark. Frightened myself. I'd been half-convinced there was some monster in the basement after the pinprick in my foot. But now I had the needle in my pocket. No monsters. No blood. No bodies. Just an old needle and a hangover.

I fingered the needle in my pocket.

Had I really imagined it all? It had felt so real.

Gingerly, I turned my aching head to the wall I shared with my neighbour and listened. She was quiet again today. It was strange. That first night I could hear every creak and groan in that place as if it had been my own house.

Now this morning, silence again.

I got up and listened. Nothing.

I pressed my ear to the wall. Still nothing.

She was alright, right? Probably just sleeping off last night's pub visit. She hadn't looked like the type that got out often. Maybe she was just hungover in bed, like where I should have been in that moment.

Or maybe she's lying cold on the floor of her basement.

CHAPTER 18

I STOOD OUTSIDE her front door. The air was still, the sky was overcast and that early-summer-late-spring clamminess was already starting to cling to my clothes. My tacky, unwashed, post-drinking skin felt thoroughly gross. I was minging. Bogging. I wished I'd had another bath first. A planter full of tumbling begonias had been added to my neighbour's window sill. Surely that was enough evidence she was fine.

Unless she put it up yesterday after I left for the pub.

I peered through the window into the living room. The net curtain occluded much of what I could see. A shadow of furniture here and there. But no neighbour.

I backed away from the two houses and looked up to see if I could spot movement from the upper windows. Again, I don't know whether it was the curtains or the reflection of the light grey skies, but I couldn't get a sense of life within.

I checked my phone. It was eleven in the morning. She'd be up by now.

I wiped my face with my hands.

I should probably do something. Break down the door? Smash in a window?

Could try knocking first.

I raised my fist and then wavered over the wood. Just like I did last night when I decided not to invite her to the pub.

When you decided to ditch her.

Shut up.

Even though you knew what that felt like.

Shut up.

Hypocrite.

I stepped back from the door.

If I knocked and I got no response, I'd have to break the door down. I didn't want to break the door down. I didn't even know if I could. Especially in my hungover state. Also, just because she didn't respond didn't mean she was lying on the floor of her basement with an axe wound in her face. There was every chance she'd left the house early. Yes, gone into town for a restorative fry-up at one of the pubs. Or perhaps she'd never made it home. Maybe she'd got lucky and copped off with someone else for the night.

I remembered her awkward stance, her lank hair and strange expressions. Not to mention that weird grin. It didn't feel likely to me that she'd got laid.

I scratched the back of my sweating, itching neck

Better to wait. Yes. Wait and see if my neighbour emerged or returned home.

I went back inside.

It was deathly quiet without the sound of her rummaging about next door. I tidied the splintered wood into the boiler and set it going. Once the water had a chance to heat up, I went upstairs and washed last night off my hair and skin, hoping it would help give me some clarity or soften the churning in my gut. It did neither, but I felt cleaner. In body at least.

I threw my ruined Aran jumper into the ancient washing machine in the kitchen, only to remember that I hadn't bought any washing tabs yet. I didn't have the headspace to worry about that right now. I'd sort it later.

As my hair dried, the cool humidity rediscovered my skin, replacing the post-drink sweat with a sticky gleam. I sat wrapped in my towel on the living room windowsill and watched the driveway.

No one left. No one came.

I checked my phone. No notifications. No emails. No calls. No sound from next door. The house beside me stood silent. The house around me stood silent, too. The sun was hidden behind thick grey clouds, so I couldn't tell whether it was morning or midday or afternoon or evening. Everything was still, so very still. Not like in a sense of waiting, but in a sense of there being nothing to wait for. There would never be anything to wait for ever again. That this was existence now: sitting in this house, watching out the window, until the dark came.

I checked the time again. It had been an hour. She could still be out.

Or she could be lying on the floor of her basement with an axe wound in her face.

I stood up. I should call the police.

And say what? 'Excuse me, officer, but I think I hallucinated that I brutally murdered my neighbour with an axe and now she's not answering her door. Can you go in and check she's alright?'

I could already see the sideways looks, the concerned conversations, the gentle suggestion that perhaps I should speak to someone.

Or they could go inside her house and find her lying on the floor of her basement with an axe wound in her face.

A trembling grew in my limbs. My hands fidgeted in an attempt to release the uncomfortable build-up of energy, but it was no good. My stomach cramped and my thoughts darted about my skull as if each one was a bee and my head was an angry hive. I ran from the window and threw up into the kitchen sink.

Too much drinking.

It always did this to me. I was never any good at it. Now it was filling my head with awful visions and paranoia. No more alcohol. I'd stick to cranberry juice and everything would be fine.

Would it?

I leant on the sink and wiped my mouth.

If you're not going to knock and you're not going to break down the door and you're not going to phone the police, then what exactly are you going to do?

I pushed myself up.

My neighbour was just out for breakfast or visiting a friend or doing her shopping or a million and one more likely things than lying dead in her basement.

I would go into the village, find her and then everything would be fine.

CHAPTER 19

I PUT ON fresh clothes, grabbed my key and left.

The vibrating energy racing up and down my spine converted itself into a swift march up the lane. Good. Exercise it off. That's what the magazines recommended. Cut down on alcohol, and do more exercise. And eat healthy. I thought of the dry crackers I'd had for breakfast. Another thing to fix. If I was going to check around the village for my neighbour, I might as well pick up some proper food, too. Vegetables. Wholegrains. Fish. Eat myself healthy. Yes.

The thick air pulled at the scraggly locks I'd failed to gather into my ponytail. The green hills rose around me. The trees in the distance stood at attention, as if they were ancient guards or bars on a cage.

I found myself thinking about all the murderers I'd ever read about in the news. How they'd tried to cover their tracks and how clumsy and stupid they'd been. Going back to the scene of the crime. Keeping the weapon. Heading to a petrol station, plastered with CCTV cameras, to get a packet of Rolos afterwards. I'd always thought that was just a symptom of their character. If you're the kind of person stupid enough to murder someone, then you'd be stupid enough to get caught. Now I could understand why they did the stupid things they did. Because in moments like these, reality splits. In one reality you've permanently snuffed out a life, the individual spark of a person, never to be seen again by anyone they've ever loved and who ever loved them back. And in the other reality, you're still just an ordinary person, going about your day, making cups of tea, telling people about the dream you had last night, stepping in dog shit and trying to wipe it off in the long grass.

And what would happen if, say, you're not sure which one is real? How long would you last in that no man's land between the two realities? How long before you'd beg someone to tip the balance and give you the gift of horrible certainty?

But that's not what was happening to me, no. Because I was going to the village and I was going to ask after—

Wait, what was her name? I still didn't know her name. Who would I ask after around the village? Fuck's sake.

A high bleating broke me from my thoughts. I started at the sound. In the field next to me was a lamb. No, two lambs. White bodies, sweet black faces, side by side, reflecting each other perfectly. I could have put a mirror between them and got the same image. So perfect, so still, I wondered if I was looking at models, stuffed toys. A breeze licked the sweat off the back of my neck and a shiver ran a finger down my back. I don't know whether it was the hangover paranoia or the horrible uncertainty I'd been carrying all morning, but the animals felt off. Like finding a straight line in nature. I stepped up to the dry stone wall to get a closer look.

The lambs bleated in unison. Strangled and in stereo.

My heart leapt in my chest at the sound.

Their identical amber eyes stared at me.

My skin itched in their gaze. What was it with sheep and staring? Dogs, too. Whenever I'd reached out a hand to pet a dog, it had always just seemed to stare at me.

They just don't know you, their owners always said.

But they do know, don't they? Animals and small children. I figured it was because they hadn't learned shame. They hadn't learned that it was better to swallow down your instincts. They hadn't learned to worry about being rude or unfriendly or unkind. When they felt that someone was 'not quite right' they would just stare.

The lambs stared right at me.

They knew. They could smell it on me.

I pulled down my sleeves and looked out over the field. It was empty except for the two lambs. The paddock rose to a small hill then dipped back down and out of view. Perhaps the rest of the sheep were hidden over the other side. A line of crows waited along the hedgerow ahead, watching the lambs intently.

"Where are your parents?" I asked the lambs.

They bleated at me again in unison. As one, they turned inwards, one flicking their left ear and the other flicking their right at the exact same time. Then they trotted away, left and right, right and left, in perfect synchronicity, like the world had folded in two. They toddled up over the hill and out of sight. The crows on the hedgerow cawed in delight and took to the skies, floating their ragged, shadowed selves over the crest of the hill after the tiny bodies.

A new wave of nausea swelled into my chest. My back and neck flushed, suddenly hot and sweaty. I forced the feeling down and continued along the road. I'd dallied long enough.

I needed coffee. And a bacon roll.

CHAPTER 20

THE FIRST THING that caught my eye as I crossed Bodach's Brig and walked into Carlinsrest that morning was the Celtic cross war memorial.

At the base of the memorial was a carpet of flowers. Pansies danced gaily in the breeze. Bold nasturtiums tumbled in verdant, virulent vines from polished terracotta pots. Proud fuchsia bushes shook their bright pink heads, though not a bee seemed to want to go near them. From the rood, pink, blue and purple lobelia spread in a wave down the little steps, tendrils creeping closer to the line of cafés and shops.

A young man stood staring at it while holding his squirming toddler in his arms. He saw me looking, raised an eyebrow and nodded in the direction of the flowers.

"Eye-catching, isn't it?" he said, dodging chubby fists reaching for butterflies.

"Who did it?" I asked, staring at all the sudden flowers. "Was it the WI or something?"

"I don't think so," he said. "We don't have one of those, uh, branches up here. Someone must have done it overnight. One of those guerrilla gardeners you hear of. Y'know the types. They throw seed bombs onto abandoned demolition sites and the like. Though I've never seen anything like this!"

"No," I said, hangover curdling in my stomach. "Me neither."

There was something in the brightness of the flowers, an enforced cheeriness, that felt a little… unreal.

"Someone's repainted the sign over the community centre as well." The woman who'd served me at the café—the eponymous Maggie, perhaps?— wandered over, arms crossed, apron tied round her waist. I tucked my head down, hoping not to be noticed. She frowned at the flower display. "Community centre's been closed for months, mind. Must be a newcomer."

Must be a newcomer.

I crossed my arms. I could feel eyes on me even if I couldn't see them.

"It's like something from one of those American movies," said the man.

"Aye, I could pure murder the Hallmark channel," muttered Maggie. "My pal lives in a village in the Cairngorms and not a year goes by without some melt turning up looking to open a guesthouse or a cupcake shop. Never mind the locals already have B&Bs and cafés. But dreamers don't care about that. They're so busy recreating the fantasy in their heid, they don't care about the place or the people who already live in it. Dinnae want to get involved with what's actually here. Then they get all affronted when no one's welcomed them with open arms. The locals get told they're cold and unfriendly. But who wants to be the backdrop in someone else's movie, eh?"

She shook her head.

I took in the uneasy mood around the flower display.

"Is this the first time it's happened here?" I asked.

She tapped her lips with her fingertips.

"It does remind me of something. God, must've been about twenty years ago. There used to be a playpark where the Tesco is now. It suddenly got spruced up overnight. The slide and the swing set were brightly painted, right over the rust. And there were footballs everywhere. Something felt odd about it, so no one let their kids near it. I remember my mam telling me it must have been the pixies in Doon Hill over at Aberfoyle. I told her she was being stupit, but she insisted it had happened before, during her grannie's time. She said the minister back then had a habit of poking around Doon Hill. Said he'd met the faeries that lived inside. He must have wronged them somehow because one Sunday, the kirkyard suddenly got covered in flowers. Everyone was so busy looking at them, it took them an hour to realise the minister was lying dead inside the kirk."

"Aberfoyle's a little far from here," I said.

"Eh?"

"Could it have been another hill?" I swallowed. "Closer to home?"

Maggie shook her head. "I'll tell you what I told her: there's no such thing as faeries. It's just some bampot with too much time on their hands. Funny the stories we tell to try and explain something so..." her eyes scanned the display before alighting—pointedly?—on me, "...deranged."

I broke eye contact, face flushing. Looking over the flower display I suddenly felt very glad for my earlier shyness. What would it have been like if I'd confidently sprung into my fantasies? The flower shop. The library. The gardener. I imagined the eye rolls and the awkward pauses, those small unspoken signs that I'd overstepped. I'd beaten myself up for my past hesitancy. Perhaps a little self-doubt wasn't a bad thing.

But then who else could have done this? I imagined a shadowy figure sneaking about at night with a wheelbarrow full of clinking flower pots. Then I remembered the hanging basket swaying beside my neighbour's door. The begonias on her windowsill. I snatched at the hope in my mind. Yes, that sounded plausible! My neighbour was the village's volunteer gardener and had gotten up bright and early to decorate.

And maybe gone a bit overboard with it all, but that was beside the point.

She was alive. She was fine!

But then, why were the locals so surprised by it all?

And why did this cheery display feel like a haunting?

I LOOKED OVER the faces along the river, trying to read the expressions I saw. I spotted more flower arrangements further down the main street. Maggie tutted and headed back into the café.

I slipped away while the other onlookers were distracted by the flowers. I skirted round the tourists and the hillwalkers, and returned to my task of looking for my neighbour.

CHAPTER 21

After a quick bacon roll at one of the other cafés—I couldn't bear poking my head into Maggie's after my abrupt exit the other day and the flower chat this morning—I extended my search to the back streets. I had no idea where my neighbour might be. I hadn't found her in any of the shops and eateries along the river. She didn't have a car, so she couldn't have gone that far.

Eventually, I found myself peeking inside the hardware and supplies store. Perhaps she'd stopped in for more gardening supplies. What I hadn't realised was that beyond the display of tools and sundries in the windows, was a clear view to the counter. Rowan clocked me immediately. I froze upon being seen. His face broke into a toothy smile, and he waved me in.

I shook my head.

Rowan rolled his eyes and waved me in more enthusiastically, mouthing something I couldn't hear. I weighed up whether it would be more awkward to leave than to go in. I figured it was best to go and find out what he wanted. I might even get some info on the whereabouts of my neighbour.

The electronic bell announced my entrance.

"Sorry for just peering through the windows like a creeper."

"Eh, don't worry." He chuckled. "How's your head after last night?"

"Oh." I put a hand to my scalp. "I think I threw most of it up on the way home."

Jesus, you didn't have to tell him that!

He laughed. "I did worry when you started off with the two pints, but you seemed so much more relaxed afterwards."

My shoulders inched up toward my ears.

Oh God, what did you do?

"Don't worry." He leaned on the counter. "You didn't dance on the tables or anything. We just had a good chat. If it helps to know, you're a ranty drunk."

"I am?" I braced myself.

"Yeah, in a good way. It was funny."

What did you say?

"You talked about your work a lot."

My blood chilled. Did I tell him what happened at the office?

"It's so weird to think that behind all those emails from big multi-national companies there's just some person sitting in a room writing away, pretending to be them."

Oh, thank Christ. I'd just talked about marketing emails.

Rowan shook his head.

"It sort of reminds me of the folk in suits pretending to be Mickey Mouse for photos at Disneyland. Does it feel weird pretending to be someone else all the time?"

"No." I imagined myself sitting in a Mickey Mouse costume at my desk, hunched over my keyboard. "I mean, that's just what everyone does at work. Pretend."

Rowan gave me another of those hard-to-read looks.

"Anyway, my sister told me I should start a Facebook page or a newsletter for the store, but I really can't be bothered with it." He shrugged. "If you're as good as you say, maybe you could work something up for the store. Just don't pretend to be me, alright. Be yourself."

I was trying to imagine myself taking off the costume when I registered what Rowan was saying. This was a lead. A job! I hadn't heard back from any of my old clients. I'd started to worry the whole freelance thing just wasn't going to happen for me. But now Rowan was asking for help marketing the store. I could make him a website, social media profiles, emails. I could use the hardware and supplies store as a case study. There was probably a whole heap of businesses in Carlinsrest that could do with some help. I could even start helping businesses in other villages further afield. This could be a living. A career. Out in the countryside. My God, it was actually happening!

"Absolutely! Yeah, I can chat you through some things I could do for the store—"

If only I didn't have a leaden feeling in the pit of my stomach.

"Before I bore you with all that, um"—I said, hoping I wouldn't regret asking—"you haven't seen the woman from last night, have you?"

I nonchalantly picked through some cannisters of midge repellent trying not to look too bothered.

"Which one?"

"The woman who lives next door to me." I gestured in reference to her long lank hair. "She kind of… she came by the table but didn't say anything. Wore a blouse."

Rowan frowned. "I don't remember seeing anyone. To be honest, you're the only person I know who lives in Sgàthan Sìth. I didn't even know those cottages were split until last night." He shrugged. "Why do you ask?"

I realised the mistake I'd made. I shouldn't have said anything. He hadn't even been aware of my neighbour until I'd mentioned her. What if no one had known about her until now? Now that I was drawing attention to her existence—

And her disappearance.

"How's that shadow of yours doing?" a voice asked behind me.

I spun and backed into the shelves, rattling the tins. The old man from the pub peered up at me. The sheepdog sat at his feet, staring just as intently. His wife snored in the wheelchair.

Rowan reached out to steady the shelves.

"Ah, afternoon, pal." He raised his eyebrows pointedly. "If you're done scaring the other customers, I can get your order from the back."

"Perfect, lovely." The old man smiled, oblivious.

Other customers.

Rowan nodded kindly.

"Back in a sec," he said then jogged to the door behind the counter.

"Well?"

I blinked at the man.

"Sorry, I don't—"

The old man rolled his eyes. The dog at his heels whimpered, although whether it was expressing sympathy with the man or me, I couldn't tell.

"Did you manage to fix the stitching? That house of yours has a bad habit of catching one's seams."

Another fool's tale about my damned house. I took a calm breath.

"If this is about the house being haunted or—"

"Haunted!" He barked a short sharp laugh that startled the dog. "What nonsense. Haunted, my God."

Thank Christ. Some sanity at last.

"That's what I thought, but—"

"That house isn't haunted. It's a mirror."

My breath caught in my throat.

"I'm sorry?"

The old man peered at me closely.

"Oh dear," he said. "It's got away from you, hasn't it? I tried to warn you"—he shook his head—"back when it was hanging off you by a thread. Now it's got free, climbing the shelves of the pantry, running across the roof, hiding in the basement—"

"Here's your order." Rowan appeared suddenly to my side. He handed over a small plastic postal bag. A lump gently weighed down one of the corners. Rowan nodded at the sleeping woman in the wheelchair. "Though you might want to tell the missus there are better ways of ordering embroidery thread."

The old man took the package and tucked it into one of the giant, rustling pockets of his coat.

"She insisted I order through you." He winked at me. "I'm just the messenger."

The wheels on the chair squealed to a start, as the old man shuffled toward the door, dog pattering in tow. Outside, he wandered away, dog dancing a zigzag in the wake of his sleeping wife's chair. Inside, I was still trying to process what he'd just said.

My house is a what now?

CHAPTER 22

"Okay," said Rowan, eyeing me in confusion. "What was that about?"

I shook my head.

"I don't know."

The alert on Rowan's phone went off again. He checked the screen then looked at me.

"It's okay," I said. "I've got… stuff."

Rowan watched me carefully.

"Sure. Good to see you." He got down onto the floor into his plank position, then looked up at me through the hair that fell over his eyes. "I'll keep a look out for your neighbour!"

I flinched at the mention of her, guilt crawling over me like ants, then marched out of Rowan's store and ran after the old man.

Looking up and down the back road, I heard the squeak of the old woman's wheelchair. My head jerked in the direction of the sound and I caught sight of the sheepdog just as it turned the corner.

I chased after it.

I thought again about what Fergus had said last night. The old man was weird, probably mad. But he was also smart. Biggest-biological-breakthrough-in-the-last-hundred-years smart. Sweat slicked the palms of my hands. And he clearly knew something about my house, so he probably knew my neighbour. If only I could—

I turned the corner and ran straight into him. The old man looked up at me expectantly. Behind him, the sheepdog stood guard by the old woman. All three of them looked posed, like they'd been waiting for me.

"Can I help you, young lady?" He stared at me through those thick glasses, his eyes large and insect-like, all-seeing. He waved a hand toward the flower display at the end of the road. "Silly question, I suppose. This is going to be a bugger to clean up, let me tell you!"

I regained my composure and tried to think of how to start the conversation.

"Sorry, I just heard a rumour that… ah… you worked on Dolly the Sheep."

It sounded idiotic the moment it came out of my mouth. It was like asking the delivery driver if they were Doctor Who.

But he looked at me over his glasses and sighed.

"I guess we're talking about that," he muttered. Then, "What do you want to know? Hmm?" He glared at me with gleeful accusation. "Were they trying to clone humans? Make armies of obedient slaves? Hmm? Is that it?"

"No, actually I—"

"Well, they weren't!" He huffed. "They were only trying to increase the amount of milk a ewe could produce. The cloning was just a side product of that. They didn't realise what they were doing until they were right at the point of doing it."

He suddenly took the handles of the old woman's wheelchair and started walking again toward the main street. The old woman snorted as he jolted her back into momentum. I quickly followed after them.

"They found a way to create new, healthy tissue from just a few cells. Imagine the things they could have done with that. Spinal cord repair, liver transplants, Parkinson's treatments. They only cloned the whole sheep to see the limit of what could be done. To show it *could* be done." He pointed a finger. "But there was the problem: Clone a bit of tissue and no one bats an eyelid. Clone a sheep—well, now you're Victor Frankenstein. Ended up spending most of their publicity fund fighting questions about clone armies."

He shook his head. We walked alongside the river past the memorial.

"All that potential, all those people they could have helped, lost in a matryoshka doll of whataboutisms and straw men." He tutted. His sheepdog whined at his feet. He reached down and scratched the spot between the dog's eyebrows. "There was nothing to be frightened of. Dolly was her own sheep. She just happened to share the DNA of another. That was all. What those scientists did was no different to the creation of the first vaccine, antibiotics, surgery, and no one pitches a fit about those. Well, they do at vaccines these days, sadly…"

I nodded like I was listening, while I thought about how to direct the conversation back towards my neighbour, who she was, what she did, and whether she had a habit of sneaking into other people's homes in the middle of the night.

"That's fascinating. So, are you some kind of scientist or something?"

"Oh, I'm something, alright." The old man's eyes twinkled at me.

I forced a smile.

"How long have you lived in Carlinsrest?" I asked. "I've just moved in, and I don't know many of the locals yet. You must know everyone—and all their business—by now. Speaking of, do you happen to know the lady who lives next door to me? I've been trying to hunt her down"—*ooft, wording Tamsin!*—"and I'm not having much luck."

He sighed.

"I'm not telling you this for my health, m'dear."

The breeze dropped and the flowers around town stood still.

"I'm telling you this because of your…" his eyes quickly skirted around the street as if wary of eavesdroppers, "issue."

I shook my head, but I was a terrible liar.

"I don't know what this has to do with my—"

He gave me a pointed look and continued.

"What was it about Dolly that made all those people so afraid?"

He stared at me silently.

He can smell it on you.

"Um, cloning?" I offered.

"Doubling." He put up two fingers, side by side, then spread them apart. "Copycats taking up your space in a group. Reflections that don't do as they should. Shadows that start moving on their own. Meeting your doppelganger on a misty day. Humans don't like it. Why?"

I shifted on my feet. It felt like he was playing with me.

"I don't know."

"Yes, you do," he insisted.

I shrugged. "How do you tell who is who?"

He clapped his hands. The sheepdog barked at the sound.

"People are more than their DNA, how they look, what biological build they've been dealt. It's your experiences, your decisions, your actions that make you who you are." He leant forward, dropping his voice conspiratorially. "And you know who you are, don't you?"

A yellow kite. Neon pink fingernails.

Do you think you're a—

The old man straightened up and looked out over the river.

"And that's your lot for now."

The old man wheeled his wife toward the bridge, closely followed by his spritely trotting sheepdog.

I chased after him.

"Wait. What do you mean?"

"When you're ready, she'll be the one to help you." He gently patted the shoulder of the woman snoring in the wheelchair. "I hope I see you again. I really do." Then after a pause, he added not unkindly, "If you are who you say you are. Good luck."

And he disappeared out over Bodach's Brig, pushing his still snoring wife over the bridge, ploughing on steadily and unhindered by the cobbles.

I watched on as they left, the old man's words repeating in my mind.

If you are who you say you are.

CHAPTER 23

I CHECKED TO see if my shadow was still attached to my feet. There it was, short and stubby in the midday sunshine, like a puddle on the cobbles.

Shadows that move on their own.

No shadow-ectomies or faeries or sheep clones here. Just me.

Be yourself.

And you know who you are, don't you?

The old ringing buzzed through my skull and my head ached.

I couldn't get what Rowan had said out of my mind. About the costumes. About pretending to be all those different companies. And now all the old man's talk about clones and doubles and…

My hangover wrenched my insides.

This had been a mistake. I should have stayed back at the house. I hadn't found my neighbour. And if anything *had* happened in my basement last night, I'd only made myself look even more suspicious.

But nothing had happened. My neighbour was fine. She was up and out early this morning. She'd been busy with the flowers in town. She wasn't lying dead in the belly of her home. Because I didn't do that. I *wouldn't* do that. That's not who I am.

I felt the memory of a wet crunch of bone shuddering up my arms.

If it didn't happen, how could I remember the sensation so well?

You know why.

I felt sick. I needed to think. I needed to calm down.

I did my best to look like I wasn't freaking out. Head high, arms at my side, definitely not hunching over myself and glaring at people. I found a bench looking out over the river and hastily sat on it, resisting the urge to tuck my knees into my chest. Then I focused on the sound of the gentle rushing water and tried to breathe.

The old man was just talking nonsense, I told myself. *Everything is fine, so stop freaking out. Be fine!*

A group of women had stopped at the waterside nearby, phones up, taking pictures. I arched my neck to see what they were looking at. There was a small family of some kind of water bird dabbling in the weeds at the edge. One large parent and a troop of fluffy chicks streaming after her. The women threw crumbs of the pastries and cakes they'd bought at the café into the river. Small bills whisked the water in the hunt for flakes of croissant and red velvet. I wondered if pastry was bad for ducks, but that didn't seem like a very popular thing to ask strangers. Especially strangers just out for a nice photo with cute animals. Why did we find the babies of other animals so cute? Ducklings. Kittens. Puppies. A lot of the time the behaviour we cooed over was just early play versions of hunting behaviour. Playing with ropes was practice for breaking small necks. The squeak of a toy mimicked the panicked cry of prey. Somewhere in our mammalian brains we see this and think 'aww!'

The ducklings paddled after their mother along the river and the women left, swiping through photos, picking which ones to post. Only I was left watching the little duck family after they were gone. Only I watched as the clouds came over and the mother led her brood away. Only I saw as the line of ducks began to pull away from the last and smallest duckling.

I looked around. I was the only one who had noticed the straggler. I turned my attention back to the ducks. Perhaps the little one would catch up. Ducklings had that sudden burst of speed they could do, that little skipping across the water like a thrown stone. As I thought it, the littlest duckling did just that. But bit by bit the gap was still growing. I looked around again, to see if anyone else had noticed the tragedy unfolding before me. Perhaps someone I could lock eyes with. We'd nod and head down river. We'd stop the mother duck. Or maybe rescue the family together. Or perhaps just adopt the small duckling. Have it live at my house. Paddling in my sink. Waddling about my garden.

But there was no one to lock eyes with. No one else could see what was happening. I turned back once more and watched quietly as the gap grew and grew, and the duck family pulled further and further away from the smallest duckling. The mother duck darted round an embankment, turned and led the family toward a bed of reeds on the other side of the river. It was as if she—no. No, she wouldn't deliberately leave the duckling behind, would she? I'd heard of it happening, though never seen it until now. When a mother senses something wrong, smells a weakness, an oddness, in her child, she's driven to abandon it. No point wasting effort on something that's just going to fail anyway. Or worse, infect her healthy babies.

The duck family disappeared into the reeds, but the smallest duckling carried on in a straight line. It chirped loudly, desperate, as it kept going along the river, alone, until I could see it no more.

I pressed my lips together. See, this is why you have to pretend. Otherwise, everyone smells the sickness on you. And then you get left behind.

That's why I'd come here.

To be better.

To pretend better.

My fingers, hands, limbs felt fuzzy and incorporeal, as if I was lifting up and out of my body, as if I'd never been in it in the first place, as if 'I' was a lie I'd told myself to stop the meat of my brain from going totally insane.

Why couldn't I tell myself a better lie? Why couldn't I pretend better?

You know who you are, don't you?

I rubbed my eyes. The ringing had left and in its place was a hollowness, a nothing, like I was just an empty suit of skin, ready to be blown away at any moment.

If you unzipped me, I'd disappear.

CHAPTER 24

A WARM BREEZE stirred the muggy air, fluttering the fly-away hairs around my ears and hushing through the leaves in the trees on the other side of the river. I wiped my face. It was barely afternoon and despite my hangover I found myself desperately needing a drink.

Perhaps I could ask after my neighbour at the pub. She'd been there last night, after all. And if that didn't work, I could have a drink to calm my nerves.

And dull all these uncomfortable feelings.

I turned away from the river, up into the back streets and toward The Curtyard.

The smell hit me first as I turned the corner into the cobblestone courtyard. I halted where I stood and took in the view, open-mouthed. The wall of the pub was now veiled in fragrant greenery. A coarse coat of flat, thin leaves climbed and covered the old stones of the pub. Along the barrels-turned-tables, tubs of long-stemmed herbs ending in fringed sprays of delicate greenery gathered in pungent crowds. The smell of the plants, a rich perfume, hung heavy in the humid air. I approached carefully, tiptoeing up to the herbs in case some green-faced figure leapt out from among them. I imagined brushing my fingers through the leaves and luxuriating in their scent. Reaching out, I stopped as I identified the smells. Fennel. And rosemary? I withdrew my hand. Sprigs of rosemary unbelievably climbed and knotted through the broken Curtyard sign. I didn't think they were there last night. I didn't think rosemary was a climber.

I pulled my arms up to my chest. A bubble of voices greeted me as I stopped at The Curtyard's door. I tried to work out if heading back to the pub would incriminate me or set me above suspicion. Do guilty people go to the pub?

They certainly skulk around outside taking forever to decide.

I was here to ask after my neighbour and then *maybe* have a drink. That was a perfectly normal thing to do.

I opened the door with unearned confidence.

Pubs always have a different feel to them during the day. They reminded me of the old country pub my parents used to go to when I was small, all sticky maroon carpets, dark tacky wood tables, and fruit machines with their brightly dancing lights in the corner. I'd be plied with bottles of cold, sweet cola and packets of salt and vinegar crisps and sent out to play on the rough-hewn climbing frames and hot metal slides in the pub garden, while my parents avoided the sun and the wasps at a table inside. I'd remembered feeling lonely, pushed outside with the rest of the kids and away from all the people my parents wanted to talk to.

Of course, that all changed a few years later when the Graysons divorced. They were friends of my parents. While they went to mediation, my mum and dad looked after their daughters, Lucy and Laura-Ann. Golden-haired girls with perfect dimpled smiles. After that, when I was sent out to play at the pub, my parents came with. My mum stayed smoking at a table with all the drinks in the shade while my dad pushed the two blonde-haired girls in tandem on the swings. Their giggles rang against the red bricks while I stood and waited my turn.

"Their parents aren't together anymore," my mum explained, "so you should let them share your dad for a bit."

My parents got called saints a lot back then.

When it was my turn for the swings my dad played with the girls on the slide instead.

Later that summer he bought them a yellow kite. The same one I'd been asking for since my birthday in the spring—

I smacked the back of my own hand to snap myself out of it.

Look at you, I scolded, *drowning in self-pity. Get a grip!*

The Curtyard was surprisingly busy. There was a crowd gathered on the right-hand side of the bar. Funny. Last night most people seemed to gather on the fireside edge. Every so often the crowd would cheer and tap the air with their half-filled pint glasses. I shuffled into the mass of heaving bodies, carefully stepping into the spaces people left empty as they shifted about. Through a parting in the crowd I spied the centre of the commotion.

A woman stood on one bare foot with a tartan scarf wrapped around her eyes like a blindfold. She sipped a pint with one hand and aimed The Curtyard's plastic 'o' with the other. The beer was the same rich, rusty red colour as mine the night before. She failed the first sip with a snorted laugh. The crowd laughed in turn.

"Stop it, you bastards!" she cried out. A wide open-mouthed smile puckered two perfect dimples upon her cheeks. I caught more glimpses of her between the spectators. She wore a perfectly tailored, white silk blouse and a pair of tight black trousers that were at once edgy and fashionable. Her hair was that healthy kind of bouncy, cut into one of those styles that looked effortlessly chic. She had a pleasant-looking face, what I could see of it around the blindfold, but something about it gave me an odd feeling. I craned my neck to try and get a better look at her.

She wobbled a little then waved her pint as if entreating her audience to silence. All the while, despite the wobble, her raised foot stayed perfectly pointed. Her toenails were painted a tasteful shade of burgundy.

"Now shut up. I'm doing very busy and important things here."

She grinned at her own self-deprecation, then put the pint back to her lips. The crowd waited in anticipation. I scanned their watching faces. Every eye was locked on her. Even the line of zebras above the bar seemed to be watching. She raised the 'o' in her hand, tilted back her pint glass to gulp, then flicked her wrist. The hoop flew, silent and true, right onto the neck of the finest, most expensive looking whisky behind the bar.

The crowd erupted in delight. She brought down her raised foot.

"Did I do it?"

She whipped off the scarf with her throwing hand.

"Oh my God, I did it!"

She screamed in delight and bounced on her feet, straight into the nearest arms. Other hands reached to her, patting her shoulders, her bouncing hair, her straight back.

I stood frozen to the spot, staring at her face, not quite believing what I was seeing, my whole body turning cold.

The barmaid shook her head—this time she was wearing a long-sleeve top covered in waves of smaller surfing zebras—and reached for the expensive looking bottle.

"Alright, hen, will that be a double?"

The woman extricated herself from her adoring audience, her bright eyes sweeping the ceiling for a moment.

A white scar shone along the left-hand curve of her forehead.

I backed away toward the door.

"Ah…" She pursed her lips, her eyes alighting on her existing drink, then back to the bar. "Just another one of these please!"

She raised her red pint and grinned.

She was different, yes, very different. Polished up till she looked like a whole other person.

But it was definitely her.

She smiled at passing well-wishers who'd gathered up her shoes for her. Wellingtons, the posh ones, with a tweed trim, practical but still stylish. Then her eyes tracked straight onto me.

My stomach dropped.

Her face went eerily static for a moment. Then her mouth pulled wide.

Wider.

Wider still.

Until I could see every one of her teeth.

It was definitely her. Alive. Transformed. Looking right at me.

"Good to see you," she said, "neighbour."

CHAPTER 25

I LEFT THE Curtyard in a rush. Just slipped out the door while no one was watching. It was easy to do. Everyone there was gathered in one crowd around the bar, listening intently while my neighbour enacted some fascinating story from her life.

My heart pounded. It was her. She was alive.

I pressed both palms to my chest.

Thank fuck! I hadn't killed her! I was free! No one would hunt me down and lock me up. I could live my life. My new life.

I should have been relieved.

Why wasn't I relieved?

I couldn't stop thinking about what I'd seen in the basement last night, her appearance today, the scar on her forehead. My mind obsessively picked away at the scab of it all. None of it made sense.

The bridge and the road out of Carlinsrest were quiet, thank God. No one to see me scuttling home. No one to see me muttering to myself. No one to see me picking at my skin until the small spots on the outer edge of my arms bled.

She'd looked so… different.

The hair, the expression, the voice. The way she'd moved her hands. So confident. So at ease. Where was the nervy, strange woman from the other night? The lank hair. The staring, watery eyes. Maybe I had caught her on an off day. Maybe she'd always had that scar.

The afternoon sky stretched long and high above my lonely walk back.

I thought of the way everyone had gathered round her at The Curtyard. How they'd watched her, intently, genuinely. How they'd laughed at her jokes. For a brief moment I remembered when I'd felt like the confident one, looking on at her shyness, her awkwardness, as if she were a problem to solve, or a contagion to avoid.

Now we'd switched places.

Or the world had righted itself back to its true order.

That certainly makes more sense.

As I walked back along the empty road, I thought of all the parties I'd slipped out of over the years. The family get-togethers, the school reunions, the work dos. It had always felt better to remove myself before I grew tired of pretending to be normal, before I gave myself away, before people sussed me out. But even with all that history against me, I had tried to be different back at my last company. I'd really tried.

After shrugging off the first pub invitation from Issy, I was very careful to make the next one. But finding out about the next one had been more difficult than the first. I kept coming in on Monday to tales of what the team had got up to the Friday before. Stories of shots, of hook-ups, of bouncing between bars until folk ended up at the casino or the jazz bar or whatever was still open in the early hours of Saturday. I'd make an effort to listen in, to join in the conversations about those nights, to remark—positively, I'd thought—on the 'crazy' adventures everyone had been up to without me.

And I'd ask, each Monday morning, that they let me know next time they were going out, even though doing so made my heart beat loud in my ribcage and my palms turn slick with sweat. But still the Fridays brought no invites and still the Monday mornings brought plenty of stories. Maybe people aren't so keen to extend invites when they feel the first one's been snubbed.

Then one Friday, I just watched the team carefully. Waited until I saw the flurry of shared looks, and the messages on phones and the not-so-secret chat group I was not invited to and everyone pretended didn't exist. I waited at my desk when end of play hit, to see when people would get their coats, to see if the others came down from the other floors and asked, 'Where to tonight?'

I could have just asked them. I sat there in my shame, knowing I could have just asked them. But I didn't. I couldn't.

Maybe you deserved to be left out if you insist on going about things in such a hidden, sneaky way.

If I was honest, it was because I didn't expect them to tell me. I should have paid attention to that feeling. I should have listened to that part of myself. Taken the hint. Stopped engaging in what was clearly some social version of self-harm. But it's hard to have a spine when the people you're stuck with eight hours a day are your only socialization, even if they don't want anything to do with you. Or when loneliness is not a good enough reason to leave a well-paying job.

Or when part of you believes no one in their right mind would want to include you anyway. Not once they know what you're really like.

But anyway, I waited. And it paid off. One of the devs came down and asked, "Are we off then?"

"Where to?" I'd asked, coat already on, ready to go.

I'd noticed a small look flash between some of my team.

"Just for a drink. Probably only one."

"Cool, I'll come with," I'd said.

As they let me follow along, I actually felt good. Like I was finally doing it, getting over whatever this thing was that separated me from everyone else. Maybe I just needed to give people a chance. Maybe I just needed to open up a little. Maybe they would help me find my better self.

I followed them to a pub set in an old whisky bond, all glass and hammered copper set against old beams and time-blackened stone. They talked among themselves as I followed them up to the bar.

I ordered a glass of wine. It was the second least expensive one on the list, even though I'd been told that was the one bars and restaurants made the biggest mark-up on, knowing that everyone buys it. I was already breaking one set of difficult social conditioning; challenging the order of wine prices would have to wait.

I found a seat at the table, making sure to sit in the middle so that I could have my choice of conversations to join. Unfortunately, both sides quickly turned away from me, lost in talk at their own ends, leaving me like Moses parting the middle. I tried a couple of times, leaning in, making those active listening nods and 'ah's' and 'yeah's'. But even if I had been included, I could barely make out a word anyone was actually saying. Everything was so loud.

So, I drank my wine to give my hands something to do.

And then I got up to order another glass, to give myself something to do, to fit into the surroundings, to be part of the machinery of the place and not the one dead cog stuck on the outside.

And then I drank that glass, too fast.

And then I got up to go to the bar again. I offered a round out to the table, but everyone was still halfway through drinks. Somewhere along the way, pinballing through people back to the bar, I decided to buy some fizz for the table. I bought a bottle of the second least expensive prosecco. I tottered back with it and a handful of glasses. My arrival won a small sound of surprise, raised eyebrows, a few 'oh's'.

Some eagerly reached for a glass, while others thanked me politely but refused.

I drank two glasses, again too quickly. It was a little warm and sweet. Not the best. But I was drunk enough to slug it down anyway.

And then there was a tray of shots.

And then I remembered talking to someone. They were watching me talk, but even in my drunken state I could tell it was in that humouring way.

Nod and listen to the monologue and hope you can catch eyes with someone else and pass the role of listener on.

And then I remembered stumbling home.

And then I remembered waking up on my bed and vomiting over the side.

And then I remembered remembering and I curled around myself wishing I could sleep forever.

I was full of dread on the walk to work the next Monday. What would they think of me? What had I said to them?

I needn't have worried. No one said anything about me. They were too busy talking about the club they'd gone to after I'd left. I sat at my computer, not even bothering to try and join in this time.

The girl I'd drunkenly talked the ear off of caught me in the kitchen later. She asked about my father and whether I'd spoken to him about all that stuff I'd mentioned on Friday. I pretended I didn't hear her and went back to my desk, leaving my tea unfinished on the kitchen counter.

A few months later, another new girl started with the agency. She was invited immediately to Friday drinks. I see photos of her hanging out with my old colleagues all the time on social media. She was confident and happy, too. Just like my new neighbour.

Or my *new* new neighbour.

I thought again about how effortlessly she'd held everyone's attention in The Curtyard. Her hair. Her clothes. Her confidence. It seemed to come to her so…

Naturally.

I halted in the middle of the road. The sparrows in the hedgerow stopped their bickering. The breeze died and silence descended as the realisation hit me.

All those different people I'd imagined myself being. The stoic gardener. The talkative librarian. The magical florist. It was the same thing I'd always done. The new outfit for my first day at work. All the different ways I'd tried to engage my colleagues at the pub. How I'd tried to impress the director with my work. All the false smiles.

I'd moved here to become a better person, but I've spent my life trying to be better.

And it never worked.

So why did I think things would be any different this time?

My whole plan for this escape into the countryside, my new life, my new *me*, it was doomed from the start.

CHAPTER 26

I RETURNED TO the overgrown, gravel path leading up to the Sgàthan Sìth cottages and tramped up the hill to my house. I put my key in the door—my door this time, very much my door with its new lock and strange scratches down the front— and returned to the darkness within.

I stood alone in the living room. My living room. Though it didn't feel like much living was done here. There was no warmth. Not even literally at that moment, as the fire in the boiler had died. There was nothing that said 'home'. Just layers of shadows and not much else. Oh, and a rug that didn't fit it. I turned on the light. The bare bulb illuminated the wooden floor in blue light. Not the golden hues I remembered growing up, when everything was coloured in terracotta and sunshine yellows. There was a cold greyness to it all, like how I imagined skin looked after the heart stops pumping. Pallid. They say the kitchen is the heart of the home. Does that still count when your kitchen isn't much more than a fridge, a hob and a few cupboards? I guessed not. This place was heartless.

Bloodless. Nothing to bleed. Everything I'd wanted. It should be perfect.

Down in the basement I set the boiler going with more wood, then I headed back up to the kitchen to make dinner.

As I heated up some beans on the stove, I turned my head to the wall I shared with next door.

I wondered again what the inside of 1a looked like. My earlier idea of neat doilies or dusty newspaper piles was replaced by a warm fireplace, tartan cushions, a nice rug. One that's the right size for her living room, of course. She'd have a handknit blanket across the couch. The sofa would be second-hand, but expertly chosen. Warm wood legs and plush velvet cover. Upcycled, perhaps. A carved, wooden room divider would lazily separate the space between the kitchen and the living room. Her kitchen would have more than a fridge, a hob and a cupboard. There'd be a tidy range cooker. Copper pans hanging from the ceiling. A kitchen island. Lord knows how she managed to fit a kitchen island into such a tiny room, but she'd manage it. Herbs growing on the windowsill. A suncatcher hanging from the ironwork latch. No white PVC for her.

I ate the beans at the hob, dipping slices of sandwich bread into the saucepan to soak up the sauce.

Next door, *she* would dine, back through in the lounge, on a beautiful round table. Wood again, of course, on a single polished pedestal. Just like the one I've always wanted. With a chess board. No, a handblown vase, ribbons of coloured glass, holding pink peonies and only pink peonies. Shelves up the side of the fireplace would hold a few books, some boardgames, perhaps a wooden box of trinkets, or scented candles or wax melts. The wax melter, or whatever it's called, would be on the tiled fireplace, lit and smelling wonderful. Not that garish cookie scent or fake washed linen smell, but something gently perfumed. Baltic amber in winter. Jasmine in spring. Maybe something retro like sunflower in the summer. There'd be pictures on the walls. Photos. Candid photos. Of all her friends and family. In tasteful frames with that white card thingy that went around the border to make them look classy. She'd probably need to change the photos out regularly, to make room for new ones. She would stare and tut and rest her chin on her palm and puzzle out how she could possibly fit more on the wall.

I thought of the old man and Dolly the Sheep. And Dolly's donor. Did Dolly's donor even have a name? I imagined her seeing herself in that cloned ewe, feeling envious of the attention, the care, the food Dolly got. This younger and more special sheep that looked just like her. Maybe she wondered what Dolly was doing that she didn't.

Maybe she was secretly glad when Dolly died.

I shuddered and broke out of my imaginings. Goose pimples ran along the topography of my arms.

The sky outside had darkened to a hazy, inky blue, like fountain pen ink had bled into the white air.

Bed, I scolded myself, *now*.

Obedient, I turned off the lights and went upstairs. I brushed my teeth, mechanically and quick.

I put my phone on to charge, then stripped unceremoniously and put myself to bed.

I pulled my dressing gown bedsheet up to my neck, rolled onto my side and tucked up my knees. After a moment, I wrapped an arm around my shoulder, and rubbed my own back until I was too sleepy to feel embarrassed by my need for it.

I woke in darkness to the sound of 1a's front door opening and a jangling of keys.

My eyes blinked open at the sound. My neighbour let the door fall shut behind her and the whole house shook with the slam. I bolted upright.

What the hell?

Had the front door always been that loud?

Oh God, she'd probably heard *me* come and go like that.

I sat there quietly listening. At least she hadn't tried to open my door by mistake, har har. At least this meant she was definitely fine. I flopped back down onto my bed, but relief still didn't meet me there.

She was fine. Demonstrably fine. Then why was I still so—?

Clump clump clump.

I could hear every footstep she made in that house! It was even worse than the first night. I mentally followed her from the living room to the kitchen as if she were walking around my own home. It was uncanny. Maybe that's what had triggered my vision of her in the basement. Maybe it was just like the other night. I'd just heard her and my mind had filled in the rest.

Cupboard doors creaked open and clapped shut. What on earth was she looking for? I rolled onto my side and wrapped my hoodie-turned-pillow over my head and squeezed my ears between my elbows. It was no use. I could still feel the vibration of the cupboards opening and closing through the floor and through the mattress and into my ears. I rolled onto my back.

Just calm down, I thought to myself, *you're making it worse by letting it get to you.*

I tried to remember what that therapist had suggested. The one the police made me see after the incident. I'd gone to one session, just to try it, then noped out soon afterwards. There was a breathing exercise she'd suggested. In through the nose for four. Hold for four. Out through the mouth for four. I tried that for a few cycles, counting out the numbers with my fingertips as I breathed.

In, two, three, four. Hold, two, three, four. Out, two, three, four.

Or was it for five?

I couldn't remember.

It was four or five.

There was also something about naming things I could see or feel or hear. Well, I could hear plenty just now. It sounded like my neighbour was sorting through her recycling. Bottles and cans clanked and rang through the walls. I thought about moving my mattress into the bathroom. Perhaps I should have gone back for that second therapy session after all. No, I definitely *should* have gone back. I wondered if the therapist had reported my absence. No one had come looking for me, so I assumed I was fine.

But that's the problem with assuming. You're never quite sure if you're really off the hook or if the line has just got slack enough to make you feel like you'd got away. You can never relax. You'll always be looking over your shoulder, waiting for the line to pull taut.

Music started from next door.

I glared at the wall in the dark as some beat I did not recognise reverberated through the plaster. I scrabbled about for my phone, yanking it from its cable, then squinted in its glare. It was gone midnight! What the hell was she doing playing something like that so loud so late?

I lay back and tried to think about what to do.

Back in Edinburgh this kind of thing was a bimonthly occurrence as someone in the red brick tenement opposite my flat share brought the party home from their latest rager. I'd be woken by the *unce-unce-unce* echoing off the brickwork and across carparks until someone yelled for them to 'shut the fuck up' or just called the police. I thought I'd escaped it out here in the countryside.

The worst part was always the powerlessness of it. The many times I'd tried to talk myself into heading across the street to the flat making the noise, to ask them to turn it down. I knew what would happen, was convinced of what would happen. I could already see the shiny, happy faces laughing me out of the flat.

Leave us to have our fun. Not everyone is as wasted and joyless and heartless as you are.

Or maybe they'd get angry at me. They'd be *that* kind of person, sharper and harder than I was, confident in their bodies and what those bodies could do, especially to small, soft bodies like mine. Perhaps it would just be asking for trouble, a long grudge, a stream of abuse, rubbish through my letter box, dog shit on my front doorstep, because I couldn't be chill. Couldn't live and let live.

So, instead, I would just lie awake and silently steam, fantasising about bricks through windows, lit bottles of vodka following shortly after, speakers melting in a fire. I'd dream of myself, larger and stronger, wielding a hammer and knocking on their door all nonchalant. At first, they'd scowl at me, ask me what I wanted, then they would notice the hammer and their faces would drop. In a hushed voice I'd say something cool or chummy-sounding but most definitely a threat. I'd soothe myself with images of their faces—faces I'd never seen—full of fear. Fear of me. 'Certainly,' they'd say. 'Of course. Sorry to have bothered you!' They'd tiptoe to their flats, they'd step out of my way on the street, and they'd certainly never play their stupid, awful music late at night ever again.

The sounds of a crowd of people came through the wall. She must have invited half the town over! They filled the lower floor and—from the sounds of it—spilled upstairs. I imagined the group that had surrounded her at The Curtyard, cheering her on, now continuing the party despite me trying to sleep next door. I saw Fergus's face in my mind, with that dismissive scowl, now lit up, welcoming, friendly. I saw Rowan, dancing in the kitchen. No, he wouldn't have gone. Not without asking to invite me, too, right? I remembered the face he'd made back at the store when we talked about my job, when he asked about taking the costume off. And then I thought of how I had left my neighbour behind yesterday evening, how when she had come grinning at me I'd hidden in my seat in an attempt to shrug her off. I couldn't really blame Rowan for doing the same to me now.

Someone drunkenly fell into the wall above my head. A shower of old plaster fell onto my face and into my eyes. I sat up and swore. My eyes stung. The thundering tone in my ears reached its crescendo and all hope of control was lost.

"That's it," I said. "That's fucking it!"

I threw off the dressing gown, pulled the bedroom door open so hard I ripped the latch out of the wood. I marched down the stairs and pulled open my front door.

"Shut the fuck up!" I screamed up at the house.

The dark and empty house.

I wiped my eyes with the back of my hand. The throbbing rush of blood calmed away suddenly at the sight of the quiet windows above me. No revellers in the living room. No dance music pounding into the night. Not a light. Not a sound. Just the house, stood as quiet and as still as the hill beneath it.

The loudest, most disruptive thing was me.

I shivered. Then I slunk back inside my half of the house and went back to my bed.

But despite the calm and the quiet outside, I couldn't sleep a wink.

CHAPTER 27

I THINK I am going mad.

That's what I thought over and over, lying in bed, watching the dawn creep round the blue horizon, slowly turning pink and pale before climbing up the ceiling beams of my bedroom.

I had to be mad. What other explanation could there be for what I'd experienced last night? Not to mention the night before. I'd heard the music through the floor, felt the house shake when she let the front door slam. But the house had been silent. Empty.

I ran my hands through my hair. Plaster board powder came away on my fingertips. I shook it off my skin as if it were fungal spores. Maybe I was hallucinating the plaster in my hair as well.

This wasn't the first time I'd ever wondered if I was going mad. Every time there would be some all-hands announcement at work and my colleagues would nod with approval at speeches that just sounded like corporate nonsense to me, I would wonder if maybe I was mad, out of step with reality.

I checked my phone for messages. Nothing.

Of course not. When was the last time you messaged anyone? No one knows what's going on with you. No one from your old life even knows you moved away. That was the point, remember?

I threw my phone out of the bed and looked up at the sloping ceiling. I lay there in the stillness of late morning with the pale light creeping round the walls.

If it wasn't madness, how else could I explain what was happening? The figure in the basement. The phantom party next door. It's not like the place was *actually* built on a fairy hill. There weren't pixies and sprites running around playing tricks on me in the night. I huffed at the thought. Fergus would love that. 'Rich English cunt' chased off by scary stories.

I wasn't even English. Or rich, for that matter.

I thought for a moment. Then I rolled onto my belly and reached for where I'd thrown my phone. I opened the browser and searched for "Carlinsrest fairy hill". My palms went slick as the little coloured buffering dots danced on the screen. There were no results exactly for that term, but my phone was clearly still sharing my location, so I got a screed of "Scottish monsters" and "Scottish mythical creatures". I clicked on the first result that wasn't an ad.

An etching of a face sprang up at the top of the article. It was pretty and youthful and charming, except for a too-wide smile. My finger hovered over the picture. Then I scrolled down:

Faeries, Pixies, Fair Folk, Tylwyth Teg, Changelings, Hidden Folk. This race of mythical creatures is known by many names, but can be found throughout the British Isles and, in fact, most of the world. Theories vary on the origins of these strange humanoid creatures. Some believe they are angels; others, demons. Folklorists speculate that perhaps they were the spirits of the ancestral dead, or a prehistoric race living across the Earth before humanity, or ancient pagan deities worshipped as elementals, nature spirits or the anima of special places in the landscape e.g. hills, large rocks, caves etc.

I looked up and thought of the door in the basement below and Fergus's story about the hollow hill. I shook my head.

They are believed to have supernatural qualities including long life, the ability to change their appearance and a penchant for illusions. It is debated whether they are benign or malicious, but in Scotland faeries are said to be feared—

I pushed my phone away from me in disgust. There had to be another explanation. Something simpler. I squeezed my eyes shut.

Two different versions of my neighbour. Dolly spinning on her stand at the museum. The old man's talk of doubles—

Maybe it's her ghost come to punish me for what I did. Come to drive me insane.

I balled my fists into my eye sockets.

So those were my options. Either I was mad, or I was a murderer.

A cold, heavy sensation spread out from my chest and into my arms and legs.

It was beginning to feel like I had come here not to start a new life, but to die.

My grandmother died of combined liver and lung cancer. I remembered the day she called my father to her house because she felt unwell. Her lovely home, decorated with her crafts and her photos and all the porcelain houses she liked to collect— stained with cigarette smoke over the years. My grandfather's oil painting of a bridge hung above her chair. Two cats sat in front of the fire. Her neatly kept gardens the main view from the living room window.

My father took her to the hospital that day. She left that house thinking she'd be back in the evening. Or perhaps a few days later. They gave her the diagnosis and moved her to a hospice an hour away up north. She never saw that house again. All her things, the collected mementos of her life, the afternoon light in the garden, the steam lifting off a hot cup of coffee in her kitchen.

She never saw her home again.

In my worst hours, those quiet dark passages in the night, I wondered what she must have felt like, moving to the hospice, that unfamiliar place, knowing it was the last place she would ever see, that she was only going there to die.

The cold heavy weight in my chest changed into a freezing tremor. Ice cold panic traced down my spine and my hands shook. In my mind's eye, I saw it, a creeping darkness, inching up from the foot of my bed, climbing over the dressing gown I used as a bedsheet, clutching at my toes—

Knock-knock-knock

I sat up and gasped, hand to my throat. I gulped air like the drowned.

The knocking came again. There was someone at the door. I had no idea who, and I didn't care. I'd cling to anyone like a life raft in that moment.

I calmed my breathing, quickly threw on some clothes and headed downstairs.

CHAPTER 28

THROUGH THE MOTTLED glass in the door was a silhouette I didn't immediately recognise. I peeled the door open, chain still on, and peered out.

Maggie—or who I assumed was called *Maggie*—from Maggie's Café was on my doorstep.

"Alright, hen," she said without a smile.

"Oh, hi."

How did she know where I lived? I wondered if she'd come to formally accuse me of planting all those flowers around the village. *This is a citizen's arrest! I am charging you with the crime of grand illicit gardening. Anything you say or think or might think or might possibly be perceived to have thought will be used against you in a court of your own head.*

Parked behind my car on the driveway was a muddy, navy flatbed truck with the hardware store's name along the side and a learner's 'L' stuck in the windshield. Rowan was examining my smashed windscreen and politely ignoring the vomit next to the front wheel. He spotted me looking and waved.

Oh God. There's no hiding it now.

I undid the chain.

It was startling to be visited. By someone from the village. At this house. I didn't know what to say, who to be. The house and the village had been two separate realities to me. Having someone from there here felt like universes colliding, like when you see your police-recommended therapist at the big supermarket on your exodus out of town.

"Sorry to bother you"—she squinted inside the house—"but Viv said you left this at the pub last night."

She held out a tartan scarf.

"Viv?"

"Aye, Viv. Owns The Curtyard. Loves a zebra."

"Oh, right."

"Anyway, I thought you'd come by the café this morning, but when you didn't Ro offered to drive me over on my way home so I could drop it off. And now I have."

She pushed the tartan scarf toward me.

"That isn't mine," I said.

Maggie's face somehow found a way to be even less smiley.

"Really? She swore it was yours."

I took it from her. I recognised it now. The last time I'd seen it, it had been tied over my neighbour's eyes as she aimed a hoop.

"Oh, this belongs to…"

Definitely not a ghost then. Unless ghosts go to the pub. In the middle of the day.

"You alright, hen?" Maggie took a step back. "You've gone awfully pale."

I didn't know what question to ask so I asked them all.

"Were you there last night? At the pub? Did you see her?"

I prepared myself to hear Maggie go on about *her* being the 'sweetest thing' or a 'good laugh'.

"No. Who're we talking about?"

I squeezed the scarf in my hands.

"Did you hear about a party? A house party. Anyone go to one last night?"

Maggie shook her head. "I'm hardly the partying type. Though we have the odd poker night at Viv's…"

Rowan appeared at her shoulder.

"Hey, mate, you doing alright?"

My head swam.

"I've had the weirdest night. I was kept up by—"

I looked up at the quiet house next door. I shook my head and pinched the bridge of my nose.

"Sorry, I'm fine." I nodded toward 1a. "I think this is my neighbour's. I can drop it off."

I stumbled out my door and took the four steps to her door and went to push the scarf through the letter box. I stopped. Thought better of it. This was my only concrete proof. Proof of what, I didn't know yet, but I didn't want to let it go so easily. I tied it onto the door handle instead.

"Hey, do you happen to know who lives here?" I asked.

"I thought it was empty, like yours," said Maggie, watching me carefully. "Have you been eating alright?" Her voice was suddenly soft. "You should come by the café. Get a macaroni pie. I saw you didn't get a chance to eat the last one."

I am a capable woman. I can chop wood and work a boiler and move house all by myself.

"I'm perfectly alright," I said, tucking my escaping hair back behind my ears.

Rowan gave me one of his assessing looks again.

"Well, if you're perfectly alright then you can give me a hand. Remember we were chatting about maybe getting your help on some things at the shop?"

I straightened up. Oh yeah! That job! I fought back the anxiety and forced a smile.

"Um, sure! Yeah. What do you need?"

"You can drive, right?"

I blinked. A driver? I'd hoped he'd wanted help with a website, some emails, maybe a little social media work, not a lift.

"Uh, my windshield—"

"I don't need your car. I just need someone who can sit with me while I drive the van." He knocked a thumb back toward the truck behind him with its 'L' in the windscreen.

"Oh, I thought you…"

He frowned, then sighed and slapped his forehead.

"The email thing! God, yeah. Sorry. Should have thought about that. I am totally going to ask you about all that, but right now I just need a co-driver as I go up the hillside. I got a tree delivery, but the root bulbs are going to dry out if I don't put them in the ground soon. And Fergus's too busy with the store to come with." He grinned. "I was going to make Maggie chum me up in return for driving her over."

"I said I'd be happy taking the bus," she huffed.

Rowan gave her elbow an affectionate squeeze.

"And miss out on your sparkling company? Never." He turned back to me. "I'd let you have a go driving the truck."

I looked up and down the driveway littered with papery elm seeds.

"I'm not sure— I mean, is that legal? I'm not on your insurance."

Rowan shrugged. "Eh, it's only a problem if we knock into someone, but the roads are quiet once we get up there and it's not far. You could walk it if you had the time. And weren't lugging several trees with you."

I bit my lip. A cool breeze ruffled my hair.

Rowan seemed to notice the thoughts buzzing around my head.

"If you're not comfortable with it…"

He'd asked me for a favour. I wanted to be someone people could ask for a favour. That was part of building friendships, wasn't it? And this favour could turn into a bit of paid website work. Maybe the whole new-life-new-me thing wasn't completely out of my grasp after all.

"Sure," I said.

"Great!" His shoulders relaxed. "Thanks, Tamsin. You're a lifesaver. A tree lifesaver, but a lifesaver, nonetheless!"

I smiled, genuine this time. It would be good to get out of the house for a bit. Get away from whatever was happening and gather my thoughts.

"Let me get my stuff," I said.

I went indoors and grabbed my hoodie—despite sleeping on it, it was the only clean top layer I had left—and my house key.

As I tucked the key in my jeans pocket, my fingers caught against something heavy and metallic and sharp. Spring traps flashed through my mind and my hand quickly retracted. Then I remembered. I took out the needle I'd found in the basement. Still in my pocket. Still as vicious as ever. I hooked the eye of the needle onto the key's ring. It felt like a fitting keyring for now. Then I popped them both back into my pocket and left the house.

I headed down the steps to Rowan's truck, kicking through the papery seeds from the elm tree. For the first time in a long while, I had a feeling that perhaps today was going to be alright.

CHAPTER 29

THE SUN BURNED away what remained of the morning mists and by the time we reached Maggie's house it was a glorious day.

I sat shotgun, window down, arm out, fingers combing the breeze as Rowan drove us along a quiet country lane. After enquiring about my breakfast—and then the lack thereof—he directed me to a box of oatcakes in the glovebox and wouldn't let up until I ate at least three. The hedgerows sped by in a blur as the sun arced high in the hazy sky.

I was feeling better. A lot better. It's criminal how much sunshine and a bite to eat can change a person's mood. Maybe that was the problem. I wasn't mad, I just had a Vitamin D deficiency. Seasonal Affective Disorder. Could that make someone hallucinate a whole party next door or smacking an axe into someone's face? I'd google it later.

We dropped Maggie off at her house—a converted barn between two barley fields, with a greenhouse full of neglected tomato plants.

"Cheers, pal," she said to Rowan. Then she got out of the truck and casually slammed the door behind her. Before she could head up the gravel path to her door, I stopped her.

"Sorry about the other day," I said.

Her eyebrows scrunched together even more, which was impressive.

"At the café," I explained. "I made a bit of a scene."

"Oh that. Pah." She batted the notion away with a lazy flick of her hand. "I just thought you were getting frustrated with your computer. You should see me with mine. Turn the air blue when my niece asks to video chat." She leaned in the window. "Whatever it was, it's probably not worth the stress. You take care of yourself, alright? Make sure that one"—she pointed to Rowan—"feeds you properly for your labour."

Rowan saluted. "I consider myself telt."

"Aye, good," she said. "Go on to your trees then."

Rowan pulled away. She waved, we waved, and then we got back on the lane. Rowan drove further up the hill and the whole world felt light.

Not far from Maggie's house, tucked in amongst other farm buildings, we pulled up at a squat, long garage made of cinder blocks and a corrugated iron roof. A plastic sign with a simple green icon of a fir tree and poorly kerned text read: CARLINSREST FORESTRY (CIO).

"Here we are," Rowan said. "Are you ready to dive into the exciting world of tree planting?"

I laughed and followed him up to the building. There was something exciting about being invited here, like being shown around backstage at a theatre or brought into the teacher's lounge at school. Rowan lifted the painted garage door with a grunt, first pulling it up from the ground then shunting it into the ceiling space. Inside the cave of cinderblocks and cobwebs was a tiny forest of deciduous saplings, wrapped in netting, spindly branches sticking out the top, neatly stacked against organised shelves of ropes, cables, bags of compost and firewood. On the other wall hung various shovels, spades, hoes and rakes. It had the same lovely, musty, earthy smell as a garden shed. Tourists never saw this place. Only staff. And their friends.

Rowan hefted one of the saplings up onto his shoulder.

"You alright to help me get the trees in the bed?" He nodded back toward the flat bed of the truck.

"Sure," I said. I hadn't done any sort of manual labour in my life, but I was surprised how keen I was to try. It took me a few tries to balance it right, but I eventually got a sapling on my shoulder. The next time was easier. We wordlessly traipsed back and forth, carrying our trees out into the sunshine.

Once we were done, Rowan gently tossed the truck keys to me, underarm. I caught them with uncharacteristic ease.

"Really?" I asked.

"Like I said, it's not too far up the hill. I can give you directions."

I hopped up into the driver's seat. I'd never driven a vehicle this size, but I wasn't about to admit that to Rowan. His easy trust in me inspired a little in myself, and I didn't want to break whatever spell he was casting.

I got the engine started and smoothly pulled away from the garage. Rowan closed it up and hopped in the passenger seat. He smiled, not a cloud of concern blemishing his sunny expression.

"Okay, let's go," I said.

Driving the hardware and supplies truck, I felt more at home than I had in a long time. Walkers stepped back from the road to make way for me. A passing lorry driver flashed his lights to let me through and offered a friendly wave, which I returned in kind. I briefly thought about what it would take to retrain as a lorry driver. Those long, lonely hours would probably suit me. And it was an important job. I wondered why I had never tried driving a large vehicle before. I supposed it had always felt wrong in Edinburgh to take up so much space. And the petrol use! It couldn't be forgiven. But here it fit somehow. This was a working truck. And I was a working driver. I needed the space, so I got it. What a feeling! To just get space you need. No questions asked. Maybe I needed a vehicle like this if I was going to live in the country. Perhaps I would get my own. Perhaps I would offer to drive Rowan more often.

I looked at him out of the corner of my eye. He sat relaxed on the passenger side, arm resting out the window, enjoying the air as we shuttled along. I cleared my throat.

"Hey, so, uh, do you mind me asking why you're only just learning to drive now?" I indicated and checked the corner, getting the hang of the tight country turns. "Seems to me that not having a license is a bit of a handicap out here."

Rowan was quiet for a moment. Long enough for me to realise I'd stepped into sensitive territory.

"I mean, you don't have to tell me if you don't want to. Not like I know anything about living in the country," I quickly added.

"No, it's okay," he said. He took a big breath through his nose, as if he were gearing up to a big jump or to lift a heavy weight. "I lost my license a few years back."

"Oh, sorry."

"No need to be sorry. It was my fault. Road rage."

I did a double-take, then forced my eyes back on the road.

"You? Road rage?"

"Yeah, me." He nodded. "Road rage."

I hesitated to ask.

"Like?"

"Like…" He bit his lip, clearly weighing up whether to tell me or not. "Excessive use of the horn. Threatening other drivers. Driving irresponsibly." He paused. "That's what it said on the report. What that means in practice is," he sighed, "driving at speed after another car, forcing them to pull over and then banging on the driver-side window until it cracked."

"Christ." I adjusted myself in my seat, suddenly very aware of the space between us. "What had the other guy done?"

"*She* hadn't done anything," he said. "I was late for work, and I thought she'd cut me off. The traffic police ran the footage back for me after I'd been taken in. Turned out she'd had right of way. I'd been wrong. Boom. Done. Lost my license."

"How long were you banned for?"

"Six months."

"Six months? How come it's taken you so long to retake the tests?"

Rowan paused again.

"Eh, you don't want to know."

I gripped the steering wheel.

"You don't want to tell me?"

"I do"—he nodded—"but it's a long story. Let's wait until we get to the forestry."

I stared ahead.

Oh no, I thought to myself. *Not Rowan.*

He'd never given me a reason to feel uneasy around him. He was kind to Fergus and to me. He'd let me rant at him in the pub. He'd invited me, a stranger, to join them just to be welcoming. He was the most nonthreatening man I'd ever met.

But still, in that moment, I immediately found myself thinking about how I could crash the truck just right to knock out a passenger and save myself.

CHAPTER 30

Rowan pointed me up the hill and into the forest.

Shadowy pine trees crowded in around the truck as the road narrowed. Between the trunks the daylight stopped and everything was dark. I could barely see more than a metre or two beyond the road. The massive, fringed branches hung over us, as if the trees were giants peering down into the truck as we passed. It reminded me of being a child sneaking into adult parties in the dining room, before my parents would usher me back to bed so they could talk to their more interesting adult friends.

"Take that left," said Rowan.

It was an unmarked trail, barely more than a pair of tyre tracks leading further into the forest. I became keenly aware of my phone in my jeans pocket, pressed tight against my thigh. Would I get reception up here? Could I hold the truck keys between my fingers?

Rowan grinned at me, seemingly oblivious—as most men are in these moments—to the alarmed whispers in my head.

"Get ready for this," he said.

I turned along the track. After a moment of shadow, the trees opened out on a large clearing sloping down the hillside, looking out on a beautiful vista of the surrounding hills. Dramatic cliff edges cut the landscape while soft rolling fields undulated out to where the horizon disappeared in the early summer haze. Forests, all various patchworks of green from lime to emerald, shimmered in a breeze I couldn't feel, while up above two birds of prey circled like guardian angels. My mouth fell open. Rays of sunlight broke through the soft cloud cover, as if the fingers of God himself brushed over the forests and brassy slopes, illuminating them with a spectral fire. Down below us, sitting pretty like a toy town next to the glittering river, was Carlinsrest. I pulled the truck over and stared.

"It's my favourite view," said Rowan. "Too bad it'll eventually get covered up by the trees we're planting up here, but it's a fair trade-off in my opinion."

He got out of the truck and headed round the back, but I stayed to look out over the view for a little while longer.

The silence struck me the most. I'd heard that the countryside was quiet, but I'd never been anywhere *this* quiet before. There had always been the background noise of far-off traffic, the hum of a fridge, the gentle shift and murmur of other people. But up here, when Rowan wasn't dragging saplings out of the truck bed, it was truly silent. I had thought true silence would be terrifying. Like a void. A lack. A horrible nothingness. I was surprised to find it was sort of alright really. Calm. Peaceful. Like nothing else needed my attention for once. All my thoughts and the high ringing in my head were far away, and now I could hear the sounds from within my body. The soft rustle my clothes made as I inhaled. The gentle rush of the air through my nose. The wetness redistributing in my mouth and throat. The thrum-thrum-thrum of my pulse. I'd always thought of my body in relation to what it should look like, what it should be able to do. Pushing myself toward another deadline. Ignoring the hunger pangs when I felt I ought to slim down. The ache of feet that just wouldn't walk in high heels. I rarely thought of my body as a living thing, gently humming with blood and electricity. I held myself in that moment of nothingness, just listening to my body. And for a second, I thought I might levitate out of my seat and—

"Hey, did you hear me?" Rowan appeared at the window.

"Sorry, I sort of lost myself there."

He nodded. "Yeah, it'll do that to you." He lifted a sapling up to the window. "I was asking if you wanted to help plant these babies."

I nodded, the earlier tension forgotten.

Yeah. I did.

Two by two we carried the saplings further into the clearing to where a line of young trees had already been planted. Their springy, sparse limbs reached up in exultation to the sky. After the first load, my arms were already burning, but it was a good burn. The burn of something achieved.

Rowan showed me how far apart to dig the holes, what fertilizer to scatter in the bottom, and how to firm the soil back in around the base of the sapling before covering it with a layer of unprocessed wool. I spent the next hour digging. Blisters on my palms. Mud under my fingernails.

And I felt the best I'd felt in years.

So much of my work back in the city had felt ephemeral, unreal. Back in the office, I'd get a brief through for my emails, spend an hour or so writing something up, then send it back, never to hear anything about it again. Every job felt like it came from nowhere and disappeared into nowhere. There was just me at my desk, between two portals into nothingness. I sometimes suspected it was all made up, one of those bullshit jobs that never really needed doing. Just something to keep the over-educated and under-employed occupied enough to stop us realising it was all a farce. But still I kept doing it. The brief coming in. The email going out. No word before, no word after. Silence. And I learnt that silence was the goal.

Early on, as an experiment, I left mistakes in my work. The odd typo at first—*specail, thier, teh*—then out-and-out misspellings—*competishun, redused pries, perfekt*—then strange phrasing—*Merry Easter, grummy snacks, totally goatily!*—slowly working my way up to something more absurd—*our new dishwashing tabs are also great for whitening your teeth!* I got the odd comment back but most of my transgressions were quietly dealt with elsewhere. It was only after a stupid quiz I'd written for a popular nappy brand—*What's the best way to keep your little one warm? A) a blanket B) sand C) a toaster*—that I started getting more regular feedback. Only ever negative, mind. It was then that I realised the silence really was better. In fact, the less I interacted with anyone, the better. So, the briefs continued coming out of the void and the work went straight back into it. No reply. No reaction. It was easy to forget I had done anything at all.

But looking back at the row of trees I'd—perhaps a little haphazardly—planted it was difficult to miss what I had done; to see the change I had enacted on the world.

Look, here there used to be just grass. Now there is a tree.

With good care and good luck, these trees could well be here long after I was gone. It was like reaching into the future and tapping someone on the shoulder.

I was here. You are here. We were both here by the same tree.

It would outlive me, Rowan, and future generations, until someone so totally blind to the absurdity of trees cut it down. Or maybe a storm would come. Or a fire. But even then, that was still part of the shift and change of the landscape of which I was now a part. Here. Visible. Tangible. Very much not void.

At the spot where I was about to dig next was the small corpse of a mouse. It curled stiffly around a red gash where its innards had been. Its eyes were shut as if sleeping. Its tail was broken. I didn't say anything to Rowan, but dug the hole for the tree all the same then tipped the tiny body in with my spade. I scattered fertilizer over it and set the sapling on top, gentle this time with the soil, and pressed the tree in place, sending the mouse into the tree's hopefully absurdly long future.

"Nice work," said Rowan. He stood close by with his arm resting on his spade. "Stop for a bite to eat?"

We downed tools and found a patch of grass short enough to sit in. Rowan brought over two bridies in a paper bag— picked up from the pie counter at the butcher's that morning. I bit into the flaky pastry and the flavour of salty beef mince instantly filled my mouth. *My God*, I thought. *I hadn't realised how hungry I was*. How long had I been this hungry?

I smiled over at Rowan to express my gratitude. He smiled back, but this time it felt forced. An awkward silence descended on us.

An alert sounded on his phone. He silenced it without even looking.

He pressed his lips together, looked out over the view, took a deep breath, then said:

"I didn't retake the tests when the driving ban was over because I was in prison."

CHAPTER 31

A BREEZE FUNNELLED through the clearing, hushing through the pines and rustling the leaves of the saplings behind.

"At least you're not stuck in the truck with me," he said, giving me a small half-smile.

Yes, but I am now out in the middle of nowhere with you and you have a spade, I thought.

"But how did *you* end up in prison?" I brushed crumbs of pastry from my mouth. "You are, like, the nicest person I've ever met."

He bit back a laugh. "There're plenty of nice people in prison, believe me. Nice people do stupid things all the time."

I pulled the spade laid on the grass closer to me, gripping it for support.

Maybe he was wrongly convicted? Maybe it wasn't that bad?

"Was it for the driving thing?"

He shook his head.

"Is it something…" I leant back.

"No, nothing like that. Sorry, I should have led with that."
He scratched the back of his head as if the discomfort of the
situation was making him itch. "I mean, it wasn't great. I went
to prison for it. But I…"
He wiped a hand down his face and exhaled.
"From the start?"
I nodded.
"Okay, from the start." He leant back onto his palms in the
grass. "I am the youngest of three. My elder brother, my elder
sister and then me—the surprise." He put out his hands in
a ta-da motion. "By the time I came along, my parents were
a bit more hands off with us kids. My sister was 'The Girl',
so my elder brother was never allowed to play rough with
her. It was always, 'play nice with your sister' or 'we don't
hit girls'. Me, on the other hand… well, I can only assume
they thought it was good for me, or it was natural for boys
to fight. My brother used to poke or pinch me, not hard, but
just enough to get me to lash out at him. Once I'd done that,
he'd put me into headlocks or sit on me or what have you.
It used to make me so angry, but the angrier I got the more
it encouraged him. He'd just pin me down and laugh. The
more I fought, the harder he'd laugh. My parents, too. They
thought it was funny. I'd scream and rage until tears were
streaming down my face, and they'd all just laugh like it was
the funniest thing."
He looked out to the view, took a breath.
"But I wasn't little for long. By the time I was sixteen I had
a good foot on my brother. The last time he tried to pin me
down, I threw him over my shoulder like it was nothing. God,
I remember the look of surprise on his face. He looked to my
parents, but they just said it served him right. They only ever
stood up for me after I'd already stood up for myself."
"That must have felt good," I said, envy bristling my skin.
"It felt amazing," he said, a sad smile briefly lighting his
face. "But it didn't fix all the years when I'd been helpless.
It just taught me my anger was always righteous—my anger

was the only way to keep me safe from being that helpless kid again. So, I leant into it."

"Hence the road rage incident," I said.

"Hence the road rage incident." He nodded. "After I lost my license, it just sort of got worse. The anger. It felt as if the whole world was laughing at me. Little things set me off. Getting a sleeve caught on a door handle or not being able to open a packet of something on the first try. I went off crisps for, like, a full year. I'd just rip the thing apart. God, I couldn't even hold a conversation with my friends without losing it over something that annoyed me. I used to recognise the point I'd gone too far because their faces would…" He waved a hand around his mouth. "You know? But that didn't shake me up either. Didn't make me stop and think, *maybe this is a bit much now, maybe I should sort myself out*. It just made it worse somehow, like I couldn't talk to them, like I was some kind of—"

"Monster," I said.

He nodded and smiled. "Yeah. Don't get me wrong, I was a mess. They were right to feel uncomfortable around me. I would have felt uncomfortable around me." He stopped. "I *did* feel uncomfortable around me. There was this one time, I was over at a friend's place for dinner. Y'know, couples and wine glasses. That kind of thing. I don't really come from dinner party people, so I was already on the back foot. Then, as I was opening a bottle of wine, the corkscrew I was using broke in my hand. The"—he twiddled a finger—"screw bit snapped right off, still stuck in the cork."

I stifled a laugh at the image.

"Yeah, in retrospect it did look pretty funny. So, everyone laughed. Only I didn't think they were laughing at what it looked like. I thought they were laughing at me. So, I threw the bottle at the wall. Red wine and glass everywhere. The laughing stopped. And so did any invites to my friend's place. I was out of control, and it was horrible. It doesn't feel great knowing people feel that way about you. And not really knowing how to stop it."

He shook his head.

"Anyway, so after my ban, I was having to get the bus to work, like I was back in school again. I was so embarrassed about losing my license. I thought people could see I wasn't a real adult, that I was still that kid struggling under his brother's pin hold. I kept reading every look as a judgement, as ridicule."

He stopped and picked at his fingernails. Then after a moment he continued.

"I was at a pub in Glasgow, visiting my sister. While we were chatting, I said to her that I would have to go catch the last train soon. I mean, I'd been drinking. I would have had to catch the train home anyway. But this guy in the booth next to us laughed. Young guy. Shaved head. Track suit. And, I don't know why, but I just got it in my head that he was laughing at me. And my whole mood changed like that."

He snapped his fingers.

I knew exactly what he meant. Though I didn't hear it just then, that high-pitched buzz in my ear never felt far away.

"My sister saw it. I think she tried to stop me, but I honestly couldn't tell you what she said. I couldn't hear it. But I remember what I did next. Like it was in slow motion."

Rowan placed his hand out, gently slicing the air as he marked each of his actions, as if cutting up a reel of film.

"I got up. I picked up the beer bottle in front of me. I raised it up as if I was taking it back. I remember thinking I could make it look accidental, like you'd see in a movie or a TV show. Y'know, where one of the main characters pisses off one of the other main characters and they"—he mimed a slap—"and they say 'oops, didn't see you there'. And the other character rubs their head, and the audience laughs and applauds. At least, I think. I don't really know what I meant or what I wish I'd meant." He shook his head. "Anyway, I got up and picked up the beer bottle, like I said, and then I swung it at the back of this guy's head."

A cricket sang in the grass close to us. Clouds rolled over the far hills. A fly landed on Rowan's eyebrow. He sniffed and it flew away.

"I didn't think I hit him that hard. I don't think I'd meant to, but I'd been drinking so I probably wasn't fully in control and… well, the bottle smashed, and I remember being surprised by the sound, like so surprised all my anger just left like it was never there. And everyone else in the bar stopped talking and turned to look. And the guy just folded over. He collapsed as if I'd hit the off switch and whatever made him human left and now it was just a machine of blood and bone. And his mates were staring at me. And my sister had her hands over her mouth. And I realised my hand hurt. One of the guys tried to rouse his friend and the other was getting his phone out. And one of the barmen was running over to me. And someone was yelling at me. And all I could think was I'd cut my hand on the broken glass and I hoped there wasn't any stuck under the skin. Isn't that stupid? I'd glassed a guy and all I could think about was glass stuck in my hand. All the way from the police turning up to court to prison, I was obsessed that there were shards of glass in my hand."

He showed me his right hand. Running down from his smallest finger to his wrist was a pale white line.

"It's because I couldn't go near what I'd done. I couldn't think about what that made me, or how every time I felt angry afterwards this cold wave would come over me. So instead, I thought about the glass in my hand. I swear I could feel something in there all the time. I'd lie awake imagining it floating around my body, a lost raft bumping about a river basin, with the potential at any moment to snag on some outcropping, maybe blocking up a vein in my lungs or my brain, or tearing a series of holes in my gut or my liver and like that, I'd be gone. Done. Those first few months I barely slept, waiting for this glass shard to pop out somewhere and kill me. I got the nurse inside to have a look once, but she couldn't find anything." He shrugged.

I felt the imprint of the needle in my pocket.

"Y'know, he hadn't even been laughing at me. One of his friends had just shown him something on his phone." Rowan looked up at me. "He didn't die, thank Christ. But he was out for a while. Swelling on the brain means he has some permanent memory loss and, uh, issues with mood regulation. I think that's what the doctor said at sentencing. I pleaded guilty. I mean, how could I not? I'd done it. And the loss of my license didn't help make me look any more innocent. I was given four years, but I got out in two with some extensive anger management courses and counselling. I reached out once, not to the guy, but his pal. To see how he was doing. Took a while but I got a response back. The memory issues had cleared up, but he was still having trouble with his moods. He's more irritable than he used to be. Gets angry easy." Rowan looked at the ground soberly. "I don't care what anyone says. It doesn't matter how many doctors I go to, how many years I spent inside, how many trees I plant, nothing's going to undo that. Just like that splinter of glass, it's floating about out there, a timebomb, out of my control and completely my fault."

He looked at me pointedly. My skin prickled. I suddenly felt alarmingly exposed sitting there in that clearing.

"Why are we talking about this?" I asked.

He looked at me with that expression I couldn't parse again.

"It's just… back then, I wish someone had talked to me, y'know."

I frowned.

"What's that got to do with me?"

He sighed. I realised what the expression was. It was pity.

"I'm sorry," he said. "I don't want to push if you're uncomfortable, but—"

The alert on his phone went again. He silenced it, fingers faltering for a moment on the screen.

I forced a smile and laughed.

"I think there's been a miscommunication here." I felt my cheek flicker under the strain. "I must have made a terrible first impression to make you think…"

I paused. This was where he was supposed to backtrack. Blush. Wave his hands. Anything to reassure me that he hadn't just insinuated that I had some kind of problem.

But he did not.

He let the silence hang between us. That look didn't leave his face. Heat grew in my neck and my cheeks and my eyes. I turned away to give my expression a break.

"Okay, I see I'm not changing your mind," I said as lightly as possible, calculating how quickly I could turn the conversation to me getting back to town. I stood up. Perhaps in a minute I could fake an important email on my phone. "But thank you for raising it. If I'd needed it, I'm sure I would have appreciated it. You're a very kind person."

He sighed.

"After what you told me in the pub, I thought you could do with hearing from someone who's been there—"

My whole body went cold. I knew I'd done something that night.

"What did I tell you?"

His eyes searched my face, slightly confused.

"About what happened at your old workplace."

Panic spread through my chest.

You told him? Idiot! Stupid idiotic girl!

All that time I'd spent worried about my neighbour and that hallucination in my basement. I should have been worrying about—

I turned away and bit the inside of my cheek, to focus, to calm down.

I heard Rowan getting up behind me.

"I just… after what happened with that guy and how things ended up, I thought if I could just stop it happening again…"

I spun round a little faster than I'd wanted. "Nothing is happening."

It came out harsh and sharp which annoyed me further. I wanted to stay calm, otherwise I'd be proving his point. But then the way he was pushing me—and he *was* pushing me—

how else was I supposed to react? This was gaslighting! Or something like it. When someone drives you crazy, so they can point at you and say, 'Look how crazy she is!' I couldn't let that happen. I had to fix this.

I took a breath and fought to calm myself, despite the rising pitch in my head.

"It was nothing. I probably made it sound worse than it is. You know how people are when they're drunk. Mountains and molehills and that. I'm fine. Really."

He put his hands on his hips, unconvinced.

"Really? You snap at nothing. You bristle at your own shadow. Dave says he saw you look pure murder at his boy the other day."

"What?" Then I remembered the teenagers at the memorial. I rolled my eyes and performed a thin high laugh. "Those kids just surprised me, and I felt…" I shrugged, playing things down, scrabbling about for something to take the attention off me. "You don't understand. You probably never get hassled by anyone. Big tough-looking person like you. They'd never jump out and try to humiliate you."

Rowan pulled a face. "I find looking like this tends to bring its own trouble. There's always some arsehole who wants to fight you."

I fought the grimace in my face. "I get that. I'm just saying I feel like"—*breathe, Tamsin, breathe*—"I'd get a lot less hassle if I was bigger, stronger looking. That's all. No need to interrogate it."

Rowan shook his head. "I don't think there's a magical state of existence where you'd get hassled by no one, where you'd not meet any arseholes, where some insecure stupid kid won't try to spook you to look cool to his insecure stupid mates."

"So, what am I supposed to do?" The words came out clipped and sharp again, my hands shook. "Just put up with it? Never get angry ever?"

Rowan sighed and pinched the top of his nose.

"No, no, that's not what I'm saying. I'm not saying don't

feel angry. That's impossible." He looked out over the view again as if for inspiration. "I learnt the hard way that the only way to win when you're seeing red is to walk away. Or if you can't do that, punch a wall instead of a face. Doesn't matter what anyone thinks of you or how angry they made you or how stupid or weak you think you look. Because the only other outcomes are leaving in the back of a police car or in an ambulance. It's not like the movies. There won't be a slow clap. No one's going to think you're cool. Well… some idiots might. But no one who's got any sense is going to look at you and say, 'Wow, that person knows how to handle themselves.' They're just going to think you are dangerous and unstable and they will be right. Because that's all this is. It's not strength. It's weakness in disguise. It's fear and loneliness and self-hatred, and bouncing between all of that while you spin out of control." He turned his head to one side. "For what it's worth, I think you're a decent person, and I'd really hate to watch another decent person lose themselves." He nodded. "I'm sorry if I overstepped."

I crossed my arms and looked at the ground, my skin vibrating itself to a humming fuzz.

"Well, you did."

"I'm sorry."

"Good."

The wind whipped around us.

"I'm going back to town," I said.

He gestured feebly toward the pines. "You can take the truck if you want."

I turned to walk back down the road. "No, that's alright."

"It's a long walk."

"I like walking."

He said something else, but I didn't hear him as I marched back down the mud road.

CHAPTER 32

MY EARS RANG and my vision blurred.

All I could think to do was keep marching forward, feet beating to the pulse throbbing in my temples, back down through the dark corridor of pine trees.

As soon as I was certain I was out of sight and out of hearing, I ducked onto the verge of the forest track, overgrown with weeds and nettles, pulled a large thistle out of the ground, tearing it roots from the earth, and whipped it against the nearest tree. Furiously, I flogged the gnarled trunk, teeth gritted, hands stinging from the spines up the thistle's stalk. Dirt flew. The crack of the greenery on wood echoed through the gloom between the trees. I kept hitting until the plant fibres severed and the flower head flew off into the forest, spiralling through the air like my clotheshorse had done a few days before.

The high whine in my head popped at its crescendo and stopped. A pathetic sob escaped my throat. I put a hand up to my mouth as if to catch it, put it back. But it was out now, if only in gasping, silent, fish-mouth cries. I fell onto my backside in the tall grass of the verge as tears poured down my stupid red face.

Small flies drifted in and out of the sunlight. My palms burned. I wiped my face with my filthy, burning hands.

Oh God, he knows. He knows! He knows what happened at the office!

I sniffed. I thought we were friends, or at least becoming friends.

It's only been a few days. Did you really think anyone would like you that quickly?

I groaned. How could I be so stupid?

I looked at the remains of the destroyed thistle and the marks on the trunk of that unfortunate tree.

I sat with what he'd told me. I tried to imagine Rowan— gentle, dorky, calm Rowan—smashing a bottle over a stranger's head. The fear I'd felt in the truck hadn't been entirely paranoia. The discomfort shifted about under my skin. I thought of the puncture on my foot. I thought of the needle in my pocket floating around inside my body, waiting to snag on my internal organs. I'd give him one thing: looking at that mangled thistle, he'd been right about walking away before succumbing to rage.

No, fuck him. Where does he get off telling me to be careful with anger?

I stood up.

I had a one-off lapse in judgement. A wobble. That's hardly a track record. It's men who have a problem with anger. That's been proven, hasn't it? Women don't take their anger out on the world. They don't beat up their partners. Well, except the ones who do. Or start fights on nights out. Well, no, some do that as well.

I resumed my march back down the hill.

If anything, women aren't angry enough. That's what people say. *If you're not angry, you're not paying attention.* Anger was the antidote. Being angry meant I was on the right side. Being angry meant I was safe from anyone who'd do me harm. How was anyone supposed to survive otherwise? What with all the things we have to be afraid of, all the monsters we've been told about. Shadowy men poised around corners, waiting in parked vans, hiding in the spaces the streetlights don't reach. Toxic people that take advantage of you, looking to steal your money, your time, your emotions. Workplaces that abuse your labour, that demand gratitude, that make you spend all your time slaving away for not-very-much-money-at-all-actually, that sink you into exploitative environments like frogs being slowly boiled alive.

You have to always have your trigger finger resting on your anger. Always be ready to let rip. It would be a good thing if women let rip more often. That would teach the rapists and the wife beaters and the kidnappers and the misogynists and the bad bosses and the bullies.

Smack. Fuck you. *Slap*. Fuck you. *Punch*. Fuck you.

So what if I'd imagined breaking the knees of the white sleeved arsehole who groped me once in a bar? So what if I'd thought about running the catcaller in the park through with a broadsword? So what if I'd daydreamed about smashing in the skull of whoever owned that flat that played loud dance music at three in the morning?

What was the alternative, being afraid all the time?

What if I wanted to be angry instead?

That was better, right?

Right?

I was nearly jogging back down the hillside. I stopped and took a breather.

A blackbird landed on a fence post near me and sang, suddenly loud.

"Fuck off!" I screamed at it.

It leapt from the post, a black fluttering, crying its warning call to the rest of the pine forest, and disappeared into the trees. The world was silent around me. No crickets. No insects. No birds. Nothing.

I rubbed my arms in the ensuing emptiness on the lonely hillside. My throat hurt.

That was the conflict. To take your finger off the trigger and risk getting hurt. Or to hold onto it and let it push everyone away. Where did the line lie? How much good faith did I owe other people? I'd always felt stuck somewhere between getting taken for a ride on the off chance someone might be genuine, and spotting threats around every corner and mockery in every comment.

I sat in the grass. God, I was tired.

I was so tired of trying to read the minds of the people around me, to see if they were safe, to see if I was safe. I could never know their thoughts, never see the world as they did, know it as they did. My brain, the seat of myself, sat in its castle of bone, completely encased, a wall separating me from everyone else, never to touch, never to meet. I and everyone else, in the very physicality of what makes me 'me' and them 'them', were alone.

I lay down on the verge.

All the assumptions I'd had about my neighbour when I'd first arrived, when I first met her, and then when I'd met her again, none of them had been right. It was me trying to read her mind. When all along there was just me on my side of the wall. Her on the other.

Who was my neighbour? My neighbour was unknowable, unfathomable. Another country. A whole other alien species. Just like every other person I knew. Everyone I met.

Everything else was translation.

Translation!

I sat upright. Of course, why hadn't I thought of that earlier? I pulled out my phone and woke the screen. I had a weak signal, but it was signal. I opened a new browser tab from my earlier research and opened up a Scots Gaelic to English translator. I typed in 'Sgàthan Sìth.'

The answer came back and my eyes widened.

Fairy Mirror

The old man had said the house was a mirror. Maybe he wasn't as mad as I thought. I had to find him.

I got up and reached into my pocket to check my things were still with me. I found my key, needle still hooked on its ring.

And then I found the keys to Rowan's truck.

Fuck. Of course.

I hissed through my teeth and looked back up the hill. The pines blocked my view of the forestry. No, I wasn't going back up to give them to him. There was nothing worse than backtracking after an argument to pick up a coat or a bag. I wasn't going to throw them in a bush either, no matter how much a part of me wanted to.

I marched back down the hill. I would drop off the keys, then I would find the old man and ask him again about the house.

CHAPTER 33

By the time I got to Carlinsrest, it was late afternoon. My legs were heavy and my feet were covered in the dust of dirt roads. I kept an eye out for the old man and his wife on my way in, but I'd have to complete a quick chore before I could properly go looking. I forced myself back toward the hardware and supplies store, hoping I'd beaten Rowan back down.

Fergus looked up at the ring of the electronic doorbell and barely concealed a huff of disdain. He returned his focus to a box he was sealing up with an industrial stapler the size of his head. Of course. Rowan had said Fergus was busy at the store. I thought he'd meant the antiques shop. Rowan must have got Fergus to cover for him so he could corner me into his little 'discussion'.

I marched past the rows of wood paint, twine and work gloves and dropped the truck keys on the counter. Fergus raised an eyebrow and looked behind me.

"Where's the rest of the truck?" he asked.

"Up on the hill," I said.

With your wanker boyfriend, I wanted to add.

Fergus frowned at me.

"I had to leave. Forgot I had them with me," I said and felt like a coward.

Fergus shrugged and I turned to go.

"How are you getting on with your haunted house?"

I stopped.

I should have just left. I knew even then I should have just left. I was tired and already annoyed. I had better things to do, finding the old man for one. And Fergus had done nothing but tell lies and tall tales. Nothing he could say to me would do any good.

I turned around and considered him.

He was either pretending not to look at me or he was genuinely very interested in whatever items he was boxing up.

"I'm not falling for it," I said.

"Falling for what?"

Either he truly believed he was innocent or he was a damn good actor.

"Another one of your stories."

He put up a hand. "Only the truth this time."

Fairy Mirror.

I sighed and stepped back up to the counter.

"What's wrong with the house?"

He looked down at me, unblinking, and grinned. He reminded me of the Big Bad Wolf in an old collection of Fairy Tales I'd once had, smiling down at Red Riding Hood, mouth wide and charming and hungry. A bit like *her* smile.

"Do you really want to know?"

I didn't break eye contact with him. After realising I wasn't going to flinch, he huffed a little air out of his nose, as if laughing at some secret joke I wasn't in on, then looked over his shoulder.

"Okay," he said, leaning onto the counter, lowering his voice. "But don't say I didn't warn you."

He hadn't warned me. He had done the very opposite of warn me, but I didn't care. I leant forward to hear him.

"I knew a kid at school here. He moved to the area for a brief time when I was about nine, ten? He was from one of the cities, too. Like yourself. He and his mum. I didn't know the whole story about why they were here, but they arrived quick and didn't stay long. Didn't even last the whole year. My mum thought there'd been some trouble with debt collectors. Or maybe a fella. Like I said, I never got the whole story, and they kept themselves to themselves for the most part. I only ever saw him at school, and the only time I ever saw her was when she'd come to pick him up and drop him off. Quiet people. Not really looking to stand out. Except, he had this birthmark. A port wine stain, I think it's called."

He traced a finger over the right-hand side of his face.

"From the corner of his eye, across his cheek and over to his ear. Easy to recognise. Probably why they came out all this way rather than to another town or city. Couldn't hide a birthmark like that for long. Anyway, after a few weeks he and I got to talking. Started with schoolwork, then TV, what our favourite show was: *The Demon Headmaster* not that you're asking. And before you know it, we were pals. Well, as much as we could be within the hours of school. He wasn't allowed out after class or even over the weekend. I had my mum ask his mum if he could come over one night. She was polite about it, but it was clear a sleepover was never happening. Every weekday she'd drop him off in the morning and be there to pick him up at the bell in the afternoon. It was a real shame, because I thought he'd be quite popular if he was allowed out a bit more. He had a dark sense of humour and nothing much seemed to scare him. Not the spiders in the supply cupboard. Not one of the farm dogs when it got into the school yard. Not even when Micky Campbell had a seizure in maths class. In fact, he was the one putting his jumper under Micky's head and telling the teacher to call an ambulance. For a kid who was bundled away as much as he was, nothing much seemed to faze him.

"Except for one Monday, when I got into school after my

paper round—I was always the first one in on Mondays—and there he was waiting at the school door, face pale, bags under his eyes and this thousand-yard stare. His uniform hadn't been washed. He still had the grass stains on his knees from Friday's football when he'd slide-tackled me off my feet. I called out to him, saying if I'd known he loved school so much I'd have set the two of them up weeks ago. Poor kid nearly leapt out of his skin. He saw it was me and then ran straight into my arms. Back then, my dad would have looked at me funny if he'd seen me hugging another boy, but I could tell something was wrong so I just rubbed his back like my mum would do and waited till he was ready to start talking.

"After a while, the school receptionist arrived and let us into our regi class to warm up. Once we were alone, he told me what happened. His mum had been a bit distracted lately. She wasn't telling him why and he was worried that—"

He stopped suddenly. I looked behind me, wondering if another customer had come in or—God forbid—Rowan had returned already. But there was no one. Fergus continued.

"He didn't tell me what. I was thinking, *oh shit, they've been found by whoever it was they were running from.* I told him they could hide out at my place if they needed, but he cut me off. He said things were tense all weekend, she was snippy and forgetful. He had to sort out dinner himself Sunday evening because his mum had conked out on the sofa. She'd been up at all hours, acting antsy. Eventually he put a blanket over her, headed up to their room—first I'd heard they'd been sharing a room—and packed his bag, just in case, and settled in for the night."

Fergus looked about again and leaned in closer.

"At about two in the morning he was woken by a sound. A creak. After jumping awake he remembered where he was and figured it was just his mum in the living room. He thought she'd woken up in the dark and was making her way up to bed. Then he heard a different sound. A voice. His mum. She was calling for him, but her voice was hushed slightly.

Y'know, like when you're trying to get someone's attention in class but without alerting the teacher writing on the board upfront. He got up and listened at the bedroom door. She was quietly calling him to come downstairs. His first thought was that they'd been found, that they had to go, now. He quickly, quietly, got dressed in the uniform he'd left hanging on a chair, grabbed his bag and opened the bedroom door.

"The landing was dark and it was dark down the stairs in the living room too. He thought she was keeping the light off so as not to alert whoever was looking for them. They had to be outside. At this point his heart was pounding already, so when the bathroom door opened behind him it took everything in him not to cry out."

"What was in the bathroom?" I asked.

"Not what, *who*. It was his mum, hiding behind the door. He said it felt as if his brain had broken. He was sure he'd heard her call him from downstairs. As if answering his question, he heard his mum call for him once again. From downstairs. All while he was looking at her hiding in the dark of the bathroom. 'Come down to the kitchen,' the voice downstairs said. The mum peeking out from behind the bathroom shook her head and mouthed, *There's something in the house*. Then she reached out a hand to pull him into the bathroom with her."

I gripped the edge of the counter so hard my knuckles turned white.

"What did he do?"

"He went back inside the bedroom and barricaded the door."

"He didn't go with his mum into the bathroom?"

"He said he couldn't know for sure which one was her. So, he pushed one of the beds up against the door, then he opened the bedroom window and escaped out over the roof. Winded himself landing in the back garden. He ran to the only other place he knew in the village. He ran to the school and waited for daylight.

"After he finished, I gave him one of the sandwiches from

my packed lunch and thought for a bit. Maybe he'd had a nightmare or something. Maybe someone had come to the house sounding an awful lot like his mum. Either way, I told him he was coming over to mine after school and he wasn't going to argue. He agreed. Too knackered to fight, probably. He was quiet all day in school. The teacher could tell something was up, but he was done talking about it, so she let him sleep in the classroom through lunch. I kept guard. After what he'd told me, I didn't want to let him out of my sight. I thought maybe after talking to my parents, we could figure out what to do.

"But then, right as the bell sounded to let us out of school, who turned up but his mum. Right on time, like she always did, as if nothing had happened. I didn't know what to do. I wanted him to come home with me, but I knew I couldn't overrule his mum. He stood frozen next to me. Probably thinking the same. She stepped forward and lowered her voice.

"'It's okay,' she said. 'It's all going to be okay now. It's over.'

"I'd no idea what that meant, but it seemed to mean something to him. He took her hand and away they went, back down the lane, back to the house.

"Next day, he didn't come in. Nor the day after. Or the day after that. I asked the teacher where he was. She said they'd moved on again. I was a bit miffed he'd just up and leave like that, especially after how much he'd worried me with that tale of his. I'd hugged him while he shook in my arms and then he'd disappeared without so much as a 'See ya around'. A few weeks went by and it was another Monday, just before school closed for Christmas break. Must have been close to midwinter because the sun didn't come up until just before the school bell rang. I'd arrived early, like every other Monday, and I saw someone waiting at the gates. It was him. He was back. But as I got close, I saw he was missing that birthmark. So instead of the 'Hello' or 'What the hell were you thinking leaving without saying goodbye?'

I was planning on shooting his way, I said, 'What's happened to your face?'

"'I changed it,' he said, 'so Mum could be safe.'

"I stopped approaching at that. Made up some excuse like I'd forgotten my PE kit or something, turned around and ran home. When I came back to school, as I inevitably did as my mum chucked me back out of the house, he was gone. No one else had seen him that morning. And I never saw him again."

My stomach clenched.

"His house was my house, wasn't it?"

Fergus stared at me, stony and cold for a moment.

Then the skin around his eyes cracked into wrinkles and he heaved a creaky laugh.

"Got you," he said. "Got you proper that time."

My face flushed hot. He was making it up. He'd made the whole thing up to mock me. And like an idiot I'd believed him.

He kept laughing, mouth wide, wide enough that I could see all of his teeth at once.

The high ringing in my ears grew.

My eyes locked onto the loaded, industrial stapler on the desk, his hand laid close by.

Then there was a real ringing. The electronic bell.

Rowan stood in the door, face flushed, mouth gaping with words that would not come. The sight of him shook the thundering blood from my ears. He must have chased down after me. Every vengeful imagining left me and my cheeks burned.

"Tamsin, I—"

Fergus interrupted him before he could finish.

"Your new pal is a gullible one."

"What?" Rowan frowned.

"I just told her the old my-not-mum-called-me-from-downstairs urban legend and she believed me. Have you never heard that one before, pal?"

Rowan rolled his eyes. "Ferg—"

"What?" Fergus grinned horribly. "You know what these tourists are like. They all think we believe in fairies and goblins, like we're fucking idiots."

I turned and wordlessly walked for the exit.

"Tamsin—"

Rowan's voice followed me out the door, just audible over the screaming blood in my ears.

212

CHAPTER 34

I STUMBLED DOWN onto the main street, focusing my gaze on the pavement, my head abuzz with that high ringing. Cars and people passed me as if in a dream, fast flashes of colour and faraway sound. The whole world was drowned out by that dreadful high whine. I tucked my chin down into my chest and tried to avoid any eye contact, any hint that something was wrong, any chance of being noticed at all. I clenched and released my fists, trying to shake off the growing inferno shuddering through my limbs. To shake off the thoughts of violence from my seething mind.

I marched alongside the river. My reflection refracted and jerked on the rushing water like a glitching screen.

Moving here had been a mistake. What an idiot I'd been, thinking I could get a quiet, rural life, flitting about in the background of village fetes, becoming a regular at the local pub. My gut turned in on itself. Forget the old man, forget my neighbour! I would go back to the house and pack my things and leave today. Fuck the smashed windscreen. I'd knock it out myself if I had to. Then I'd drive to the nearest train station, report the car to whatever garage was close enough and have them take it. For parts, for scrap, I didn't care. I couldn't go back to Edinburgh. Not after everything. I'd get to the nearest town and pay for a hotel room on my credit card and figure out what to do after that. The only thing that mattered right now was that I was leaving.

That's right. Run away again. Coward.

"Fuck you," I hissed at my thoughts. "Why are you never on my side?"

Oh God, I'd said that out loud. Fine, whatever.

I suddenly became aware of Viv, the barmaid—no, landlady—a simple sweatshirt with one neon pink zebra in the centre of it today—sashaying over to me from Maggie's Café.

"Hullo, hen, did you get your scarf back?"

I kept walking.

"Not my scarf."

Viv kept pace with me.

"Yes, it is. You were wearing it in the pub last night." She searched my face for a moment. "Oh, have you changed your hair?"

"No."

"Oh." Viv shook her head, slowing down. "Sorry, hen. I must have mistaken you for someone else. Though I swear I've seen your sister. You look uncannily like—"

I briefly heard the giggles of the Grayson girls in my memory. My dad pushing them on the swings.

"I don't have any sisters," I said sharply.

"Sorry," she said sheepishly. "I really thought you were someone else."

I pulled away from her. Why had I thought I'd be any different in the country than I was in Edinburgh? Why had I thought it would be easier out here where I couldn't hide among the crowds? Why couldn't I just be normal? What was wrong with me?

I was so wrapped up in my thoughts, I barely noticed the calls from across the road.

"Alright, pal? Wet your knickers again?"

Braying laughter. It was the group of teenagers from before. They stood around the flower display on the war monument, laboriously moving the tubs and planters into a crude cock and balls arrangement. They had plenty of material to work with. Somehow there were even more flowers today than yesterday. The same boy who'd jumped out at me and yelled on my first visit was snarling my way, surrounded by his court of lanky, pallid mates.

Him.

That high-pitched noise screamed in my ears. It was as if my body had been taken over by another force. I stepped out into the road, causing a car to screech to a halt, horn blasting the air with annoyance. I marched across to the boy and his friends. I saw his expression freeze slightly. Was I blinking? I don't think I was blinking. The high-pitched buzz pounded in my ears. The teens laughed nervously around him.

"What do you want?" he said, all puffed up insolence.

I realised up close, he wasn't that big at all.

Good.

In my pocket my hand closed around something long and sharp: the curved needle from the basement attached to my keyring. I envisaged myself plunging it deep into his cocky sneering eyes. One-two, pop-pop. Like two jellied balloons. Like a staple through Fergus's hand. Like a hammer through the unce-unce-unce flat-owner's skull.

"What?" the kid demanded, though his fear was palpable now.

Delicious.

My fist trembled around the needle.

Stab him in the eye stab in the eye stab in the eye cocky little shit little shit stain little fucker little twat little no-eyed twat.

"What?"

Do it!

No.

I pushed the needle through my hand. A stark blooming flower of pain.

Then I leaned right into his face and barked.

He startled backwards and fell right into the shaft of the cock and balls flower arrangement. I didn't stop. I barked, loudly, madly, like a rabid dog, a woman possessed, right there in the street. I didn't have the words anymore. Only sound. Only the great animal fuck-you and leave-me-alone uproar, exploding from my lips and leaving my throat ragged. I stopped only when I ran out of breath and coughed.

The high-pitched buzzing sound in my head had stopped.

"What the fuck?" One of the other teens stared at me, the whites of her eyes bright.

Over my shoulder I saw people coming out of the café, ready to intervene, to help, to stop the danger.

To stop me.

Before anyone could say or do anything, I straightened my back, looked away from the onlookers and marched over the bridge and out of town in the silence I had made. I took my hand out of my pocket. The needle had punctured the webbing between my thumb and forefinger, key dangling on the end. An impromptu piercing. A self-maiming. Flesh throbbing, the adrenaline kept the pain at bay.

I slid it out in one short, sharp movement. Then I tucked the needle back in my pocket and kept walking.

CHAPTER 35

ABOUT HALFWAY FROM Carlinsrest to the Sgàthan Sìth cottages, the wind changed. I barely noticed at first, I was so wrapped up in my anger and the growing pain in my hand.

It blew from the north, bringing cold Highland air down into the Lowlands. The earlier humidity of the day seized up in the rapid chill, wreathing the trees and hedgerows with a fine mist. The blue skies paled into bright white clouds. It wasn't long before they descended, and the previously shimmering roads disappeared behind a veil of cool white fog.

It was suddenly very quiet, as if all the birds in the trees could sense the change in the air and went hiding in the places they flew to when it stormed or hailed.

The tumult of my mind fell into a rare silence. As I marched on, I took my hoodie from around my waist and wrapped it around my shoulders. Then I put it on properly, pushing my arms through the sleeves, gently tucking the cuff around my fresh puncture, cold now with the hanging damp in the air.

The mist drew closer, until I could barely see a few feet ahead of me. I worried about passing cars. There was no way they'd be able to see me in time in this weather.

Would that be so bad? I thought. No one would know. The driver would think you were a deer. You'd barely have time to realise what had happened. One sharp shock and it would be over.

I shook my head as if I could dislodge the thought out of me. It wasn't the first time I'd thought something like that. Back when I was working at the office, on those days when it felt as if I were a ghost invisibly haunting that place, I'd purposefully cross the busy road outside without checking first. Just step out. I thought at worst I'd get a few weeks off in hospital. Maybe someone would realise something was wrong and I'd finally get help.

At best…

I tasted the tears before I knew they were rolling. Salt and iron. I wiped my cheeks with the backs of my sleeves, pulled down over my cold hands. The burn of the tears on my skin was overly familiar. I'd moved here, upped my whole life, to get away from the daily crying. And yet here I was, crying again. Maybe it wasn't Edinburgh. Maybe it wasn't cities. Maybe it was me. Maybe I wasn't built for these times, like an animal that had failed to evolve with the rest of its species, left behind, proof of the changing environment. It was nature. Some got the right mutations and some didn't. Some ducklings keep up, some get left behind. Some kids get to be pushed on the swings, and some have to push themselves. I was just one of the unlucky ones. That's why I couldn't escape it. It was nature—my nature—and it would be with me until I died.

Maybe a quick collision on a misty road would be kinder.

A sound broke me out from my circling thoughts.

Light rhythmic crunching came from up ahead. For a moment I thought of a mouth, snapping nut brittle between its teeth, wet half-chewed pieces tumbling down a pale chin.

When I saw the faint outline of a person, I realised it was footsteps.

A shiver raced involuntarily up my legs.

A shadow was walking toward me on my side of the road. The country lanes out here were narrow, so I tucked my head down and crossed to the other side to let the stranger pass.

The shadow crossed with me.

I slowed my pace. The hairs on my arms stood on end.

Making sure to watch the figure, I crossed back to my original side of the road.

The shadow moved as well, only where my steps were slow and deliberate to communicate my intention, theirs were quick and impish, as if they were playing a game.

I stopped. They stopped.

It was so quiet I could hear my heartbeat thrum in my ears. A different kind of beat than the impulsive thunder of before. This was the tremble of a hummingbird, a rabbit scrabbling against the walls of a box trap. My throat went dry despite the dampness of the air.

Maybe they were blind, I thought, or had some other kind of sensory issue. Perhaps they'd half sensed me out here and were now waiting for some confirmation before they could continue. Maybe they were a lost tourist. I wet my lips, still salty from the tears, and summoned up my friendliest tone.

"Hello there," I said.

My voice wavered slightly, belying the cheery tone I'd attempted.

There was no reply. They must not have heard me. I kept my eyes on the shadow and got my phone out of my pocket.

"Hello?" I said again.

After a second my voice echoed back at me from the shadow through the mist.

"Hello there," it said.

I flinched, eyes staring, feet frozen.

"Hello?" it said again.

It was my voice! I shuffled backwards and fell onto the hedge. I tried to steady myself, but pain shot through my injured hand and I dropped my phone. I looked down to see where it went, but it had fallen into the long grass under the hedge.

Fuck fuck fuck.

When I looked up, the shadow was walking towards me.

Stuck in the hedgerow and nowhere to run and no one to call, I ducked my head and clung onto the brittle branches behind me.

As the figure approached, their face came into detail. Bright, unblinking eyes, outline of beautiful, bouncing hair, that wide, tooth-filled smile. I recognised her before I saw the crescent scar on her forehead. My neighbour was walking toward me in the mist of this lonely, quiet road. I avoided her eyes. Something deep in me told me not to look in her eyes.

I watched as her feet stepped into my personal space.

"Where are you going, neighbour?" she asked.

I said nothing and shrank back into my shaking shoulders.

Those feet stayed stood in my space.

I kept my eyes on the ground. She was so close, I could feel her breath on my forehead.

Don't look up don't look up don't look up.

After a few agonizing seconds, she backed up and laughed, gentle as if I'd just told her an amusing story. My shoulders relaxed away from my ears.

Before I could stop myself, my eyes flickered up.

Her head was twisting back to keep facing me as she walked away. The wrinkling in her neck was red with torsion.

But it was her face close up that frightened me most.

I ducked my eyes back to the road.

I'd seen too much! She knew! She must know!

She kept walking. And laughing. I waited until she had disappeared into the fog on the way to the village, then I pulled myself out of the hedge and ran. I just left my phone. I didn't care about it. There was no way I was turning my back on her unless that was to run.

Up close in the fog, I now understood Viv's confusion.

I swear I've seen your sister. You look uncannily like—

The eyes, the nose, the mouth—even pulled wide. Now I knew what had bothered me so much about her face, why she was so familiar.

I realised I'd never had a proper look at her until now. Hidden in the dark at her front door. Spied through the crowd at The Curtyard. Painted and coiffed until she looked like someone new.

I'd read somewhere that none of us really know what we look like because we only ever see ourselves mirrored. Even our phone cameras present us with a mirror image because that's what we're used to. If anyone ever saw a double of themselves, they wouldn't immediately know it because everything would be—to them—inverted.

I knew now why Viv had wondered if my neighbour and I were related. Because under the make-up, the hair style and the brighter, more confident expression, my neighbour looked just like me.

She was my perfect double.

INTO
THE WOODS

CHAPTER 36

I RAN ALL the way back to 1b Sgàthan Sìth. By the time I reached the elm tree at the base of the driveway, the sky had turned murderous.

My neighbour looked just like me. How was that even possible? What was she?

Fairy mirror

The mist had soured and spoiled, and the sky had curdled into thick clouds, casting the world in a foreboding, violet light. I looked up at the symmetrical frontage of the Sgàthan Sìth cottages perched upon their tiny hill. The bedroom windows stared down like hollow eyes; the shared awning over the front doors gaped open like the mouth of a corpse.

But it's just a house, I told myself. *Just bricks and stone and mortar and roof tiles and wooden beams and copper pipes.*

I clutched my sore hand close to my chest. I couldn't urge myself any further toward the house, not even for fear of all my belongings abandoned inside. I'd planned on packing and running, but now I couldn't even bring myself to go in. Not after what I'd seen on the road.

But I couldn't turn back either, couldn't retreat to Carlinsrest to Fergus's laughter, to the sneering children, to all the horrified faces, to Rowan's pity. But I couldn't stay here in the drive. She would be back soon enough and I couldn't be here when she did.

I had to escape. I had to run.

I urged my feet to move. I didn't care where. I turned a sharp right and marched away under the trees.

Once I'd elbowed my way through the thick criss-cross of younger branches, the going became a little easier and soon I was threading between tree-trunks, trampling the carpet of ivy beneath. I sniffled pathetically as I walked. I felt like I was a child again and walking away from my parents in the supermarket to purposefully make myself lost, hiccupping slightly through the tears, arms crossed tightly across my pudgy chest. They'd laugh when I was brought back to them, usually by a concerned onlooker or a member of staff trying to be helpful. Perhaps I never wandered far enough to really worry them. Maybe they were never that worried about losing me at all. I always went back with them anyway.

I walked straight through a small thicket of bramble, thorns catching on my clothes and skin.

I used to think all children—at some level—wanted more love than their parents were able to provide. That it was normal to grow up feeling you were loved, but only because someone had to. To be dissatisfied with it. But to accept it anyway. Because what else are you going to do? You're not able to leave. If there're no bruises and your belly is full, what's the harm? So, of course, I always went back.

I had that same sense now of wanting to run, to get lost on purpose.

Only this time, I didn't secretly want to be found. I had no deep desire for the person I was walking away from to come and hunt me down.

Because it wasn't just that dull ache, that hunger for something I couldn't verbalise, that drove me out this time. It was terror.

I walked deeper into the trees, vision foggy with tears, breath a rasping see-saw, the animal of my body heaving under the weight of me.

CHAPTER 37

A WREN TRILLED in the branches above. A blackbird rustled through the undergrowth below.

Remnants of the mist snaked through the trunks and the grasses, like pale fingers clutching at the air. I pulled my hoodie around me. The light was dimming and I felt cold, but not cold enough to go back. It was time to admit it. I wasn't a good person. I was barely a person. My neighbour had done a better job of it than me, and I had no idea what the hell she even was.

Maybe it was better if I stopped pretending to be a person at all.

Maybe it was safer if I just left humanity altogether. Let the thing that was my neighbour take the house, take my life, my identity. I'd disappear into the wilderness never to be found, never to be seen again. Pinkie promise!

I hoped that's what she wanted.

I hoped that was *all* she wanted.

I trudged on, forcing myself through ferns and fine saplings, cursing my jeans each time they caught on bramble or hawthorn.

I imagined myself slipping out of my clothes and casting them aside. I imagined letting the hair on my legs and my arms grow long. I imagined it spreading over my body, a fine grey pelt. As the light dimmed, I imagined myself crawling along the forest floor, the skin on my knuckles and my knees growing thick and leathery. Instead of words I would grunt and bark and howl. I'd never have to think of the right thing to say again. No more tripping up over my words. No more worrying if I'm saying too much or too little.

I wiped my forehead with the back of my hand. Despite the evening cool, I was drenched in sweat. Well, I could sweat and stink as much as I liked now.

What a joy it would be to shrug off all the layers of structures built to reinforce an order I clearly did not fit into. School, jobs, offices, hen parties, football matches, social media, timesheets, spreadsheets, active listening, wellness programmes, disciplinary meetings, sick notes, questionnaires on how often you feel like punching your supervisor right in the teeth, official cautions, red cards, court summons, prisons, block buttons. They were all casts upon splints upon bindings upon a bone that would never straighten.

The further I walked, the darker it got. I couldn't tell if it was because night had fallen or if the canopy above me was so densely packed no light could make it through. Either way, the forest floor slipped into a silvery half-light. Everything—ivy, boughs, trunks, creeping things—was cast in a monochrome of shadows and the soft light of the unseen moon. I've been told I shouldn't be so black and white, but look, the world is black and white here. Goosebumps prickled where the soft down of my secret fur covered my skin. My chattering teeth felt pointed and broken. My fingers, rubbing my arms, now sported a set of sharp claws. I gazed at them in feverish wonder.

Oh, there I am. That makes sense.

I didn't know if it was the cold or the lack of sleep or the mind-numbing fear, but my vision started to swim and the world shifted.

Suddenly, I got a sense of others in the forest.

I dropped down behind a rotting tree stump, the chill and dread shaking my limbs.

Fading out of the darkness, I saw figures coming in dribs and drabs into a dim clearing ahead. Their movements were loping and strange. They twitched and sniffed and made guttural grunting sounds.

As they wandered closer to my hiding place, I shuddered with surprise.

I recognised their faces!

I saw Fergus rooting through the undergrowth, tusks protruding from his wide smirking mouth. I saw the teens from the village, screeching from the trees and throwing branches at the others below. I saw Viv, the landlady from the pub, an actual zebra now, with Maggie from the café riding around on her back, pecking at her mane. I saw my old colleagues, squirreling together along the forest floor, tails flicking up and down in some secret code I couldn't understand. I saw the Grayson girls, their golden arms and cheeks covered in soft white feathers. A crane came down from the canopy wearing my father's glasses and spread his wings over them. I saw an elegant woman on deer legs, hooves painted a bright pink, long ears flicking back and forth despite her fearless countenance. I saw Rowan, his ears pointed and his eyes red. They were a herd of humans, picking their way through the forest, digging up the earth with their clawed hands, sniffing the air.

The wind shifted and then the woods felt airless. A shadow circled them from the trees on the opposite side of the clearing. It flickered, just in the corner of my eyes, shifting and changing. Watching the human herd.

One of the teens threw a rock at Fergus. He reared up and with one swift move pulled the kid from the branch and thrust him onto the floor. The teenager screeched and clawed, but he was nothing compared to Fergus. Fergus ran his tusk into the kid's stomach as easy as plunging a spoon into whipped cream. The forest floor erupted into screaming as the rest of the teens descended upon Fergus, tearing at his hair and face. One of them plucked out an eye.

The crane lifted off into the air and left the two feathered girls to be poked and prodded by my many fingered colleagues. They investigated the pitifully cheeping children, bending their arms and fingers to find how far they would go. Once bored of their exploration, they bit down on the girls' necks and started to eat them.

My body trembled at the violence, half terrified, half thrilled.

This was how most animals go. Eaten alive. I'd always been convinced that we, humanity, were little better. That this was what was hiding underneath all of our civility. That's why I never trusted it. I knew that under all of the forms and the processes and the laws was that quiet pressure to be productive.

Produce or be the product.

Be the food.

Eat each other alive.

The shadow on the edge of the clearing cackled. Cackled with a too-wide grin.

Fergus cracked open the teenager's ribcage and reached his hand into the meat inside, while the teen gnawed at his attacker's exposed calf, tearing mouthfuls of bloody flesh that would appear again in Fergus's hands, gathered from the boy's stomach.

My scrambling thoughts snagged on the sight.

Wait, Fergus wouldn't actually eat someone alive.

Rowan pulled the head off one of my colleagues, bloody froth around his mouth.

I'm not sure I want to be out here.

The deer-legged woman placed her painted hoof into the split of a splintered tree.

I don't want this.

I backed away, out of my hiding place, picking up speed.

I don't want this!

I ran, chill forgotten, hoping beyond hope that the bloodthirsty creatures wearing the faces of the people I knew wouldn't come chasing after me. My heaving breaths echoed in the darkness. I didn't dare look back. My route was scattershot through the trees. But whatever direction I went, it wasn't long before I was back at the clearing again.

Only now the forest floor was an open grave filled with skeletons and rotting corpses. At the top of the heap, on the hill of bones, sat that shadow.

It perched on its haunches, mouth wide, feeding off something from the pile.

I cast my gaze about, desperate. Where could I run to?

I couldn't be in the city. I couldn't be in the countryside. I couldn't be someone new. I couldn't be human. I couldn't even be animal. Everywhere I was, so was this. Gnawing away in my guts. There was no escape.

You know who you are, don't you?

I was the disappointing progeny nudged from the nest. I'd been cast out from the tribe at the office. I had lost the competition for the Sgàthan Sìth cottage. The cuckoo removes the warbler's egg, the crow pecks out the lamb's eyes, the runt is left behind.

A crack of bone. A neon pink fingernail.

You know who you are, don't you?

Yes. I knew what I was. I was a fucking monster.

And I belonged here.

I clambered onto the hill of corpses and lay down among the bodies. The air was still and cold, but the hairs on my arms fell flat. Up above me was the wet click and suck of the creature feasting on those who had come before. Death crept up my toes into my feet and my legs. My arms went slack and numb. My sphincters loosened, my bowels emptied, my stomach acid started to dissolve my organs. My eyeballs shrivelled up into their sockets, my gums receded back from my teeth, my brain slowly turned into a brown soup, all the connections that held my thoughts and memories and fears and hopes lost to rot, a jigsaw puzzle never to be put back together. The rot crawled up my limbs and soon I was covered in moss.

All the while the shadow slurped and crunched and smacked its lips.

At least she would not eat me alive.

She.

In the corner of my eye—vision blurred from its wrinkled rotting—something glimmered. I turned my fleshless head to look. The skeleton next to me had something in its mouth. A glint of something metallic pierced the darkness between its broken teeth. I turned and reached out with my rotting, moss-clothed arm and creaked the skull open. Inside the mouth was a key. Another Yale key, but older than mine. I checked the next skull, prying open the teeth, and it, too, held a key, though older again this time. The eating on the top of the pile stopped and the creature went silent. Arms still rotting, ligaments barely holding my bones together, I searched through the other skeletons around me. Each one held a key in their mouth. I kept searching until I came to a smaller skull still partly fleshy, with a birthmark over one side of the face. Inside the brown glop between his shrunken lips was another key. Every skull around me held a key, getting older and older as if going back through time. Square-head keys became small brass keys became sturdy iron keys became simple picks of metal became a slab of wood.

All these bodies. All of them suffered the same thing I was suffering now. This wasn't just me. This was something bigger. Something older.

A screech came from the top. Then a spark of light caught the corner of my eye.

The old woman from the pub sat in her wheelchair at the base of the pile.

Only now she was awake. And watching me.

I reached out to her, offering the key in my hand.

Help me, I thought, as loud as my brain soup would allow, *I want to stop this, but I don't know how.*

The old woman huffed.

"Enough," she said to the creature on the pile. She'd barely raised her voice and yet it shook the trees and rang through the hill of bones.

The shadow screeched then scampered away into the darkness.

I turned my withered skull to face the old lady.

Now she was sat by the fire of The Curtyard. In her lap she had a spool of red thread. She wrapped it round her finger, pulling a scarlet end through the loop.

My bones were barely holding together.

"Time we had a chat," she said.

Then she pulled the knot tight and I woke.

CHAPTER 38

I was woken with a nudge. Cold, I rolled onto my side. It was freezing. I must have left a window open.

"Here." A voice spoke gruffly. "Are you alive?"

Barely, I thought. Everything ached with cold. I became aware of a god-awful stabbing pain in my hand.

I pried my eyes open. A woman in leather boots and a wax coat leant over me. A quiff of reddish curls shook in the breeze.

Can't even rot in peace, I thought.

"If you're not dead," she said, "then you're trespassing in my orchard."

Achily, I looked around me. Sure enough, I was lying between two rows of stout trees, pink blossom dotted among the leaves. No skeletons. No skulls. Just roots and hardened earth. I must have passed out here after running away into the woods.

"I'll give you some time to gather yourself," the woman said, not unkindly. "But if you're not gone in an hour, I'll be calling the police, alright?"

I tried to answer, but something caught in my throat. I gagged. The woman backed away in disgust.

"For God's sake, get some help," she muttered then stalked away down the row of trees.

I fished about in my mouth for what I'd choked on. With my good hand, I pulled out my house key covered in spit and phlegm. And the curved needle, still attached, still brutal-looking. Especially now as it sat in my painfully swollen palm next to the black-blood-crusted tear between my thumb and forefinger. It was a small miracle I hadn't swallowed the thing, let alone choked.

I remembered all the skulls with the keys inside them, then lay back down on the earth.

What happened to me? Another hallucination perhaps. A fever dream brought on by everything from the last few days.

I'd been so convinced I was dead. It had felt like everything, my body, my spirit, my mind, had gone, and all I had left was this awful ghost of myself, this last imprint, haunting these hills, waiting until I faded away. All hard to believe now, of course, lying on the floor of this orchard with my bruised body and my throbbing punctured hand, feeling very fucking visceral.

The breeze fluttered my hair.

In the dream forest, I'd found myself wishing I would fade away faster just so it could all be over. But at the same time, I'd found myself clutching onto all of this awfulness, because at least it meant I was here and that I existed. I chuckled. How fucking terrible. Holding onto a living deadness because it's still better than being dead.

The leaves above me swayed in the breeze, hushing me as if I were a squalling child.

But I wasn't squalling. Not anymore.

I thought of my father.

He was the only one I talked to after it happened.

After I left my job, after that terrible day in the office, I hid in my room, terrified, unsure what would happen to me.

I spent the night browsing property sites just to give myself something else to think about. Early in the morning—I hadn't slept—I tried to think of someone I could talk to. I hadn't spoken to any of my old friends in years and I couldn't turn to my colleagues. Especially now. So, in desperation, I messaged my father.

I didn't tell him everything, but I did tell him that things at work hadn't been great, that I felt this constant drive to escape, how I always felt ignored, like I wasn't really there, like I didn't exist.

He answered back:

Can we chat later? I'm a little busy right now helping out with the Graysons. I'm sure it's not that bad.

I never replied.

I changed my search terms on the property sites to cheap and rural. The next day, Sgàthan Sìth came up in my results. I immediately made an offer and started packing my bags.

That high-pitched tone returned in my ears.

I'm sure it's not that bad.

Anger came to me, lighting fires in my brain and my body. If my father had said anything else, perhaps I wouldn't be here. My limbs felt less like lead and more like fireworks; dynamic, alive. If Rowan hadn't gone barging into my business like he did, maybe I wouldn't be in this orchard. Sensation returned. I had weight. I had mass. I had energy. And if my stupid fucking neighbour hadn't come sneaking up on me in *my* basement, then maybe she wouldn't have that stupid fucking half-moon scar on her forehead and I wouldn't be such a fucking mess.

Anger pushed my aching body off the ground and back onto my legs.

For God's sake, get some help.

I reached my arms to the sky and yelled wordlessly into the trees. A flock of starlings lifted from the canopy and flit away across the field.

I was angry and it felt like shit, but it was better than feeling afraid, and better than feeling dead.

I thought of everything that had happened. The disturbances in my house. The incident in the basement. The phantom party next door. My neighbour, my perfect double on the road. Now that nightmare in the woods. I'd been right. I *was* stuck between two realities. One where I was mad and one where all these unbelievable things were actually happening. One where my neighbour was the monster and one where I was. Well last night, she tipped her hand. After seeing all those skulls and their keys, I was ready to choose.

I wiped my house key on my jeans. This was my key. It was anachronistic, but it was mine. And 1b Sgàthan Sìth was my house. It was cold, and quite possibly inhabited by God knows what, but it was my house.

This was my shitty life, my shitty anger, my shitty problems. Mine.

And I was ready to fight for them.

I gingerly pulled my sleeve over my injured hand, pocketed the key and the needle, and walked out of the woods.

I couldn't remember how I'd got into the orchard, so I just kept walking until I hit the road. I found a turnstile and hopped over. I came out at a section of hedge that looked familiar. Ducking down, I found what I was looking for: my phone, spattered with mud. I picked it up with my good hand and pressed the button on the side. Out of battery. Something to be solved later. I had bigger problems to deal with first.

I looked left and right. To the right was the route back to Sgàthan Sìth, to the left was the way back to the village. I wasn't ready to face the house yet. I still wasn't exactly sure what I was facing there, though after last night I was convinced this was no ordinary dispute with the neighbours. I remembered how my neighbour's head had turned, her skin pulling, her grin unnaturally wide. I needed to know what I was dealing with before I could do anything about it.

My injured hand throbbed in my sleeve. I needed to do something about that, too.

I remembered the old woman from my dream in the woods, tying knots in her lap at The Curtyard.

Time we had a chat.

It made about as much sense as anything else had so far.

Okay then, I thought. *Let's chat.*

Filthy, cold and stinking, I headed back to Carlinsrest.

CHAPTER 39

When I reached the village, I barely recognised it.

Bright pastel bunting hung from every gutter and every lamppost, casting fluttering shadows over the road and pavements. Buckets of lobelia and pansies clustered at the foot of every café, restaurant and pub, filling the air with a pungent floral aroma that caught in the back of my throat. Every window was dressed in frilled gingham. Every table sported a polka-dot wipeable cloth. It was as if the Hallmark channel had thrown up all over the place. There was no mud. All the grass was uniform. The cobbles were clean. It was so extreme that all inferred cosiness had been burned away and all that was left was a monoculture of pastel plastic. It reminded me of Disneyland. Of costumed characters. Of the brand emails I was so very good at writing.

As I crossed Bodach's Brig, I saw Maggie from Maggie's Café, all pretence of a smile gone now, trying to knock down one of the seven hanging baskets clustered around the café windows with a broom, and scowling as she did.

The teenagers were nowhere to be found.

The village was quiet.

I stared at the aggressively cheery decoration. Flowers were wound around every lamppost until you couldn't see the lamppost anymore. The planters and pots made the paths nigh-on unusable. I wanted to laugh. It felt like something to laugh at. But I couldn't. It wasn't just the feeling of threat underlying it all, the thin veneer of respectability over something truly unhinged. There was something else.

Something sad.

I reached out with my good hand to one of the flower baskets Maggie had knocked to the ground. This one was filled with daffodils, small and delicate, with white almost see-through petals and sunny yellow trumpets. The petals were cold and soft in my fingers.

Poor wee thing, I thought. *You're supposed to be cheerful, but you're just frightening everyone away.*

I straightened up. It was time I got to the bottom of this, before the madness spread across the whole village.

I picked my way through a line of sunflowers and ducked up the lane toward The Curtyard.

I stepped inside the pub and found most of the other villagers hunkering within.

Everyone jumped and turned to the sound of the door as if I'd popped a balloon. The place was packed and yet eerily quiet. No one spoke louder than a whisper. Viv stood behind the bar staring toward the rippled windows, the light from the sunny pastel colours dancing over the zebras marching across her T-shirt. The zebras on the balcony seemed to look on with much disapproval. The red-faced man—Dave, I think Rowan said his name was—was here as well, practically clinging to the edge of the bar. I found the teens, huddled together in one of the booths. Fergus saw me from the other booth and ducked his head down. The only faces I couldn't see were Rowan's—I imagined he was up among the trees, sat among the saplings, watching the clouds come over the glen—and the old man's.

"Look. The dog woman's arrived," said the boy from earlier.

For once, no one laughed.

"Shut up." Dave glowered in the boy's direction. The boy sank down in the booth and scowled.

I shuffled through the crowd toward Viv. She was on her phone, speaking in low, angry tones about when someone could come out to "hack the jungle down". The line of zebras up on the shelf seemed to cower back.

"Excuse me, I'm looking for—"

"Yeah, through the door by the fireplace." She pointed me across the room, not even looking away from the window.

Sure enough, there was a door next to the fireplace. I'd never seen a door there before. Perhaps there was a private dining room.

"She said to keep an eye out for you."

Of course she was waiting for me.

I shuffled through the crowd to the door and slipped inside.

CHAPTER 40

On the other side of the door was a small room, richly scented with wood smoke and old stone. The fireplace from the main lounge of the pub continued through the wall to this private space, dimly lighting a long table pressed against the back wall and a few chairs here and there. The curtains were drawn over the single small window, so only the silhouettes of the hanging baskets outside could be seen.

"So, you survived then."

I jumped at the sound of the voice. It was the same I had heard in my fever dream in the woods. As my eyes adjusted, a lone seated figure leant out of the shadows and into the light of the flames.

The old woman in the wheelchair regarded me from her spot next to the fireplace.

It was the first time I'd properly looked at her. Her face was a web of cracks and wrinkles, as if tracing every thought and every feeling she'd ever had. Not a single one had been hidden. My own face felt like a mask in comparison.

"Roger'll be happy to hear you made it through."

I flushed, embarrassed. I'd never asked the old man his name.

Unsure how to address her, I held out my uninjured hand, suddenly aware of my slept-in muddy clothing.

"Hello, I'm Tamsin."

"I know who you are." The old woman smiled. "You can call me Callie-Ann."

She shook my hand. Her grip was firm and strong, like shaking hands with a forest.

I searched the room.

"Where is Roger?"

"Visiting some old pals in the north. Giving me a bit of peace."

She pointed to the chair on the other side of the fireplace to her. I took the seat.

"I thought he was waiting for me to prove that I am who I said I am or solve a riddle or something."

She chuckled.

"He is a bit of a trickster, isn't he?" She shook her head and looked into the fire.

I sat on the edge of the chair, body coiled tight. The old woman was still and calm. I looked into the fire, too. Looked at her face. Then back into the fire. Tried to see something in the fire. No, just flames. I'd come here following a sense of certainty, a down-in-the-bones knowing like recognising a snake or a growl in the dark. Now I was unsure.

I watched her carefully. Fergus said she was a witch. I wondered if she would take my punctured hand and read the dried blood in the lines of my palm. Or perhaps she would reveal an ancient deck of cards from the cavernous pockets of her anorak. Or she could just be an ordinary old woman, glad of some company as she watched the fire, waiting for her husband to return.

"I heard you barked at the little shit," said Callie-Ann.

"What?" Then I remembered. The teen boy out in the main room, and what I'd done yesterday. "Oh. Yeah. I guess I did."

The old woman nodded, a ghost of an amused grin creeping up the side of her lined face.

"That's not all though."

I swallowed.

"I wanted to do worse," I admitted.

She turned to look at me, firelight dancing in her eyes. She held out a hand.

"Show me then," she said.

I pulled my injured hand out of the sleeve of my filthy hoodie. The puncture was a crusted welt of dried black blood, and the flesh between my thumb and forefinger was swollen to the size of a golf ball. It hummed with pain. In my palm, I was still holding the needle, threaded onto the ring of my house key.

Callie-Ann picked up the needle and made a small 'hmm' sound. Then she took my hand and yanked it up to her eye to inspect it. I jerked forward as she pulled the whole limb closer.

"You put it through yourself?" She handed the needle back to me.

"I wanted to put it in his eye."

"Hmm, nasty."

"I know." I sank a little into the shame of it.

"We all want to lash out at the world sometimes. It's the actual lashing out that gets you into trouble, not the wanting bit." She huffed, still inspecting my hand. "That boy is a little shit. Though the little shit has his own problems. That's why he's such a little shit. But he's not worth going to prison for."

"Rowan said something similar."

"Rowan's a wise lad." She nodded to herself. "A hard-won wisdom, at that. If only someone had intervened earlier."

She gave me a knowing look.

"I think he tried to warn me."

"It's hard to hear what you're not ready for."

I shifted uncomfortably in her gaze. Sitting with this woman felt like being caught between the shower and my room without a towel. No, worse; it felt like all my skin was see-through and my insides were visible for all to see. All my guts and lungs and piss and shit and stomach contents. And my heart, beating fast, like a bird trapped in a net, so small and so exposed. I wanted to tell her, *please let me put my skin back on.*

She straightened up and sighed.

"At least it's a clean hole straight through. Lucky you used a leatherworking needle. Needs cleaning though."

With a surprisingly quick movement, she reached over to a side table then dumped a small glass of clear liquid on the wound. Vodka. It burned immediately. White light flashed behind my eyes. I screamed.

"I know, I know," she said as she took a napkin and started to wipe the dirt and grime away from the edges. "It needs to be done. Got to clean it before we can heal it."

She sniffed the puncture then squeezed the edges. I bit my other hand to stifle a cry. A rivulet of blood and plasma dribbled down my wrist.

"No pus," she said. "That's good."

She dabbed a medicinal-smelling ointment onto the wound. It instantly cooled the stinging flesh. The relief was so good I could have groaned. My muscles relaxed and I sank back into the chair, blossoms of sweat clinging along my back, now chill on the opposite side of me to the fire. I watched as Callie-Ann gently applied a sterile patch to my now clean hand and wrapped a bandage around it.

"That should do you for now, but you'll want to go see a proper doctor." She leaned back into her chair and let me reclaim my hand. "Not today, though. Today you have work to do." She fixed me with a look. "So, now we've fixed one wound, what's this Roger tells me about you having some bother with your neighbour?"

Finally!

I leaned forward, voice barely rising above the crackle of the flames in the hearth.

"The thing is," I said, licking my lips, trying to think of another way to say it and failing. "I don't think she's human."

The old woman's eyebrows raised.

I didn't know if she thought I was crazy or what; I didn't care. I hadn't come this far to start clamming up now.

"She rustles around the house next door at all hours, even when it seems like she isn't in. She can change her appearance. One minute she was mousey and odd looking, the next she was like some supermodel. She broke into my home—"

Callie-Ann's mouth flickered slightly.

"She broke through?"

"Yes. And then I—" Oh God, how could I explain this? "I hurt her. It was an accident. I got startled. But I was also really angry at the time. And drunk. Not that that excuses anything—"

Callie-Ann waved my excuses aside. "How did you hurt her?"

"I put an axe in her head."

The old woman's eyebrows really raised that time.

"But the blood disappeared! Off my axe. Off the floor. There was nothing. And then the next day she was fine. I saw her, here in The Curtyard. As if it never happened." I wiped my non-bandaged hand over my face. "And then yesterday, in the mist, I saw her and… she looked like—I think she looks like me. But better somehow."

The old woman nodded, eyes skirting over the flames.

"Hmm, the axe. She probably wasn't expecting that. That's why it's so different this time."

"This time?" I hugged my arms around my shoulders. "This has happened before? What is she?"

"Those are complicated question that share a rather long answer," she said as she reached round the side of her chair and unsheathed an impressive-looking walking stick.

It was made of rich, dark wood and had an iron point at the end, blackened with use and age. The grip at the top had a surprisingly heavy build to it, a little like a hammer. It made me wonder how this woman was hefting it about so easily.

She drew a line into the ash below the grate of the fire, the metal tip skipping over worn layers in the hearthstone.

"James Hogg came by this way in 1802 on one of his travels. He goes on to write *The Private Memoirs and Confessions of a Justified Sinner* where a puritanical man meets the devil as his double on the mists of Arthur's Seat."

She drew another line.

"Sometime later in 1868, Robert Louis Stevenson passes through the same area on his way to the family engineering works in Wick. He goes on to write *The Strange Case of Dr Jekyll and Mr Hyde* where a genius doctor splits himself in two: his good and kind self, and his evil and murderous double."

With a screech of iron on stone, she laid another line into the ash.

"Around the same time as Stevenson's trip, J M Barrie was a boy living not too far from here. When he was young, his mother thought there was another boy living in the house. A boy who looked like him. She thought it was his dead elder brother. Barrie goes on to write *Peter Pan* about a child who'd run off to live with the faeries. A child who gets separated from his shadow."

One more line in the ash, joining the others into a squat rectangle.

"Then that psychologist came to Britain in the early 1900s. Took a sneaky sojourn up north. You won't see anything about it in his meticulous diaries, so you'll just have to believe me when I say he came this way. Not for long, but long enough to stumble across something. To suffer a strange confrontation. He became menaced by hallucinations, visions and voices. See, he'd always believed that he contained two selves, and now he'd found something that explained why. He spent years writing up his experiences with the thing he found, the thing he realised everyone carries but no one wants to be. A thing that, if ignored, has the potential to take over and frustrate even the most well-meant intentions."

She looked to the curtained window and the dancing shadows of the hanging baskets outside, then back at me.

"Starting to sound familiar?"

I leant onto my knees.

"What is it?"

Callie-Ann looked up around the ceiling, her eyes an icy blue, as if admiring the bones of the room.

"This place, like all the world really, used to be a wild place." She tapped her cane on the ground. "Thousands of years ago, people would travel across Doggerland—the land bridge between the rest of Europe and here—back and forth across multiple ice ages. Over time they collected stories. Stories of forbidding, strange places on the other side of the water. Of the creatures that lived there. Faeries. Pixies. Changelings." She leant toward me, voice deep and low. "There are strange things in the darkest corners of every country, where the land is still a little bit wild. But when you've mapped most of the mountains, chopped down the forests, drained the bogs, you don't leave much space for whatever used to live here before you. It wouldn't be too much of a surprise if some things remained, hidden in the quiet corners of these islands. Deep in the earth. In the treetops. Under the waves. Or in a remote cottage in the middle of nowhere, waiting for someone to move in." She sighed. "Whatever your neighbour was before you got here is lost to history. What's important now is how she's chosen to manifest. How she's chosen you. Now she is your *shadow*. And it is as your shadow you must deal with her."

"Okay." I took a big breath in. "So how do I get rid of my shadow?"

Callie-Ann barked a laugh. It rang off the stone walls that surrounded us. I ducked down in my chair. Something in the laugh made me think of thunder, of blizzards, of rocks falling from the sky.

"Oh child, you can't get rid of your shadow," she said as she wiped a mirthful tear from her eye.

"What do you mean?" I swallowed. "Do I have to leave?"

The old woman shook her head. "Wherever you go, she'll follow."

I threw up my hands. "Then what am I supposed to do?"

Callie-Ann looked at me, kindly, firmly.

"You have to face her," she said. "Normally this would be as simple as a conversation. But you've been running—avoiding all of this—for so long, she's not going to come to the table easy. No." Callie-Ann scratched her chin. "You're going to have to go to her."

I blinked, trying to follow.

"What, like, break into her house?"

"You won't be able to break in. She's too strong for that now. Especially with how different things are this time." One of the logs in the grate popped. "You'll have to get her on the attack. Make her the aggressive one. That's the only way to weaken the boundary. Go back to the house, alone, and wait until it's dark."

Back to the house. Alone. In the dark.

A tremble ran through my body. But Callie-Ann wasn't finished.

"Then you go to sleep."

"Absolutely not!" I said.

"Absolutely yes!" She hammered her stick on the ground. The breeze outside briefly rose then fell away. "She has to think you're weak. And you have to be in a liminal space if you wish to cross over to her side. Darkness. Sleep. The places where the mind wanders, where you can see things differently. Don't worry, you'll wake up when it's time. She'll want you conscious when she hunts you. And she will hunt you."

I saw myself inside that house. Alone. Anyone who'd known me had long moved on, tired of waiting. Not worth sticking around for after all.

"What do I do then?"

"Do not leave the house. You'll need to find the breach over to her side. Once you do, break through as quickly as you can."

"And then the shadow will leave me alone?"

She pointed to the square she'd drawn in the ash. "Once you're on her turf, that's when the real work begins. There you'll face her four times. Four for each wall, each corner of your house. Four challenges to prove you are ready to take back your home and take back your life. And four opportunities for her to tempt you. You'll have to listen, but you mustn't give in to your impulses."

I screwed up my face. "I don't think I—"

"Don't play stupid, now." Callie-Ann waved a hand toward the main room. "Your impulses, like when you've got the green eye over someone else's life, so you get the impulse to shag their husband. Or you're seeing red over a perceived rejection at work, so you get the impulse to spit in your boss' cup. Anger, envy, they're misunderstood gifts. If you listen to them properly, they're just telling you what you want out of life, or pointing out unfairness in the world. And they can give you the power to drag yourself back on your feet when the world has seen fit to bury you."

I thought of this morning in the orchard, how the ringing tone in my ears came again, but this time it felt less like I was shaking apart and more like I was coming back to life.

"But," said Callie-Ann, "if you ignore them, push them down, run from them, they'll just get bigger and louder. Because they're trying to make you listen. And if you won't listen then they'll take control of your life for you. The only way you'll get her to back off is by showing her you're ready to listen, without running away this time and without lashing out."

The clotheshorse bouncing off the windscreen. The thistle whipped against the trunk of a tree. An elegant hand with pink painted nails.

"What if I can't do it?" I asked. "What happens if I fail?"

The old woman leaned forward, and her shadow grew behind her on the wall: a giant, a mountain, an unending winter storm.

"She will devour you."

The fire crackled, sending a waft of woodsmoke up into the room. That cold, heavy feeling spread across me, the same one I'd felt when I'd lain in bed wondering if I'd come here to die. I'd dismissed it as maudlin self-pity, but I wondered now if I was right. If that itching feeling that had haunted me since I'd arrived was right. Everyone dies. Everyone. But it's always a surprise when it pops up on the horizon, wearing your own face and a too-wide smile.

Hello, here I am. I'm coming for you now.

A strong, knotted hand covered mine.

"You can do this. I wouldn't be telling you if I didn't think you could. If you hadn't already proved you could."

She pointed to my bandaged hand.

"You put the needle through your own hand before you could put it in the little shit's eye." She sniffed. "Though next time, let's try not to put the needle through anyone, aye? Speaking of…"

She produced a spool of red thread from a pocket in her giant anorak and presented it to me. It was red like veins, like a dribble of blood from a broken mouth. I remembered the old man—Roger—in Rowan's store picking up that order. The small parcel with a tiny weight in it. Embroidery thread, Rowan had said. It was wound around a yellow plastic bracket of some kind that felt uncomfortably familiar. Callie-Ann drew my attention back to the room.

"This should keep you right, and that needle of yours out of trouble." She held the thread out in the palm of her hand, and with the other she stuck up four fingers. "When she tests you, and you want to push a needle into an eye or your own flesh, make a knot instead. Remember, four challenges. Four knots."

"Four knots," I repeated and reached out to take the thread.

Callie-Ann clapped her other hand over mine.

"This is old magic you'll be working in, child. No gods, no devils. Just you and the dark. Understand?"

I nodded my head.

"You have to remember, the place where you're going, it's just emptiness. Anything that's in it, whether it's fear or pain or sadness, it's just what you brought into it. There's nothing there that you didn't already know in the first place. Nothing she can surprise you with. Nothing but what you bring with you. Just in the absence of everything else, you can see it. Clearly and probably for the first time. Look at it. Own it. And she'll have nothing she can use against you."

I held the red thread in my hands, one freshly bandaged by this strange woman. I felt the weight of it all. There was still one thing I didn't understand.

"Why are you helping me?" I asked.

"You gave the money back," said the old woman. "The notes Roger dropped that first time you crossed Bodach's Brig."

God, it felt so long ago. I remembered that morning. I hadn't been motivated by goodness, or fear of reprisal. I'd wanted to take the money and then I'd just given it back anyway.

"It's not who I am," I said.

She gave my arm a squeeze then wiggled the joystick for her chair. All the times I'd seen Roger pushing it, I'd never realised it was electric. He'd pushed her around with him all the same.

"Good luck," she said. "Now if you'll excuse me, I need another stout and a nap."

Callie-Ann went to the bar. I left The Curtyard.

Outside the sun was starting to break through the cloud cover above.

Maybe the old woman was mad. Maybe I was mad. But it was the first time I'd felt like I had some sort of grip on the thing since I'd arrived. Not so much a map, but a narrative. A story for myself that wasn't the same awful tale I'd been telling for years.

Why don't people like me? Why am I so unhappy? Why can't I figure out my life?

No matter how much I pretended otherwise, I'd been telling the same sorry story over and over. I was ready for it to end. One way or another.

I would go into the darkness, and I would look and see what was in there. After that, I would just have to figure out what comes next. It sounded like a terrible idea to be honest, but it was better than going on like this.

I took the needle out of my pocket. Daylight flashed along its sharp point. I took it off the key's thin wire ring. It was time I got a better keyring anyway. Then I took the spool of thread Callie-Ann had given me, something about it still itching at the back of my mind, and threaded the end of the red string through the eye of the needle.

I was ready.

It was time to go home.

INTO HELL

CHAPTER 41

THE CLOUDS HAD burned away by the time I got back to the house.

The air was still. Not a single breath fluttered the leaves in the elm tree in the driveway. The Sgàthan Sìth cottages stood on the hill against the sun, their scandalised face in shadow, watching me return. I thought I'd feel afraid, but I just felt numb. A cold acceptance of what needed to happen next.

I took my key, still new, still shining, and placed it into the lock for my half of the house. Once again, I noted the deep scratches sunken beneath the thick, fresh coat of gloss paint. I saw them differently this time.

How long did they last? I wondered.

I also noticed the dirt on my unbandaged hand. I hadn't washed in a while. I probably still had leaf litter in my hair. What a state I must have seemed to the villagers, to Callie-Ann. Things must have been bad if no one said anything. I turned the key in the lock and stepped back inside.

The house was quiet, as if it were holding its breath.

Dust motes were frozen in place in the beams of golden light that broke in through the kitchen window. My arrival sent them dancing, like my presence alone was enough to disrupt the peace, or bring life to this husk of a home.

Get used to it, I thought. *Because I'm staying.*

I kept my shoes on and went through the kitchen cupboards. I pulled out the remaining tins I'd bought and began to cook their contents, one by one. First the soups which I crumbled crackers over and mopped up with slices of bread. Then the second tin of chili which I covered with cheese cut thin enough to melt in the residual warmth of the pan. Once I was finished with my feast, I drank straight from the tap over the sink, splashed my face with my unbandaged hand, then picked at the remaining crackers. I felt a bit more ready now I'd eaten something.

In the corner of my eye, I spotted the metallic edge of the axe. I wiped my mouth on the back of my hand. Callie-Ann had said my neighbour would be on the attack. But she'd also said I'd be tempted to give in to my less well-intentioned impulses.

You need protection from her.

You need protection from yourself.

No, you need protection from her.

No, you need protection from yourself.

Her. Yourself. Her. Yourself.

I scrunched the empty cracker packet into the bin just to put a different noise in my head. The axe leant against the wall, all innocent. *Me? I'm just for chopping wood. No idea what you're thinking of, missus.* I bit my lip. I'd rather have it and not need it than need it and not have it.

I gathered up my axe and ascended the stairs to the bedroom.

I lay down on the bare mattress fully clothed, needle and thread in my pocket, and the axe laid heavy as a prayer across my chest. The house, 1b, lay still and empty around me in the late afternoon light.

Alright, shadow, I thought to myself, *come and get me.*

Then I closed my eyes and let myself fall into sleep.

It felt as though it had only been a few minutes, but when I woke the room was dark. Properly dark. The golden sunlight was gone and the windows were black. I'd hoped I'd feel more rested when the moment came, but I just felt… out of it. I had that sick, light-headed feeling that comes when I've slept at the wrong time of the day, crossed with the sudden jolt of adrenaline from hearing something in the shadows.

Which I had.

I hugged the axe on my chest and waited. The sound came again, the sound that had woken me.

Knocking from downstairs.

"Tamsin?" A voice muffled by wood and night came from downstairs. "Are you awake?"

It was Rowan.

I sat up on the mattress. What was he doing here? And tonight of all nights?

"Tamsin? Look, I wanted to apologise about yesterday."

A heaviness shifted in me. Guilt.

Stupid, nice, hard-won softness.

He didn't need to apologise to me. He wasn't supposed to be here. Not with what I was attempting to do. With her. I didn't know how I was going to keep myself safe, let alone another person.

I shivered in the lonely night air. It was a relief to hear him though. I rubbed my thumb along the wooden handle of the axe, polished and warm.

I realised now that I wanted help. I wanted Rowan's help. I didn't quite know how he would help. How he could help. Maybe him just being here would be enough. To have a friend. And if he was here, even after finding out what happened at the office, then maybe that's what we were. Maybe we were friends. Just having that as a possibility made the night ahead feel less dangerous.

"Alright," I said into the dark. "I'm coming!"

I got up and opened the bedroom door.

I stepped out onto the landing, ready to walk down the stairs, to let Rowan in, when I heard a creak next to my ear.

I stopped. I turned.

The bathroom door was open a crack. My eyes adjusted to the dark. Slowly, a face surfaced from the shadows.

Rowan's face.

He peered through the gap, ashen and terrified. As I stared dumbfounded at his wide, frightened eyes, not understanding, I heard his voice coming again from the front door downstairs.

"I know you're in there," his voice called out. "Talk to me."

Rowan-in-the-bathroom's eyes darted in the direction of the voice then back to my face.

Fergus was right about one thing. It did feel like my brain had broken, seeing Rowan's face here and hearing his voice there. I stepped backwards. The floorboard cracked loudly underfoot.

"Tamsin?"

The voice was in the living room now.

Rowan-in-the-bathroom looked at me and shook his head vigorously. It was everything I'd feared. I'd pulled him into my shit. Now he was in danger, too.

CHAPTER 42

WHAT ARE YOU *doing here?* I mouthed at him.

Rowan-in-the-bathroom pushed his face further into the gap in the door.

"I wanted to check in on you. Then I saw the door was open and I was worried something had happened, so I stepped inside and then I heard that… thing… and I ran and hid." His voice was hushed and shaky. "What is it? Why does it sound like me?"

My chest went tight and my hands started to sweat. This was all my fault. I had to get him out. How in the hell was I going to get him out?

"Are you alright?" the voice called from just down the stairs.

Rowan-in-the-bathroom flinched back behind the door.

"It's coming, it's coming!" he whispered. "Quick, hide in here."

The bottom step of the stairs creaked in the dark.

Rowan-in-the-bathroom reached out his hand to me.

I went to grab it, taking one hand off the axe, then stopped.

"She will hunt you."

I remembered Fergus's story. One mum downstairs. One in the bathroom. Who do you choose?

I put both hands back on the axe. Rowan-in-the-bathroom looked at me, panicked at first, then slowly shocked.

"Tamsin? What are you doing? Come on."

I stepped back.

"Tamsin! Are you nuts?"

I backed away toward the stairs.

His face curdled into anger.

"You're going to get us both killed!"

"I'm sorry," I said, "but you're not Rowan."

He sank against the bathroom door. The skin around his eyes twitched.

"You really think that thing is me?"

"No," I said. "Neither of you are Rowan. Rowan's not here."

The thing-that-was-not-Rowan stared at me from behind the door. The house was suddenly still in the way a loaded, waiting, spring trap is still. I didn't dare blink. Didn't dare turn my eyes away from the familiar-unfamiliar face still staring at me from the darkness of the bathroom. His face sagged. It was something I would have read as disappointment, hopelessness, if I didn't know better. If there wasn't still that strange twitching in the skin around his—its—eyes. It was only when the first, tiny shard of glass peeked out from under its eyelids, puckering the skin at the corners, that I realised it wasn't twitching but filling, like a coin purse.

An inky stream of splintered glass tumbled from under its eyeballs, catching in the thin skin of its eyelids. Its mouth pulled into a perfect dark 'oh', too round to feel natural in any way, and shook the walls with a piercing scream. In a scatter of glinting shards, not-Rowan lunged at me. I forgot the use of the axe in terror and threw myself away from the imposter. I slipped on the top step, fumbled on my own feet and tumbled down the stairs, down into the dark below where the voice was waiting for me.

CHAPTER 43

I FELT EVERY stair on the way down.

Each blow felt like a stick hurled against my body by a furious assailant. The final impact with the floor knocked the air out of my chest. I wheezed and splayed out my arms, the axe still clutched in my unbandaged hand. Miraculously, I hadn't gouged myself with it. After a moment of shock, I tenderly, slowly, patted my limbs with the other hand, checking for bones piercing skin and bends where there shouldn't be bends. My shins were bruised, but unbroken. My arms, the same.

Well, you definitely have her on the hunt now.

Tentatively, I raised myself off the cold, hard floor. Pain, immediate and sharp, announced itself from my side. I yelped. Then from the darkness came—

"This is not your home."

It was the voice. No, a different one. On the other side of the living room. Close, but not close enough to know exactly where it was coming from. I froze where I was, gritting my teeth through the pain in my ribs. I searched the darkness for a figure.

The voice spoke again in the shadows.

"This is *not* your home."

A figure emerged from the black. All I could make out was their outline against the grey-gloom of the kitchen beyond. Bipedal, long-limbed and slender. They were still, perfectly still.

They spoke again, voice a hissing whisper.

"You can bring all the papers and the coins and the genealogical charts and the swords and the crockery and the shields. You can pray to your gods and chant your spells and shake your charms and cite your laws and repeat your mantras and state your 'facts.' It means nothing."

A set of eyes lit up in the figure's head. I only knew they were eyes because of where they sat on their face. Otherwise, they were unrecognisable as eyes; they were round, flickering pinpricks of light.

The figure hadn't moved, but the voice spoke beside my ear.

"This is not your house."

My heart pounded insistently in my chest. Each beat implored me: *Get out get out get out! Forget the knots. Forget the breach. Just get out!*

The figure burst into life, arms raised high and wide, impossibly long, bending in all the wrong places. It charged toward me.

I scrabbled back on the floor, flinging myself toward the front door, away from the footsteps thundering toward me, louder and heavier with each step. Shapes flew in the dark. My arms moved painfully, sluggishly slow in the adrenaline fog, as I swung the axe in front of my face.

In my flailing I managed to hit something.

There was a screech.

I was on my feet, twirling out of the way, bouncing off the fireplace, pain a shout in my hip. I hunched against the wall and braced the axe in my arms. The living room was still again. Where had it gone? I searched the darkness, looking for movement, hoping for none.

Silence.

Moonlight softly lit the house around me. It was still bare. Bare as I'd found it. Bare as I'd left it. No sofa, no armchair, no dining table for dinner parties with friends. Just a single sheepskin rug. I realised how with everything that had happened I hadn't had time to get furniture yet. No soft things to buffer my fragile self from the hard stone walls built up around me. The place looked abandoned. Like no one lived here. Lonely and empty and cold.

And no assailant.

I lowered the axe a little.

This had to be another trick. The fight had only just begun. I had to push on.

"Come on." I glanced around the room, pushing as much of my bravery into my voice as possible. "Where are you?"

An explosion of wood to my right. The front door burst open. The figure rushed me from the outside. A monstrous boar. A minotaur. A fury. Limbs and claws and those bright, watery eyes.

I instinctively reached for my anger, finding it—as always—a hair's breadth away. Because that was the key to survival in this world. Always have your finger on the trigger. Always be ready to go absolutely apeshit at a moment's notice. Never be caught unguarded again.

I reared my axe and swung.

Everything went blurry, as it always does. My battle cry rang in my ears. My limbs burned with the quick, heavy chop-chop-chop. Fear and rage ran my arms like pistons, pounding the metal blade into the meat of the thing attacking me. I only stopped when my swing found nothing, and I unbalanced with the force and weight of the axe.

I let myself tumble to the floor, panting hard, my side now screaming in pain. But I kept the axe close, clutched in my sticky, wet fingers. I searched the floor for movement.

A sickly coppery smell cut over the scent of trees and pollen blowing in from the open door.

Moonlight pooled on the living room floor, casting Rowan's battered face in cool blue light. Puddles of black liquid spread around his head.

CHAPTER 44

ROWAN'S CHEST WAS patterned with slices and gouges. Half of his face peeled away, opening up his skull and spilling gore onto the sheepskin rug.

I'll never get that out of the wool, I thought stupidly.

He sputtered and shook, a marionette whose strings were snagged and caught, as a dark froth foamed up from his bisected mouth. My eyes widened. This time there was no brief flash of gore, no face disappearing into the darkened doorway. The bloody horror was lying in front of me, inescapable, unrelenting.

You'll never learn, will you?

My body trembled. I thought I could hear sirens. The front door lay open behind me.

Hurting and hurting, round and round.

Maybe it really was Rowan. Did I want to wait and find out? They'll lock me up for good this time. If I ran now, I could escape to town. Why did it have to be Rowan? The one person who was nice to me. I tried to push what I'd done away.

Your very own circle of hell, spinning like a hamster wheel.

I stumbled toward the front door, hurrying in the direction of the night air, thinking of places I could hide.

Then I stopped. I leant against the door jamb, looking out onto the driveway. My car sat there with its broken windshield. A cool breeze, fresh and inviting, pulled around my sweat-sodden clothes, and I found myself aching to be outside, to be anywhere but this house of horrors.

Callie-Ann's words came to me on the breeze, suddenly cold and hard.

"Stay in the house. Find the breach."

I inhaled a deep breath of that sweet, night air, let it cool the sweat on my arms and brow, then I turned around and went back into the house, back past the twitching body on the living room floor, back to the door under the stairs, and headed down into the basement. Down inside the hill.

CHAPTER 45

MORE STAIRS. MORE darkness. At least I wasn't falling down these ones. No, I was choosing this descent. God, I hoped I wasn't going mad. Would I even know?

At the base of the stairs, my feet found the concrete floor and I waited in the black. It was dark all around. I stepped away from the staircase.

Without any light, the room felt as if it were spinning, no discernible up, no down. Just floating in space. It was like what I'd always imagined death to be like. An unending darkness, a void, and me alone in it for all eternity with no escape.

Normally, I would run from this. I would drink or flick aimlessly through TV shows or scroll on my phone, anything to get away from the awful nothingness I was sure awaited me at the end of it all. But this time I stayed in it, though every nerve told me to run back up the stairs, that no monster skulking in the living room could be worse than this one thought, this one inevitability, that just by standing here in it I was making it true, wishing it to me, letting it find me.

I waited.

And then I realised there was something here. There was fear.

I held onto the fear as a something.

I felt the rise and fall of my chest, the beat of my heart, the shifting of my clothes—just like I had in the forestry on the hill.

My eyes adjusted. And I saw the basement. And I saw the door.

Faint lines, plastered over.

The breach.

The house was quiet again. I'd half expected the door to be barricaded shut with planks and nails. But it was just like how I had seen it the first time.

I sat on my knees in front of the door. Now the real test would begin.

"What are you doing? Splitting or chopping?"

That's what Rowan had asked me. Back when I first arrived. When I needed help with my boiler. He was so happy to help me. I felt the weight of the axe in my hands. I thought of the firewood mashed to splinters. I thought of my neighbour's face, blade sunk into the curve of her forehead. I thought of the vision of hopefully-not-Rowan upstairs, face halved.

When I'd raised my axe in wrath, in fear, I'd hacked one thing into two. Could an axe ever cut two things back into one?

I looked at the door ahead of me, shutting me out of 1a, keeping me in 1b, splitting the houses in two. It occurred to me that it was entirely possible to chop two things into one.

"What are you doing? Splitting or chopping?"

Chopping, I answered and swung my axe into the door.

The destruction was organised this time. Less adrenaline, more precision. My axe crashed through the wood. Each hit sounded like the beat of a drum. I ignored the ache in my side, the bruises up and down my body, and focused on the work. Splinters and chunks tore away reluctantly. I squinted my eyes against the flying wood. At least it wasn't blood and gore this time. I had a good steady rhythm, swinging like a metronome, breaking down the barrier in my way, bringing the houses together, making them one home once more.

Suddenly, light poured through the growing gap.

I stopped mid-swing, panted and wiped my forehead.

I tried not to think about where all the light was coming from.

I pushed the axe through the breach and used it to lever and rip away long thin panels. Once the hole was big enough, I barged my shoulder against the gap and pushed my way through.

Into my neighbour's house.

CHAPTER 46

I wiped the dust from my face, looked about, then leant back against the wall to bolster myself. It took me a moment to realise where I was.

Why is she sleeping in the basement? I thought.

Then I noticed the slanting ceiling and the window set into it. My head spun.

I was in her bedroom.

Upstairs.

I looked through the hole in the wall, then back at the room. Somehow, I had got from my basement to the first floor of 1a.

I stepped away from the hole, feeling as if the floor could disappear beneath me at any moment. Besides the slanted roof and the window, the room couldn't be any more different to my own. It was lusciously decorated. Sheer curtains dotted with little golden stars enveloped a bed layered in sumptuous fabrics; a thick feather duvet in deep burgundy sateen sheets, a tactile chenille throw, and a creamy fur tossed casually over the bottom. A dozen pillows were piled around a padded headboard shaped like a shell. A string of warm fairy lights lit the bed with a gentle halo. Sweet, little tealights in yellow patterned glasses were dotted atop a walnut bedside table and dressing table, sending flickering candlelight around the room. A wardrobe door hung open as if casually reclining, revealing ruffles and velvets and silks and wools. Draped over the door, a perfumed scarf—still body-warm—scented the air with a heady, floral aroma. It was the same tartan scarf I'd tied onto her door handle yesterday.

My neighbour had been here recently. Maybe I could find out more about her, a clue, a weakness, a key to making her stop.

I edged along the wall, not wanting to touch anything, being careful to step over a pristine sheepskin rug—which somehow looked much softer than mine. So soft and inviting I wanted to dig my fingers into it. I searched the counter tops, littered with glittering necklaces, elegant eye liners and sleek tubes of lipstick. I tiptoed round to the other side of the bed, carefully listening out for movement elsewhere in the house. My eyes caught on something tucked under the bed covers. A pair of silver lacy knickers, the kind that hug and sculpt, and a matching bra, fine and shining as if made from spiderweb. Under the perfume there was another smell, of warm bodies and sweat and hair. Rich and animal.

I felt the heat rise in my cheeks.

Stay on task, I told myself.

I backed into the space of the window, burying myself in the heavy damask drapes. I had an overwhelming urge to air the animal smell out. I pulled back the curtains and reached for the latch, then stopped.

The world outside was gone. It was as if the panes had been painted over with black gloss. I leaned against the glass so I could peer outside.

My cheek cooled on the window and my breath fogged the view ahead. That's when I realised what I was looking at.

Soil.

Dark, packed earth pressed up against the glass.

I gasped and flinched back.

I was underground. But I'd come out on the top floor. That didn't make sense. How was I inside the hill?

Hollow hill. Fairy hill.

I thought of all the earth pressing against the walls. The image came to me again of that creeping darkness, edging up and over my toes. Oh God! I was being buried alive and this was my coffin. Six feet under, alone in the dark, cut off from everyone and everything forever. I started to hyperventilate.

What the hell is this house?

A voice came from behind me.

"What about the house?"

I spun round, axe raised ready for attack.

It was Fergus, looking down at me, unblinking, grinning, like the Big Bad Wolf. He was standing behind the counter at the hardware and supplies shop. I looked around. I was stood in the aisles again. There were the hoses, the bird feeders, the decorative planters, the tool display at the back where Rowan had picked out my axe for me. It even smelled of sawdust and rabbit food.

"How am I—?"

Fergus huffed a little air out of his nose.

"Okay," he said, leaning onto the counter, lowering his voice, "but don't say I didn't warn you."

I'd been here. I remembered this. I remembered this all too well. That awful moment at the store. Why was I back here? *How* was I back here?

"I knew a kid at school here. He moved to the area for a brief time when I was about nine, ten?"

No, I wasn't doing this again.

"I know," I said. "He lived in my house. Had a port wine birthmark on his face. Here to"—I traced a line on my cheek and Fergus did the exact same thing at the exact same time—"here."

Fergus stared at me. I swallowed hard. I felt a little like I was about to be eaten.

"Did I ruin the joke or something?" I eyed the empty aisles nervously. "Ha ha ha, the tourist fell for a stupid made-up story."

"Oh, I didn't make it up," Fergus said, expressionless, eyes unmoving.

This was new. Was that good or bad?

"I really did know a kid who lived in your house. He was my best friend. He wasn't unflappable though. I made that bit up. He had this haunted look about him, always looking over his shoulders, like he was being hunted. Him and his mum."

I was pretty sure new was bad.

"That morning when I came to school and found him on the steps, that was true. And everything he told me that had happened that weekend. About his mum in the bathroom and down in the living room. And about him escaping out the window. I made up the bit about him going with his mum peacefully at the end of school, though. He screamed and yelled that he wanted to come stay with me. That the woman who'd come to collect him wasn't his mum. No one believed him. He'd been so jumpy, so nervy. Everyone was fed up of him flinching at shadows and crickets and milkmen. The teachers thought he needed a good shake. Everyone hated that kid. They thought his mum was a snooty whore and him a broken weirdo. They made him go with her. And then I never saw him again. Folk thought the kid and his mum had driven each other mad. The police didn't look too hard into it. Just thought they were a wrong sort and wrote them off."

I hugged the axe closer to me. I tried to turn my head slightly while keeping him in my eyeline. There was no one else in the shop. It was so quiet. I managed a glance back at the front windows. They were packed with dark soil as well. Just like the bedroom windows before.

"I made up the bit about seeing him again." Fergus stepped round from behind the counter. "About running away. And then I made up that it was all a story. Because I wanted him to be alright, or to come back, even if it meant he was different, not quite him. Because I wanted it to be a story. Because it's scary, your house. Only it's not your house, is it?"

The fluorescent light over the till reflected off the beads of sweat gathering at his hairline. He still wasn't blinking. His eyes continued to stare at me, his smile still a Big Bad Wolf-hungry grin.

I felt that old familiar buzz growing in my head. A hive, rattling around in my skull and my veins. Only this time it wasn't that white hot rage. It was fear. My eyes locked onto the large industrial stapler on the desk, his hand laid close by. The buzzing in my ears growing and growing.

Fergus broke eye contact. His gaze slowly drifted down, following my focus to the industrial stapler behind him on the desk.

"Oh, this thing?" He slowly picked it up. "I remember the way you stared at it."

His eyes flicked back to me. I shook my head.

No no no no.

"You wanted to press it to my hand, didn't you?" He put his hand onto the counter and pushed the head of the stapler against it. "And do this."

With one smooth, squeeze of his trigger finger he fired the stapler and there was a loud, wet *sch-unk*.

CHAPTER 47

Fergus turned back to me, grinning and sweating. He pulled the industrial stapler from his hand, its metallic mouth red and wet with its feed.

"You wanted to teach me a lesson, didn't you?" he said.

"No…" My voice was small and pathetic.

"Yes, you did." He nodded at me, teeth and gums bared. A trickle of blood ran down the side of his hand. "*Oh, he'll never make fun of me again after that*, you thought. *No one will ever make fun of me again.*"

He moved the stapler up to his wrist.

"No—!" I tried to stop him.

He pulled the trigger again. *Sch-unk!* This time with a faint crunch. He shuddered. A guttural exhale escaped his still-grinning face.

"Well," he said. "Do you feel better now?"

He raised the stapler from his wrist. I shook with horror at the blood pooling round his battered flesh. He paced closer, pressing the teeth end of the stapler to his neck.

"What about now?"

He fired the glinting payload into his neck.

Sch-unk!

I backed away.

He moved the stapler down to his collarbone.

"Or now?"

Sch-unk!

My fingers shook over the axe.

He carefully undid the buttons of his flannel shirt then placed the stapler over a hairy nipple.

"Or now?"

Sch-unk!

He kept approaching me, metal staples in his flesh catching the light, blood blooming on his clothes.

I frantically searched the shop around me, looking for something to make him stop.

He raised the stapler up to his eye. The world went white-hot.

"Or how about now?"

Before I could answer, he fired the stapler into his eye.

Vuh-schunk!

"No!" I screamed.

The buzzing in my ears shrilled like the string of a strained violin. Fergus lowered the stapler. I didn't want to look and yet I was still looking. The metal staple hovered in the centre of his eyeball. As his gaze shifted, it flickered, catching the light, a silver strand of confetti in a night sky. There wasn't as much blood as I thought there would be. But his pupil… God, it looked like his pupil was melting. It dripped down to the side, like the darkness was spilling out of his eye.

"I don't feel better," I said. "It doesn't make me feel better! It never does. It just makes everything worse!"

He froze, staring at me. Two white clouds formed around the punctures in his cornea.

"It always makes things worse."

And then I realised. This was it. I was being tested. This was my first challenge.

I lowered my axe and reached into my pocket for the thread.

"*When she tests you*," Callie-Ann had said, "*make a knot instead.*"

"That story was never about humiliating me. Not really," I said. "The way Rowan is around you makes me think that you're not actually an arsehole. I mean, you're an arsehole, but he knows why."

Fergus's body twitched, but he didn't approach.

I tucked the axe under one arm and slowly wound the thread around my fingers.

"You told that story about the kid with the birthmark living in this house. So, you grew up in this village. I don't think you've ever left it. And the way you're so antagonistic to visitors, but not just any visitors—the ones from cities— makes me think everyone you grew up with—all your friends, your cousins—they all left. For university, jobs, boyfriends, girlfriends, spouses. And they left you behind. Like this village, and therefore you, weren't good enough for them."

I twisted the thread over and under itself, my fingers finding the right loops to pull.

"You accused me of thinking the people who lived around here were dumb. Superstitious. 'Fucking idiots,' you said. I don't think that about you, by the way. But it's clear that you do. You believe it so much you assume everyone else does, too. That's why you told that story the way you did. You were shadow boxing with an assumption of an assumption."

I pulled the thread tight. A knot.

"It was never about me. None of this is. You couldn't even see me."

The store was silent. The ringing in my ears had stopped. Fergus stared at me, still with that horrible grin and that awful, punctured eye.

But then the corners of his grin began to falter. The metals shelves in the aisles rattled and the fluorescent light flickered and buzzed. Fergus's grin pulled down into an anguished scream as a tide of bloody staples tumbled from his mouth.

With a roar he rushed me, stapler held at arm's length in my direction.

I turned and bolted as the store crumbled and fell apart around me. Ceiling tiles rained down in clouds of dust, and cans of wood stain fell from shelves and rolled across the floor. Fergus's screams were close behind me, along with that horrible metallic *sch-unk sch-unk sch-unk*! I ran for the front doors and the darkness beyond. Clutching the axe close and the thread tight in my fist, I shouldered the door open.

And fell onto the landing of 1a.

CHAPTER 48

Plaster dust settled around me in the gloom. I looked over my shoulder, half expecting Not-Fergus to still be chasing me with his stapler. Instead, I saw a me-shaped hole in a plaster wall. And through the plaster wall was the bedroom from before, only now it was dark. The beautiful drapes around the bed were grey, moth-eaten dust sheets; the sumptuous bed, a stained mattress, flattened in the middle and nibbled at the edges. Where I'd fallen through the wall, the plaster was crumbling and degraded. The bedroom was dilapidated and rotten, as if decades had passed since that luxurious vision I'd seen just moments before. Even the perfume was now a dank, musty odour of decay.

As my heart rate settled, the realisation surfaced that I must have done something right. I'd passed the first challenge. I ran my thumb over the knotted thread in my hand. I smiled, with relief, with surprise. Maybe Callie-Ann was right. Maybe I could do this.

Okay, I thought. *Next.*

I looked around the landing and then down. A flight of stairs led to an open floor below.

Oh good. More descending.

A warm light was cast against the wall and the gentle sound of music drifted up. I pulled myself to my feet, bracing my side as I picked up the axe. I hoped she didn't have any other industrial-use stationery down there. Then I descended the stairs.

Down, down, down, further into the earth.

At the bottom of the staircase was an opulent living room, bathed in pools of golden light. My head swum briefly as I orientated myself. I'd come in through the basement, but there was the front door. I had to be deep underground. Through the windows was that same packed earth encompassing the house. I tried not to think about the crushing weight of all that soil against the walls, and turned my attention to the room.

Two emerald velvet couches sat either side of a chic marble and brass coffee table laden with fruit and canapes. Candles fluttered in more little coloured glass tealight holders, and a thick embroidered curtain hid the kitchen from view. Somewhere close by, music was playing. The place was done up for an intimate celebration, a party for two, which I guess this was. I thought about how the bedroom had looked upstairs. I wondered if there was more rot and decay hiding beneath this shining mirage, too.

On the coffee table, a wreath of redcurrants shone like a crown of luscious jewels round a small pile of pomegranates in a golden bowl, all garnished with a scattering of mint leaves. A bottle of champagne, as green and inviting as the sofas, stood casually off-centre, wrapped in a crisp white napkin as if it were an attending waiter. By its side, two sparkling coupes were filled to the brim with dancing, golden fizz reflecting the light from the open fireplace.

Well, that's a trap if ever I saw one.

I didn't need much knowledge of folklore to know you never eat or drink anything in… wherever this was. My neighbour clearly thought I was stupid. I eyed the corners and behind the furniture.

Where was that music coming from?

The soft gentle strains of an earnest female singer gave way to a pulsing beat and a short, repeating melody. Of all the furniture and decoration in the room, I couldn't see any radios, or record players or speakers or anything that could be playing music. Despite this, the music was getting louder.

Unce-unce-unce-unce

The baseline crept up my spine, rattling my bones and fuzzing in my ears. The repetition was just short enough to annoy. Like a story that never really starts. I grimaced as it got louder and louder. I searched with more urgency, to make it stop. There was a muffle to the sound, as if it were coming from another room, or next door in my house, or perhaps in the curtained-off kitchen. I held up my arms and pushed my elbows in around my ears, holding the axe above my head. I frowned. I was wary about what I would find in the kitchen. But this was the journey and I was committed now. The only way out was through.

I took a deep breath and pulled back the curtain.

The music hit me first. And then the cold.

I stood in a pool of orange streetlight in front of a painted door with an intercom. A low insistent buzz told me my finger was pressing the trades button. I jumped back and snatched my hand away from the buzzer. I was outside one of the red brick tenements opposite my old flatshare. I glanced over my shoulder, hoping to see my old home, but nothing was there but the darkness all around me. That and the loud dance music coming from the window next to the main door.

Oh God. I know what this is.

Sure enough, the axe in my hand had been replaced with the clean, barely used hammer from the DIY set I'd left behind during my exodus from Edinburgh. It still had that new blue tinge to the metal along the claw end.

The door clicked open. I hid the hammer behind my back.

A wiry young man with a shaved head and hollow cheeks slouched over me in the doorway.

"What do you want?"

His breath stank of old cigarettes. My throat went dry. My palms felt slick with sweat.

He frowned at me, then eyed my shoulder, my elbow.

"What've you got?"

I wanted to run. I didn't. He leant round me, quick, flitting movements like a hummingbird or a fox. He caught sight of the hammer and stopped.

CHAPTER 49

In my old fantasies, this would be the moment when his eyes would widen with understanding and then fear. He'd raise his hands, palms up, head shrinking back into his shoulders. I wouldn't have to say a word. He'd nod his head and back up and say, "Keep the noise down. Got it. Sorry, pal." Then he'd creep back inside and out of view for a moment and the music would stop. He would peer out sheepishly and ask, "All good now, yeah?" And, again, I wouldn't have to say a thing. I'd just raise my chin and casually sling the hammer up onto my shoulder. I'd turn slowly, eyes still on him, so he knew I'd be watching, and then I'd return home triumphant. Badass.

I had the distinct feeling that wasn't going to happen here.

"I've been expecting you," he said, his voice a hoarse whisper.

He pushed the door open wider, beckoned me in with a nod of his head and disappeared inside. I hesitated on the threshold, hammer held behind me, my hand clammy on the handle. The light above me on the pavement went out. I jumped inside. Darkness swallowed the space I'd inhabited. The music suddenly grew louder.

I entered a communal stairwell similar to all the others I'd seen in Edinburgh's various tenements. Concrete walls painted in two tones of gloss pressed in on either side, and an iron balustrade with a wooden handrail spiralled up to the floors above. The only light came from an open door to a flat on the ground floor.

"You thought a hammer would scare me"—the gaunt young man leant against the wall between me and the open door—"didn't you?"

Coloured lights bounced through the doorway behind him. The *unce-unce-unce-unce* rattled my teeth, yet I could still hear the man speaking, his voice raspy and hushed. His eyes, heavy-lidded and unblinking, regarded me coldly.

"I know you have it behind your back. You can't hide it."

He stepped into my space. I froze with the sudden intimacy. The heat of his body warmed my chest. His breath brushed my neck. I pursed my lips tight. He reached around me and gently, calmly, took the hammer out of my hand.

"The thing about a weapon is"—he casually tilted the hammer as if checking the balance—"if you're going to bring it somewhere, you've got to be prepared to use it."

Lights danced in the flat, but there were no shadows of anyone else. I was alone with this stranger. And he was alone with me. The stairwell felt small all of a sudden. And so very lonely.

"But you hadn't thought about that, had you?" He twirled the hammer in his hand. "You thought the sight of it would send me shaking. Because that's what would frighten you."

He tutted. The lights from the room behind him cast long, sharp flashes on the walls around me, putting the world into a slow staccato. He swaggered in stop-motion in the blaze and shade.

"That's why I kept the music loud. Because I knew there was nothing you could do about it. I had your number the moment I saw you, peeking through your curtains, tutting in your dressing gown. I know your kind. You're the snob who kicks over the cup of change while the jakey's asleep. You're the busybody who tips a noisy cat into a wheelie bin. You'll dish it out on those who can't fight back, but you wouldn't dream of standing up to the real target of your anger. Full of rage, but none of the balls to do anything about it. Too scared of losing the little you have—the job you hate, your crummy flatshare, the freedom you're too scared to do anything with— to gain a little respect."

Flash-flash-flash

Unce-unce-unce

Like the crack of a whip, his arm flew up and struck the wall next to my head with the hammer. I flinched. The old gloss-painted plaster cracked around the impact. As he removed the hammer from the wall, a small chunk came away with it.

"You're a coward."

He put his hand over the hole in the wall.

"That's why you could never do what needs to be done."

He swung the hammer into the knuckles of his hand.

The sound rang in the cramped stairway, vibrating the walls and the stairs in time to the music.

KRunce-KRunce-KRunce-KRunce

My eyes couldn't leave the violence. I was glued to it. Each flash of the lights from the flat revealed a new visceral snapshot. A finger bent the wrong way. A knuckle burst like a grape. A bone piercing skin.

I froze with the horror of it.

Flash-flash-flash

A hand caught in a tangle of metal. A painted fingernail hanging by a thread. Hot pink.

I blinked for what felt like the first time. The image was there and gone in a flicker of neon light.

Suddenly the gaunt man stepped to me, head bent to get into my eyeline. I jumped.

"Look at me when I'm talking to you!" he roared.

Hot flecks of spittle landed on my cheeks. My teeth chattered as if I were freezing. It was like all those times I'd been screamed at not to cry and yet the tears would always come anyway. *Don't cry or I'll give you something to cry about.* I desperately wanted to run, but there was nowhere to run to. The door behind me was gone. The stairs above had been taken away by darkness. And the way ahead was blocked by a man with a hammer and the will to use it.

"I-I-I don't even know you." I managed to force the words out despite my fluttering jaw.

"And you didn't care!" He threw the hammer against the wall by my head.

The ringing was so loud. I clutched my ears and scrunched my eyes closed.

"Look at me!"

I opened my eyes and now he was different. He was taller with a full head of hair, and wearing a stylish, blue-striped shirt.

"Would you have felt different if I'd looked like this?"

The lights flashed.

Now he was an older man, squat, wearing a white vest, with hair sprouting from his ears.

"Or this?"

The lights flashed.

Now he was the teen boy who'd leapt out at me in the village. Small and untrusting.

"Or this?"

The lights flashed again and now he was just a silhouette, lights flashing around him, music pounding through my skull.

I held my hands over my ears. That same ringing came to me again. I was trapped. Nowhere to run. Nowhere to hide.

Fight him! Steal back the hammer! Smash his skull! Make him pay!

Then I thought about what Rowan had said up on the hills.

"The only way to win when you're seeing red is to walk

away," he'd said. "*Doesn't matter what anyone thinks of you or how angry they made you or how stupid or weak you think you look. Walk away.*"

"You're right. I don't know you," I shouted over the music, eyeing the dark outline of the hammer in his hand carefully, "but I think I know enough."

I forced myself to look at the flashing lights in the empty room behind him.

"You always played music late at night. But I never saw anyone coming over. I never heard any talking like you get at parties."

He hit the hammer against the wall again. I felt it move through the air in front of my face. The noise was horrendous.

"I don't know what life you had. Whether you worked or you didn't. Whether you were drunk or sober. But I know you were alone."

His hand froze. The music stopped. I lowered my arms from around my head

"You were awake and alone in the early hours of the morning. My gran once said that's called the wolf hour. I don't know who came up with that, but that's when your mood is at its lowest. It's when people have their worst thoughts."

I wasn't speaking very loudly, but every word boomed through that empty, dark space.

"Maybe I'm wrong." I reached into my pocket and found the spool of thread. "But if I'm not, it would make sense that someone would want to make a noise at that hour. To drown out the thoughts, to bring some life back into the night, hell, just to tell the world you're still here."

The lights behind him flashed slower and slower, cutting our outlines into shadows along the walls. I wound the thread around my finger.

"It was never about me. You didn't even know I existed."

I pulled the thread tight.

The light stopped flashing. All was still and quiet. That loud kind of quiet you get after a long period of noise. Like your ears can't quite trust the silence.

The gaunt figure stood frozen in front of me, hammer still raised. I waited for the drop. Because by now I had learned there is always a drop.

A squeal of feedback burst through the air behind him. A piercing pain shot through my head. The lights blared bright white. The man disintegrated in the flare.

I flinched back, tumbling over my own feet.

The walls crumbled around me, raining cement dust and old iron railings.

I fell onto a dark wooden floor.

And then the axe fell beside me with a dull clang.

CHAPTER 50

I WAS BACK in my neighbour's living room. As I'd suspected earlier, it was now as dilapidated as the bedroom before.

The sofa cushions were sunken and ripped, their foam spilling out at the corners. The fireplace was crumbling and damp. The coffee table was covered in a layer of grime and mouse droppings, scattered among the remnants of a broken bottle. I briefly imagined those bitter, green shards slicing my throat as I tried to swallow them.

I shook the thought from my head and fingered the thread in my hand instead. Two knots. Two challenges down. Two more to go.

I got back onto my feet. It took a couple of tries. I was feeling worse for wear. The adrenaline wasn't keeping the pain out of my side as much anymore. I didn't want to know what all the running and ducking was doing to whatever injury I'd sustained.

I picked up the axe.

The stink in the living room was dank and oppressive, as if there was no air here. Or what little air there was had been eaten up by mould. How strange it was to finally see it. If this was what the cottage above truly looked like. After all the different ways I'd imagined this side of the house—a tidy hermitage, a hipster party pad, a luxurious temple to the feminine divine—seeing it for real was anti-climactic somehow. Knowing it was just an empty, old place left me feeling… complicated, somehow. Like when a cheating lover cries when you confront them and you can't quite feel pity for them but you're not as righteously angry anymore. There's only that creeping awareness that they're just an animal, just like you, just like everyone, all bumping into each other and trying not to fall over and choke on our own tongues.

At first, I tried to shrug the feeling off, but then I let it settle in the pit of my stomach for a bit. There would be time to investigate that later, I hoped. For now, there was only onwards. There was only the third knot.

I turned to the door under the stairs and made my way down to the basement.

This time there was no music, no inviting light and warmth drawing me to the next level. There was only the soft echo of my own footsteps and a pale grey light revealing the next few stairs ahead. I gripped the axe close, preparing myself for whatever horror I would find at the bottom. I wondered what would be next. A parade of all the women I've ever judged, poking pins under their nails? That arsehole from my math class slowly peeling off his own skin with a sharpened spoon? The tribe of barking brats beating themselves in the face with their own shoes? I could handle that. Maybe.

The stairs became soft underfoot. The carpet grew thicker and more frayed. The light grew gently until bit by bit, I realised I was no longer descending, but walking up a grassy hill on an overcast afternoon. The air grew cold and a frigid wind whipped down the slope. I rubbed my upper arms to try and put warmth back into myself, wishing I'd thought to bring a jacket with me.

And then suddenly, I could smell the sea.

The hill levelled off and I was on the cliffs above the beach close to the town where I'd grown up. Below were the ruins my family would come and explore on bright Sunday afternoons. The sun was a pale gold disc behind the cold clouds and the sea stretched out forever, slate-grey and unforgiving. Someone's tartan scarf went flying over the cliff edge.

With a sinking feeling, I realised I remembered this day.

I turned to my right and there they were. Just as I feared.

My father, wrapped in a fleece and a waterproof, was anchoring himself into the grass as he gripped a fine spool of string. Its other end flew out of the yellow plastic handle, like a laser beam, up to a fluttering yellow kite swooping and dancing against the grey skies. Sunset was coming and with it the light that made me think of endings. Two little girls, with the prettiest curls and sweetheart faces, a perfect pair, leaned into my father's legs, giggling and smiling as he passed them the kite string. The Grayson girls.

"There you go," he said. "You've got it now. Look at it fly."

An older couple passing by smiled approvingly at the sight. Perfect family picture. Total Kodak moment. My father smiled and nodded bashfully as they waved.

"This day and age, it's good to see a man embrace fatherhood."

Except neither of the smiling, happy girls were my father's daughter.

I knew that because I—his actual daughter—was also there, standing where I was now, flat-haired, dull-eyed, sullen. Watching. I'd wanted to play with the kite. We were all around the same age. I knew the girls from school, though we didn't really play in the same circles. I didn't understand why my mother had pulled me away to the side to watch instead. She smiled and made conversation with the approving passers-by. She explained to them that the girls' parents were getting divorced, so we were taking care of them for the day.

"That's a shame," the older couple said. "But how lucky they are to have you two. That's very good of you to keep an eye out for them."

My mother had explained things slightly differently to me.

They don't have a father anymore, she'd said, *so let them play with your dad. It's good to share.*

Back then I'd agreed. It was good to share what you had with those who didn't have the same, but it had left me feeling odd. It was an oddness that had stayed with me over the years as the girls had continued to come over to my house for dinner, for weekends, for birthdays, then a couple of Christmases. My parents explained their continued presence in our lives as an ongoing part of that care they'd shown all those years ago.

"We're just going to look after them while the Graysons go on a trip together."

"We're just going to have them for the day while the Graysons go to marriage counselling."

"We're just going to take them out for the afternoon while Mr and Mrs Grayson are at mediation."

"Mr Grayson and Ms Morgan are having some trouble agreeing to the girls' visitation schedule, so we're going to give the girls a break with us."

"Lucy's been having some trouble adjusting to the divorce, so she's coming to stay for a while. You don't mind sharing a room, do you?"

"Laura-Ann misses her sister, so she's going to come visit. You don't mind sleeping on the sofa for a bit?"

All the while the neighbours and my teachers and the people at church all went on about how good my parents were to take care of them.

And all the while I agreed, yes, it was good to share. It's good to share and be kind and be thoughtful.

But I also started pulling out my hair and biting the skin off my lips.

One day at school, I was in the same classroom as the older girl, Lucy. Her teacher was off sick, so we had to share a class. I pulled the chair out from under her as she went to sit down. From the head teacher's office, I watched through the window as my father arrived. He checked on Lucy first out in the hallway. He got down on her level and wiped away her tears and gave her a hug. Then he silently signed me out at the secretary's office and drove me home without a word. Lucy came over the next day for me to apologise. I think I did, though I don't remember doing it. I remember imagining I'd left my body and was flying up into a grey sky over the cliffs, a yellow kite, brilliant and free.

I noticed now that the kite string was red. A spool of red string. I reached into my pocket and pulled out the thread I'd been using to make the knots. Even the plastic it was wound about was yellow. The same as the kite.

"Fuck's sake," I said to myself.

"Such language, Tammy." My father tutted. "Don't listen to her, girls. You'd never use language like that, would you?"

The Grayson girls shook their heads sweetly, like two fucking adorable cherubs. I bit my tongue.

"See how well they share?" my father said to me. "You really should have been better to them. You've no idea how hard it's been for them."

Okay, tongue-biting over.

"Yeah, yeah, I get it. Divorce is tough on kids. But here's the thing"—that high whining buzz rang in my ears again—"they still had a fucking dad, Dad!"

All three of them looked up at me.

"Their father didn't die. He didn't leave them. Fuck, he didn't even leave the town. He moved two streets over. I saw him pick them up from school. They saw him every weekend. Or the weekends when they weren't at our house. You treated them like they were fucking orphans, when they had better shit than I did! But still, every birthday and Christmas and graduation you were there with flowers and photos. When they fucked up, you came running to dust them off. They're in their thirties now and you still run after them like they can't even wipe their own arses. And everyone thinks you're a fucking saint."

I shook as every photo of every smiling family dinner my father had attended with them came flying through the mental social media feed of my mind.

"When she"—I pointed at Laura-Ann, the smallest girl—"graduated from her nail course, you got her a car."

"She needed it. For her new business," my father said.

"When she"—I pointed at Lucy—"got pregnant you moved her into the house."

"She needed support. For the baby."

I sniffed and nodded. "Yeah, I get it. But when I graduated from uni, I just got a lecture on finding a job. And when I needed a place to stay, because the finding-a-job bit wasn't going so great, I had nowhere to go because you'd moved a girl with her own goddamn family to worry about her into my old room."

"They'd had a hard start in life. The divorce—"

"Then who was there for me when you got fucking divorced?"

The wind ripped through the space between us, a howl. I looked over my shoulder, but I already knew the hillside behind me would be empty. My mother was gone. She moved down south and remarried into a large family. I'd visited a few times, but I'd never quite found my footing amongst her new stepchildren, all of them so boisterous and busy. She never said anything, I'll give her that, but it soon became clear that things were just easier for her if I didn't visit. Though she did express surprise at how I failed to meld into her new family. After all, it had been like I'd had two stepsisters long before my parents ever split. I turned back to my father and the Graysons. The two girls stared at me innocently, hand in hand. On top of everything else I'd envied about them, through it all, they'd always had each other.

My father nodded and sighed.

"I suppose you're old enough now to know the truth."

CHAPTER 51

He stepped away from the girls. They looked up at him, confused. I braced myself.

This can't tell me anything I don't already know, I thought. *It can't tell me things I don't know.*

But somehow that didn't bring me any comfort. There were so many things I already suspected, feared. What was left to invent?

My father walked over to me, then looked back over at the two girls.

"Look at them." He gestured. "Aren't they perfect? They're tidy and neat. They're well-mannered and sweet. They play princess and tea parties. They're gentle and kind. They don't swear. They don't fight. Despite everything they've gone through, they never lash out at anyone. Proper little girls"—he turned back to me—"like your mother and I had always hoped for."

And there was the twist in my gut.

My father shrugged.

"We understood you don't get to choose," he said. "You get the kid you're dealt and you do your best with what you're given. But can you really blame someone, after all those years of dreaming and hoping, those nine months of wondering, not to feel a little disappointed when what they get is plain, sulky, lazy, careless? When they don't get what they hoped they would?"

I tried to turn the tight, hot feeling in my chest into rage, but it refused. It sat like concrete, weighing down on my stomach, choking the air from my chest.

"But it wasn't just that." My father waved a hand reassuringly. "Believe me, if it was just that I'm sure we could have pretended better. Got on with it, without you becoming aware of how we really felt. But there was that… you know, that other thing."

I frowned. My father looked surprised.

"Wait, you don't know?" He raised his eyebrows and put his hands on his hips. "You must have known. Didn't you see it, even back then? That there was something not quite right with you."

He shook his head with surprise. Then a thought seemed to come to him. He walked over to the girls with that stuttering quickstep he always had when he was thinking. He took their hands.

"Come here, princesses." He led them further up the cliff, then looked over his shoulder to me. "I'll show you what I mean."

I followed them up to the cliff edge, numb and hollow. He placed the two girls, standing side by side, backs to the wind at the edge of the cliff.

"Pose just there, girls," he said to them. "We're going to make a picture so Tammy can understand something."

He turned back to me. His hair shimmered and shook around his head, battered by the growing wind. My eyes kept flicking from him to the girls. They were a little too close to the verge for comfort.

"You know, I could read it on your face that day. So could your mother, that's why she kept you so far away from us. We'd both known there was something wrong with you, but that day we realised we'd underestimated how bad it was. We could both see it in your eyes—before the graduation gifts and the giving up your room and everything else you accused me of, so you can't blame it on all that. Right from the very first time we stepped up to take care of these poor innocent girls, you had the overwhelming desire to do this."

With a quick, sharp shove, he pushed Lucy off the cliff.

I thought I'd be desensitised by now, after the stapler and the hammer, but nothing quite prepares you for hearing a little body crack on rocks far below you.

Vomit flooded my mouth instantly. I fell to my knees and heaved.

"I know," my father said. "It's sickening. I was sickened that day when I saw the desire in your face. I thought, *I knew there was something wrong with her, but I never thought she was…* well…" He gestured toward me, as I emptied my stomach onto the grass.

"It's not real," I muttered, chanting to myself, trying to make some sound over the horrible crack that kept echoing in my mind. "This isn't real this isn't real this isn't real."

"It feels very real, though, doesn't it?" said my father.

Then he shoved Laura-Ann off the cliff.

I heaved again. My body convulsed with sickness—stomach and soul.

"No," I sobbed between mouthfuls of bile. "What the fuck?!"

"Why are you saying that?" My father tilted his head. "This is what you wanted. This is what you've always wanted."

The worst part was that he was right.

It took me years to find the words for it, but I'd spent a lifetime measuring myself against those perfect girls, and then every perfect girl who'd come after. The glossy-haired, sporty teens at school. The preppy student who'd confidently chat with the lecturers at university. The chatty women at my office always surrounded by friends. The confident, coifed director at my last position. It had all started here. And I had twisted myself into knots hating them, all the perfect girls, for decades.

"I didn't mean it. I was a kid!"

"Child or not, you had despicable desires in your heart." My father leaned close to me. "You are so full of spite. You put on a good face, professional, calm, but anyone with any sense can see it. It bubbles away just under the surface. Your finger rests on the trigger of it, ready at a moment's notice. That's why we kept you at arm's length. The strain of it all took its toll, of course, on your mother, on our marriage. It wasn't just that we preferred those girls. It was you and all that sickness you carry around with you."

He laid his hand on the grass next to me. Next to the blade of my axe.

"Look. You came to your neighbour's house and what did you choose to bring?"

With his other hand, he raised the axe head up. He hovered the blade over his knuckles. I still held the handle, but not with any fight. My wrist twisted, limp, yielding, with the turn. My father leaned in close to me and whispered.

"There's only one monster in this house, Tammy. And it's you."

This house.

The thought wriggled clear over everything he was saying, no matter how true it sounded and felt.

He dropped the axe blade.

We're still inside the house.

I caught the axe by the handle just before it hit him. His eyes flicked to me.

I moved the axe out of his reach and set it down beside me.

"I'm not spiteful, I'm angry," I said between sniffs. "I'm so angry. All the time. The moment I see anyone do better than me, I'm the crab pulling them back down into the bucket. I'm angry and I'm envious and I'm bitter. I thought for a long while my constant anger would keep me safe, give me power, help me fight back against the horrible bullshit I think about myself." I wiped the vomit off my mouth. "But all I am is tired. So, yeah." I sat back and let the wind pull through my hair. "I guess I am kind of fucked up. But if there's anything I've been learning recently"—I looked at him—"it's not all about me."

My father-not-father leaned back as well, mirroring my seated posture, sun setting behind him with that world-ending light.

"I used to look at those girls as if they were the archetypal little girl, the perfect child I was not. But they weren't. Lucy bit the music teacher at school once. And Laura-Ann made an art out of lying. Impressive really. But I don't think that mattered. They could have been boys. They could have been rescue dogs. It would have ended up the same. Because I think that perfect little girl line is bullshit."

I sat in my father-not-father's attention. There was something nice about it. How his gaze never left me. For once that open-eyed stare wasn't too bad. I continued.

"For a long time, I thought if I was just successful enough, I'd somehow prove my worth to you, then maybe you'd pay as much attention to me as you did to them. But the more successful I got, the bigger clients I took on, the higher profile stuff I got to work on, the less you cared. I didn't understand. I thought I was becoming what you wanted me to be. But I'd gotten it wrong. Because I wasn't competing with them on some ideal. It wasn't anything to do with that. It was about you." I nodded at the rightness of it, letting the realisation wash the past in a new kind of pain, but one that put out the fires of anger, one that brought a cool-headed understanding. "All the compliments down the years, all the people telling you how kind, how good you were. It was never about them being sweet or cute, it was about them being in need. They make you feel needed, like some kind of hero. And I don't."

The waves crashed below us, a low rhythm in time with my breath. Seagulls glided in the air above, alongside the kite that still hovered there somehow, its red line bright against the grey sky. I picked up my own spool from where I'd dropped it in the grass.

"That's why you always rushed in to help. That's why you keep rushing to them with every new disaster. You want to feel like the hero. You still do." I looped the thread around my fingers. "You crave it above everything else. I can see it now. You always choose the people and things that are falling apart, that would fall apart without you. Those girls make you feel needed. They continue to make you feel needed. I don't know if you ever consciously thought about this, or whether you just assume I'm tough, I'm fine, I don't need you. But the effect was the same."

I looked at this approximation of my father, now in silhouette against the sunset, wishing for a moment he was really here, really listening to what I was saying.

"I'm sorry it took me so long to figure it out."

I sighed. Time to get it over with. I looped the thread around my fingers.

"It was never about me. Even if I sort of wish it was."

I pulled the knot tight.

My father's silhouette sat frozen, the dusk seeping into the sky behind him, the sound of the sea and the wind all around. It was almost a nice day out. Almost.

"Bye, Dad," I said.

He dropped away. As did the cliffs and the seagulls and the sea and the beach and the wind and the sunset and the light at the end of everything and the past and the yellow kite. It all dropped away into nothingness, until it was just me and the darkness and the basement.

CHAPTER 52

I WIPED MY eyes and looked around. Her basement had the same whitewashed walls as mine. The same bare floor. The same barely concealed door in the wall, only flipped, of course. It even smelled the same. Fresh paint. Cold stone. Old earth. There were none of the illusions of the other rooms above. But none of the dilapidation either.

I felt for the thread in my pocket.

Three knots. Three challenges.

I frowned. After my chat with Callie-Ann, I'd expected a lot more… rage-inducing moments. But none of the interactions so far had made me that angry. Sad, yes. Terrified, definitely. Horrified, most certainly. But angry to the point of snapping? To the point of wanting to split someone's skull open, to push a needle through their eye? No.

Maybe my neighbour was losing her touch.

I looked at the outline of the door in the wall. Through there was 1b Sgàthan Sìth. One last challenge and I would be home. Done. My side ached and I was finding new bruises upon bruises. I'd seen enough horror to last me a lifetime. I was ready to be done.

I pried the edge of the door open with my fingertips, then pushed it aside and walked through.

I stepped into the foyer of a bright modern office, all glass dividing walls and funky furniture. But not just any modern office.

Oh no.

There were the same orange lilies the director liked. The pictures on the wall displayed work for past clients. I'd worked on a good few of them myself.

I walked down the corridor to the left as if on autopilot. My bruised skin and dirty clothes stood out against all the clean, bright lines of the open-plan office.

There were the red sofas where the rest of my team would gather for lunch and talk about what TV show they were watching or what trainers they wanted to buy. The secretary's liver-spotted spaniel came bounding past my legs, followed quickly by the secretary herself in one of her rainbow jumpers. I'd always hated those jumpers, though I could never quite pinpoint why. Now I knew it was because she always looked so happy. It felt like a front. A lie. I never thought that maybe she just liked rainbows and wearing one made her smile. Or that she liked her job. Or the people she worked with. I'd always assumed that everyone was secretly just as unhappy as I was, only they were better at hiding it.

Come to think of it, she'd always been nice to me. The Dev Team, too, had never seemed shy about chatting with me. Maybe I'd been a little too focused on my own misery to see it.

A happy chattering bubbled in the air. It was coming from a bank of desks in the corner. I followed the grey carpet round, knowing what I'd see.

All of my colleagues were gathered around their workstations in the afternoon light. They held bottles of beer and cans of cider. Some were wearing beanies. Some had forearms covered in tattoos. Some wore bright clothing inspired by the girls of Harajuku. Bright and talented and chatting among themselves. It was four o'clock on a Friday, or "Beer o'clock" as the team called it. They had all gathered around a top hat full of folded papers.

As if on cue, the director passed by my shoulder, shining bright in a fitted sunshine-yellow suit. Her prematurely grey bob was streaked through with neon blue, and her lips were sporting her trademark matte lip paint. She was the very picture of feminine confidence. A girl-boss. A she-ro. A grade-A leaner-inner. The director of my old work was the paragon of what a post-feminist woman could be. At least, that's what she emanated. She could tell dirty jokes just as well as the bawdiest men. Her go-to drink was a Cosmo. Her nails were short but always immaculately painted.

That day, they were hot pink.

She was everything I thought a modern career woman should be. And everything I was not. Maybe she sensed that tension coming from me. Maybe that's why I was never one of her favourites. Maybe it was because I'd been a bit of a nervy weirdo, and she had no time for nervy weirdos. Maybe it was because I overthought everything around me. Just like I was doing now.

I followed her over to her waiting audience.

Let's get this over with.

"Alright, you shower of bastards," she addressed the crowd, wide-mouth smile projecting her it's-actually-a-compliment-get-a-sense-of-humour greeting.

The congregation raised their drinks to her and brayed.

"I know what you're all gathered here for, and it's not clips from Alan's latest porno appearance. Wink wink!"

She laughed. Alan, muscular arms crossed over his barrel chest, laughed. Everyone laughed. I didn't. The me-in-this-moment probably did laugh. Wanted to 'get it'. The me-here-now didn't laugh. I didn't even pretend this time.

"You know I love you, Alan. Meet me in the car park later." This time she managed to wink without saying 'wink'.

Cut it out, Tamsin, I scolded myself. *Don't be like that. You know what we're here for.*

I knew what perceived rejection I was waiting for.

"It's Star Awards time!" the director announced. "And I've got fifty quid in digital vouchers for our lucky winner."

The Star Awards was our version of Employee of the Month. In essence, it was exactly the same though, as if a topping of cherries might change the stinking shit pile of presenteeism and poor work-life culture that usually got rewarded.

That said, I had been feeling pretty confident that month.

I'd worked with the Dev Team to come up with a word processor template for our clients' CRM programmes. Instead of having each email go through the creative department to be designed from scratch, I could use tags in a document to populate a pre-designed template complete with layouts, colours and client branding. All it would need was a quick tidy from an art worker, a check from QA, and it was good to go. I'd calculated I'd shaved twenty-five per cent off our production costs. It also saved the designers' time for more creative work than replicating the same emails over and over. It was a small idea, but it made us more competitive, more innovative and more efficient— everything the director had waxed lyrical about in our monthly all-hands meeting.

I had envisioned myself giving talks at the biannual conference in London about how innovation could be something small and clever like this. I'd already planned my outfits. At the very least I was convinced I'd be a shoe-in for a Star Award, or at the very least some amount of praise. Perhaps the beginning of a conversation about a raise, a promotion. Perhaps my standoffish-ness would work better in management. It's okay, I was never meant to be everyone's friend. But I could be a good boss.

For the first time in a while, I'd felt hope. I'd felt like maybe there was a place for me here after all.

The director picked up the top hat.

"Let's see who our nominees are this month," she announced with a smile.

God help me, I still felt the rising spark of excitement in my chest.

"We've got Callum from Creative for absolutely smashing it and working so hard for Crystal Vodka. You know he's been working late for… God, I just thought you lived here now, pal! When was the last time your wife saw you for dinner? Maybe you'll get to take her and the kids out with your winnings."

The crowd applauded. She sorted through more of the paper slips.

"We've got Felicity from Client Services for…" The director laughed that wide-mouthed laugh again. "No! You lot are so naughty! I'm not reading that out. Although I've got to say I do agree. Okay, I'll read it out. Felicity from Client Services for wearing that rather fabby pair of short shorts last week. You cheeky girl!"

Laughter from the crowd. Felicity waved her hand like she was the queen. The director pulled out another slip. My heart thundered in my chest. This must be me. The Dev team had all said they were going to vote for it. It had to be me.

"And finally, we have"—she raised her eyebrows in surprise—"Tamsin from CRM Services for"—she squinted at the paper and leaned on Alan's standing desk—"developing a template to automatically populate customer emails with tags."

She said each word as if it were the name of an exotic dish on an unfamiliar menu, or the taxonomy of some long-forgotten lizard.

The director shrugged. "Whatever that is."

I thought watching it from a distance would feel better, that time would have softened the hurt, that I would find it funny even.

I did not find it funny.

The buzzing in my ears was a fine ringing. Without even thinking my hands had tightened on the axe's handle. The director swung lazily against Alan's standing desk, her hand draped over the crossed struts beneath its crowded surface.

"In which case, this month's Star Award goes to… Felicity! Come here and bring your gorgeous behind with you, you lucky bitch!"

Felicity danced as she leapt up to collect her vouchers. The crowd was applauding. My hands were shaking.

Come on, Tamsin. I breathed deep. *You can do this.*

"I see you and I understand," I said. "You, uh… the way you try so hard to pal about with the younger ones. The clothes, the hair, the nails. When you were coming up through the ranks, the answer was to be tougher than the men. Take the jokes with a laugh and then out-do them. You never realised you were pulling the ladder up behind you."

I squeezed my fists to try and bring the shaking under control. Over the ringing in my ears, I could hear the crowd laughing around me.

"And can I blame you? You don't get many women in their fifties directing a company like this. You had to sell confidence and creativity and *now-ness* all while facing the same shit you'd had to fight through to get where you are. I don't know how much you must have worried. We all worried."

The laughter got louder. I felt the rage rising. Hot tears came to my eyes.

"It's a hard industry with new competition all the time. No one wants to be seen as stale, but no one wants to take the risks. And no one wants to admit they're scared, like admitting it means making it real."

The realisation dawned on me.

It was okay. I got it.

I looked up at the director, watched her laugh with her mouth. But her eyes darted about the other faces, nervously.

"You didn't understand what I'd made. You said it like we were putting tags into emails. You got it wrong. You didn't know what it was. You didn't understand and it scared you not to understand. So, you made a joke instead."

I looked around at my old colleagues.

"It was a tough job. You were all working so hard. You just wanted to enjoy yourselves when you could. I just wasn't the partying type."

My fists relaxed. Oh my God, I was going to do it. The sting of the memory was released and cool relief washed through me. I reached for the thread.

"It was never about me. You—"

But I was wrong. This was exactly about me.

I watched as I appeared at the back of the crowd. Not the me-watching-this-happen. The me-back-then. The me-shuffling-purposefully toward the desks.

The me-that-did-what-I-did.

Helpless, I watched as I skirted a few steps behind the crowd toward Alan's standing desk. The desk was overloaded as usual, with monitors and books and all those rattling mugs and whatever weights he repped while he marched back and forth during a client call.

The desk that shuddered under the force of his typing.

The desk raised with springs and weights and the same sort of crossbeams I'd seen in the clotheshorse.

The desk the director had carelessly threaded her hand through, fingers resting right at the crossing of those beams, the X that marks the spot.

I watched myself grab the safety latch.

I watched my face, expressionless, my mouth a thin line.

I watched myself pull.

CHAPTER 53

It happened so fast.

The desk came crashing down, monitors, half-filled mugs of tea, thick business books, the weights and all. The mechanism, a folding crossbeam of thick metal reinforced with springs, snapped shut with a bang.

The crowd fell silent.

And then the director screamed.

Alan and a few of the others rushed to try and lift the standing desk, but the mess of bone and gore had jammed the mechanism shut. No one could move her or the desk. Too heavy. Too painful. I knew from memory it would be an hour before the ambulance would arrive. Then another hour before the firemen came to cut around the mess. All the while the director had to sit next to her mangled hand, face grey, forehead beaded with sweat, as the poor secretary kept trying to keep her spaniel from licking the blood.

The director lost two fingers and much of the use of the remaining two. I can still see that bloody fingernail, immaculate and hot pink, dangling from the metal.

Back then I'd frozen with shock, unable to do anything afterwards. I'd only meant to scare her, at least, I think I had. I don't know now. I hadn't really thought it through. I'd been so angry. I'd just wanted her to stop laughing.

Everyone had seen me next to the desk, but no one had noticed me pull the latch. And it was so overloaded with Alan's things there was every reason to believe it had collapsed by itself. No one could prove I'd done it. But the police took me in, anyway, for questioning. I was saved by the director deciding not to press charges. The police let me off, but they also sent me literature on anger management courses and strongly suggested I attend one.

I'd lied and said I must have just knocked it, but I could tell in my leaving interview the director didn't really believe me. She'd stared at me, hand bandaged under so much gauze and plaster you couldn't see it, unnervingly sober.

After HR had covered all the basics and the paperwork, a flicker of something passed over her face. Confusion. Anger. Pity. I don't know. And then she'd asked me:

"Do you think you're a good person?"

Our HR rep had turned to her nervously, started to rebuff but was cut off by the director who told me to do whatever I needed to "get better".

I didn't. I saw one counsellor then bunked off the rest of the sessions, broke the lease on my flat share, and ran away to Carlinsrest. Bought some property for cheap, sight unseen, without looking closely enough at the details. Now I was here, revisiting my sins in a haunted house full of the ghosts of everyone I'd ever wanted to hurt.

I looked at myself, the me-in-that-moment-back-then, staring silently, open-mouthed, like a lemon.

Like a stupid fucking lemon.

Like a stupid, spiteful, toddler idiot.

Like a fucking moron awful piece of shit needy whiny sour-faced boring twat.

The rage returned to me with a snap.

I charged at myself with the axe and swung with all my might. Harder than I had at the monsters in my house. Harder than I had at the door. I clipped myself right in the face—Oh God, what joy! What release!—and kept on swinging.

"You stupid piece of shit you stupid piece of shit you stupid piece of shit!"

I screamed with the effort, the hate and the anger fuelling my every swing. How could I have done this? I'd hurt that woman, scared all my colleagues, seared that terrible image in all of our memories forever. And all over an employee of the month award I didn't even care about! Why had I let something so petty get to me so badly? What was wrong with me? What was *wrong* with me?

The sound of laughter beneath me broke me out of my swing.

I wiped the sweat from my face and stared down where my bloody face should be.

My neighbour lay there, gripping the axe blade away from her face, blood trickling down from her palms, eyes full of delight and hunger, her smile wide and full of teeth.

Full of victory.

"Got you," she said.

My colleagues, the director, the secretary's spaniel, had all disappeared. The office, empty now, shuddered with joy. The lights flickered off one by one.

My neighbour pushed the axe—and me attached to it. I stumbled back as the darkness swallowed up the room and I fell through a doorway. I rolled over concrete, righted myself and came to a stop where I was spat out on the floor.

The floor of her basement.

Then I watched as the door between our houses slammed shut.

CHAPTER 54

OH FUCK.

I dropped the axe and ran to the door.

Oh fuck oh fuck.

I scrabbled for a handle, an edge, anything to pry it open again.

Oh no, please, oh fuck, oh no, please, no, please.

The door wouldn't give. I went back and grabbed the axe. I'd broken through before. Perhaps I could do it again. Panicked, I swung at the wood. The metal cut through the boards then clanged against brick. Fragments of door fell away, revealing nothing but old stone wall. The door wasn't just gone. It was as if it had never been there at all.

I wasn't getting out. It was over.

I'd failed.

I sank to my knees and pressed my forehead to the wall. My home, the house I'd fought so hard for, was just on the other side. The flowers in spring. The coloured leaves in autumn. I'd come so close. I thought I'd had to understand and forgive the director, but I'd gotten it wrong. It wasn't about my anger at other people at all. I hadn't learned a thing.

And I'd fallen at the very last hurdle.

A chuckle echoed quietly from a corner behind me. I turned resignedly to the sound. My neighbour prowled out of the darkness.

"You really gave me the runaround there. First the axe. Now this."

She wore my face, wide-eyed and grinning so hard it looked painful. The crescent moon scar shone along the curve of her forehead.

"It didn't have to be this difficult," she said. "You know that's what makes the end so horrifying for some. Their inability to accept that it's here."

She circled me in the shrinking light. The beams overhead creaked under the strain of the earth outside.

"They always spend the precious little time they have remaining fighting the inevitable." She paced leisurely around me. "They wrap themselves in knots of denial and bargaining with a universe that really doesn't care. And then their very last moment is one of rage, despair and terror. Can you imagine that?" She shook her head in mocking disbelief. "A whole life reduced to that last moment. Well, you won't have to imagine it for long."

Soil tumbled down the stairs into the basement.

"You could have spent time with loved ones." She shrugged. "Or if you don't have any loved ones, gone somewhere you like to be. The beach. A nice garden. I don't know, something nice to think about in the last moments." She flashed me a look and flicked her tongue over her teeth. "Though between you and me, we know it won't work."

Rivulets of earth trickled in through the gaps between the stones in the wall. I shuffled away from the encroaching soil, tucking closer to where the door used to be, as if I could shuffle away from the awful, soul-sucking, sinking feeling that weighed heavy in my heart-pounding, panicking chest.

I was so far underground. No one would ever be able to find me.

My neighbour pouted.

"Oh, come on, *Tammy*. Don't you understand yet?" She knelt down in front of me as soil rained down around her. "I'm not the one you came here to get rid of."

I stared at her.

"It took me a bit to get it, but once I did," she whistled, "you made this all so much easier for me."

She gestured to herself.

"Look at me. Do I strike you as *the thing you have no wish to be*? I don't annoy anyone. I don't go around with that perma-scowl on my face. I'm not so fucking needy I send everyone running for the hills, like you do. I know how to start a conversation. I know how to make friends. I get invited to work drinks. I'm easy to know. I'm easy to like. I'm easy to understand. I'm not going to bristle at some stupid comment. I'm not going to hold offense or a grudge. I'm not going to force everyone to tiptoe around me. I don't pull a weird face at perfectly fine jokes. I don't look wounded whenever anyone else is hanging out and I'm not invited. I don't have to be invited to every fucking thing. I don't randomly blurt out uncomfortable details about my childhood. No one knows what my childhood was like. As far as they know it was completely normal because I have weekly calls with my loving, encouraging mum, and my dad, who just has to ask a million questions about anything I'm into because it's the way he shows he cares. They know what job I have. They know where I live. They know what matters to me. I'm not such a fucking mystery to them. I don't hide myself away. I don't have to blame them for every annoying thing I do. I don't force people into awful uncomfortable silences where they realise how fucked up I am. I don't want to push needles into people's eyes. And I don't crush people's hands in standing desks."

She tilted her head.

"I wonder how many people had odds on you bringing a gun

into the office, you fucking psychopath. '*Oh God, not Tamsin again. Oh God, not this shit again. Oh, thank God she's gone. Thank God she left before she decided to take her inability to be a person out on anyone else.*'"

I watched her silently. I had no arguments, no rebuttal.

She stared at me, eyes sympathetic.

"You know the truth, right? Deep down, you've got to know," she said. "I'm not your shadow. You are."

CHAPTER 55

SHE WAS RIGHT. Ever since I'd hit her with the axe, she'd become everything I'd ever wanted to be. It was as if we'd switched somehow. Only I was still just me. That's why I'd failed. I never stood a chance from the start.

The earth, black as night, swallowed up the walls of the basement.

And then there was nothing.

No house. No basement. Just me and her in the darkness at the heart of the hill.

"You have to remember, the place where you're going, it's just emptiness."

My neighbour stood over me, dimly lit in the half-light of this strange place. Around us an unending void. Her eyes glittered.

"Wouldn't it be better if you just, y'know"—she leaned closer to me—"didn't exist?"

"There's nothing there that you didn't already know in the first place."

It was me. I was the monster.

"Just unzip the costume and fade away," she continued. "No more pretending. No more struggling. It's not like you were doing a good job of it anyway."

The void found the edges of my feet.

"*Whether it's fear or pain or sadness, it's just what you brought into it.*"

All of this pain, this loneliness. I'd brought it here.

I saw as the outline of my toes started to fade, felt the edging loss of sensation.

"It would be a relief, right?" Her eyes were wide, wide as her hungry mouth. "A relief for everyone. Even you."

Wide in that way when you've lost all reason to pretend you're whole and happy.

I knew those eyes. They were mine.

"Don't you want this over already?" she said. "Isn't this absolute hell?"

"*Own it.*"

I closed my eyes and took a deep breath.

"Yes," I said. "This is hell."

She grinned in victory.

"*We're* in hell," I said.

And her grin melted at the corners a little.

"Shut your whore mouth."

"We're in hell," I said again.

"No." She shook her head and wagged her finger. "No no no—"

"We are in hell."

"Fuck you."

"You and me."

"Fuck you!"

"We're in hell."

"I will devour you!"

"And you'll still be here. Only now you'll be alone…"

"I will wear your fucking skin!"

"Alone in my hell."

She stared at me in fury, eyes that horrible bloodshot red, throat wrung blue. Her shoulders heaving under a weight I knew only too well.

She was me, alright. Me and all of the hell that lay inside me.

If I was my own shadow, then all this darkness belonged to me. As did the truth that came with it.

"You're right," I said. "I hate this. I spend every day trying to be someone else. Each morning, I wake up hoping I'll be different. I hate being like this. Almost as much you do."

"You're so fucking miserable," she spat. "I wish you'd just die!"

I laughed. "Join the fucking club!"

My laughter enraged her. Her face wrung itself red and the skin around her—my—lips split as she became all teeth and nails and horns. Her skin paled and cracked. Her shoulders rounded and her limbs lengthened and her eyes glowed with that awful light.

She lunged at me.

I lunged back.

I caught her hands, mirroring her in mid-air, palm to palm, claws to broken nails.

She reached her right arm back to swipe at me and I did the same.

We struck the same spot in the space between us.

Where she moved, I followed, a perfect reflection as she was to me.

I felt my rage coming out of her, my all-consuming anger crashing back over me, all the ugliness of it. And then the waves of disgust, the shame, the fear, the loneliness, the soul-crushing sadness and the emptiness. All of it I felt as she felt it as I had felt it, reflected back and forth and on and on and on.

I thought of the dilapidated house above us, the years and years of it lying empty. I thought of the nights I'd fallen asleep holding myself.

She caved in around herself, taloned arms helplessly wrapped around her scaly shoulders, her face stretched into a monstrous but silent scream.

A scream I knew all too well.

I finally saw it. Now, I understood.

And the hate and the rage and the fear and the disgust and the shame vanished.

And all I felt was love.

I gathered her into my arms like a child. She scrabbled and fought, but I held on. Just like the stories. Just like in Tam Lin. And I didn't care what she turned herself into whether it was snakes or spiders or fire. I understood it now. What it meant to love, and to be loved, that hard. She curled up in my lap and sobbed into my chest as I hushed her and stroked her hair. She was so small. Small and alone.

"Why?" she said. "Why why why?"

"A long time ago," I said, "when you were still new, someone told you a story, maybe not in their words, but in their actions, in their choices. And in that story, you were a monster. And so, you behaved like a monster."

She curled in tighter to me as I took the needle from my pocket, still threaded with the red string.

"You grew tough scaly skin that no one could pierce," I said, "or see you through."

I pushed the needle into the sole of my foot, gritting my teeth against the pain.

"You lashed out so no one could come close enough to hurt you," I said, "or heal you."

I pulled the thread through the hard skin.

"You hid yourself away in the dark where you wouldn't be found by your enemies," I said, "or your friends."

I pulled her close to me, holding her tightly, then pressed the needle to the hard skin on the sole of her foot.

"Then when you found people, good people, you didn't know what to do with them. So, you devoured them."

With one quick move I pushed the needle through her skin.

She yowled, but I held tight. She looked at me accusingly.

"Because you were so hungry for love. Because you never trusted anyone to stay out of choice."

I made a loop, guided the needle through it then pulled the thread tight between us.

The fourth knot.

Her eyes darted down to where I'd stitched us together, the other three knots sticky with our intermingled blood.

"We've done monstrous things," I said. "But I don't think that's who we are. I think it's time we admitted we're not monsters."

"But then," she said quietly, "who are we really?"

I kissed the top of her head.

"Come home, my little shadow, and let's find out."

She nodded. I threaded the needle once more and pushed it through our skins. The pain flared white hot in my mind. The soles of our feet pressed together. Like a book, or two slices of sandwich bread, or two palms. Like a prayer. Like the house.

I pushed on.

"It's okay," I said, as my fingers became slick with blood, as her face raised to my face, as her sweating chest pulled close to my sweating chest.

"It's going to be okay," I whispered to her. "It's going to be okay."

And with each okay I worked the needle and thread, passing it back and forth between us, sewing us together, palm to palm, sole to sole, cheek to cheek, bone to bone, until I couldn't feel her skin against mine anymore because now it was my skin, until the boundaries between us melted away.

"It's going to be okay it's going to be okay it's going to be okay."

And then I was sitting in the dark of her basement—the real one, not the one deep down inside the hill—alone but not alone, wet through with sweat and tears, arms wrapped around my own shoulders, needle stuck to my fingers with blood, the light of the rising sun just starting to filter down the stairs.

"It's going to be okay," I said to myself. "It's going to be okay."

Then the door between the two houses blew open and I was engulfed in a cloud of brown dust.

INTO LIGHT

CHAPTER 56

IT IS HARD to rebuild a house.

It is so much harder to rebuild a life.

But unless you're content to rot in the ruins, it is a necessary work. A work I was finally ready to begin.

I woke up, broken and bruised in a hospital bed. I didn't remember getting there. For a moment I thought I'd died and this was just what happened to folks after. Your soul is sent, battered and worn, to a soul hospital.

It's alright, the soul doctors say. *You're safe now. It's over.*

No such luck for me. Thankfully.

I was too exhausted to feel much of anything other than tired and sore. I'd been burning myself at both ends for a while and I probably would have ended up here even if I hadn't had my arse handed to me by a mythical shadow creature. The first few days passed in a blur of nurses and needles and dressings being checked and changed. The sunlight arced gently across the ceiling over a steady background hum of beeps, coughs, sighs, trolley wheels and crocs squeaky on linoleum floors.

Then on the third day, I woke from another recovery nap to find I had a visitor.

A figure sat in the plastic chair near the end of my bed, frowning at a catalogue of antiques.

I blinked, trying to clear my eyes, because it couldn't be who I thought it was.

Fergus looked up, startled a little from the noise of me shifting under the starched sheets.

"Oh, hi," he said, uncharacteristically sheepish.

I worked the spit round my dry mouth.

"What are you doing here?"

Fergus huffed in surprise.

"Tell me how you really feel, why don't you?"

"Like I got a house dropped on me," I said. "Now, what are you doing here?"

"Visiting you, you snarky cow." He pointed to the table at the side of my bed. "Even brought you a gift."

I turned my head gently, trying to pull on my aching and bruised body as little as possible. Sat on the table was a small cactus with a yellow ribbon round the pot. Next to it was a note:

A prickly bastard from a prickly bastard, F x

"See, Ro said you're not supposed to bring flowers into wards anymore. Pollen and infections and all that. So, I got you a cactus instead." He shuffled in his seat. "Also thought you might find it funny."

I was beginning to think I must have sustained a head injury.

"Rowan?"

Fergus pointed back to the doorway. "He couldn't come today, so I said I'd pop in. Don't worry; you're not doomed to my company every visiting hour." He made that same sneering, wolfish grin, though it seemed different now. More self-deprecating than predatory.

He rolled the magazine in his hands.

"Y'know, funny you should say that. About having a house dropped on you. Because that's how we found you."

My eyes widened. If I wasn't awake before, I was now.

"What?"

"Nothing but rubble left," he said. "Rowan had me drive us round to check in on you after… your conversation."

Ah, so Fergus also knew what I'd done then. That was fine. I was done hiding it anyway.

"I can't believe he did that by the way," Fergus continued. "I said to him, 'You don't take a girl up into the woods to tell her you went to prison, you psychopath.' He said he thought the quiet would help." Fergus shook his head, but there was a hint of that wolfish grin. "I swear to God, he's got to be the dumbest wise person I know. Anyway, we came round to check on you and half the cottage had come down."

I sat up, ignoring my protesting bones and muscles.

"Which half?"

"The 1a one, so your neighbour's place. Though we weren't sure which half was yours at first, 'cause there's bloody nothing in 1b. Except that sheepskin rug you got funny about." He peered at me like I was a strange new animal he'd found on an alien world. "How are you living like that? No table, no chairs. Not even a telly. You've got to get that sorted out."

"How'd you know what the inside of my house looks like?"

"Because Rambo Ro went running inside to check. I wanted to wait for emergency services to arrive, just in case the other half came down, too. But in he goes, so of course I have to go in as well. Luckily you left the front door open, which, again, you've got to get sorted out."

He shook his head and grabbed something from my side table.

My phone.

"I'll add it to the list."

"Hey!" I protested.

"Shut up. You'll thank me later." He finished typing something, then put my phone back down on the table. Then put the charger cable into it. "Anyway, we found you down in the basement, covered in masonry dust and more blood than I thought a person could make so… congratulations, I guess.”

I looked down at my bandaged limbs.

“For making that much blood or surviving losing that much blood?”

“Either. Both.” He shrugged. “Rowan told the emergency services you’d talked about having a neighbour, so they went looking for her in the clusterfuck of building violations you call next door. I don’t know who you’d seen, but they said the place looked like it had been deserted for years. They checked the blood on you, too, just in case you’d murdered someone.”

I looked up.

“But it’s all yours, so we’re calling you Blood Bath from now on.”

I thought of what had happened in her side of the house. The last I remembered I was in 1a. There was sunlight and then there was dust everywhere. I must have been blown through the door back into my side of the house.

Along my arms, I saw the line of pinpricks from the needle. The red thread was gone.

Fergus noticed me looking.

“Doctors don’t have clue what those are,” he said. “They were hoping you could enlighten them.”

I shook my head in faux confusion.

“Nails from the floorboards maybe?”

The lie would probably cost me a tetanus shot, but the truth was probably better left alone.

Fergus was quiet for a moment.

“Good thing we came round to apologise when we did, eh?”

I frowned.

“What are you apologising for?”

Fergus frowned back.

“Oh, come on. I’m man enough to know when I’ve been a prick.” He pointed at the cactus. “Hence the prickly bastard.”

“Yeah, I got that,” I said. “I’m not exactly an angel myself.”

"He told me," Fergus said, "after I—what I told you in the hardware store."

Here it is. Your comeuppance. 'We're glad you didn't die, but we don't want to be mates. Please leave us alone.'

I hushed the nervous voice inside myself.

Maybe. Maybe not. Either way, it's going to be okay.

"See, Ro has a habit of picking up strays," Fergus said, before adding, "Probably shouldn't have called you that."

"I don't mind," I said, meaning it.

"He knows what it's like to fuck up your life. I remember when he first moved up here. He looked haunted. I think he feels like if he can help other people avoid making the same mistakes he did, it'll make up for—well, everything he did before he got his act together." Fergus leaned forward. "He overdoes it a bit, though. I tell him he's got to let people sort themselves out, but he never listens…" He sighed. "I just wanted him to focus on himself rather than running around trying to solve everyone else's problems. And, well, I guess I took it out on you."

I remembered the version of him back in the house. The stapler. The store raining down around us.

"I thought you hated me because I'm from the city or something," I said.

"No, I *judge* you because you're from the city," he said, with a ghost of a smile. "But I don't hate you. And I'm sorry I made you feel like that."

My phone started to buzz on the side table. I reached over and looked at it. There was an alert.

TEXT ROWAN

it said and then listed Rowan's number.

Fergus looked over my hand at the screen. "Oh, I put that one in yesterday. In case neither of us managed to make it today."

I didn't understand.

"You're putting alerts on my phone?"

"Yeah," he said, as if I'd asked the most stupid thing ever.

"Why?"

"Alerts are great. Remind you to sort out important stuff. And have I mentioned you've got stuff you need to get sorted?"

"No, I mean why are you helping me?"

He understood.

"We're all we have out here. If you can't trust your neighbours to turn up when you need them, then—" He shrugged. "And Ro's right. You are a ranty drunk. And it amuses me."

He looked again at my phone screen then at the clock behind him.

"Ah, shit. Time's up." He got up from his seat. "I'll have a chat with my Aunt Sheila—she used to be a solicitor—about what happened with your neighbour's house. I reckon you could get some compensation or something. No promises though." He put the catalogue in one of his jacket pockets. "See you tomorrow."

I sat, pleasantly dumbfounded.

"See you tomorrow," I said.

Later that day, my phone buzzed with another alert.

It said,

    DRINK WATER.

I did.

CHAPTER 57

The whole of 1a had come down that night, collapsed like a diseased ribcage over desiccated lungs. The floorboards on the ground floor had rotted through and the whole thing was sodden with mould and lichen.

When the building surveyor called, she said the destruction was so total she could see all the way down to the basement from outside. I had braced myself for news of what they found down there; images of the boneyard I'd seen in the apple grove crept their way into my mind. But there had been nothing. It was empty now. Just lonely old stones, worn and blackened with age.

When I asked about the door in the basement, there was a small pause, then she said something about all doors being completely destroyed. So, I guess I'll never know for sure. Probably for the best.

A few weeks later, the estate agents who'd sold me the building got in touch. Apparently, the fact that the house was semi-detached wasn't the only thing they'd missed from the details. They'd sourced the original survey from an old friend and known property cowboy in the area who'd sign off on rural properties for cheap; of course, never actually making their way out to survey the place at all. I quickly got the impression they were concerned I'd take them to court for this. As a sign of good faith, they gave me a cheque for damages plus some. If I kept my expenses modest, I calculated the money would last a year or two. Time enough to figure out a new path for myself, a different way of living. Fergus's Aunt Sheila reckoned I could get more if I wanted, but I didn't. I had fought enough for a lifetime. This was one battle on which I was happy to call a truce.

Fergus started dragging me along to antiques fairs and car boot sales under the guise of getting some fresh air and helping him pick out stock for the shop. I almost always come back with some bargain piece of furniture. I have a proper bed now, a wingback chair, and a set of vintage curtains we got for a steal. I've yet to find a round dining table that fits my kitchen, but Fergus says we can keep trying.

As I recovered at home, I watched next door recover, too.

People in hi-vis jackets and hard hats came to tear it down to the bones. They ripped out the old rotten beams, floorboards, doors, countertops and plaster, and threw them into the successive skips that came and went via the driveway each week. But the stones, I noticed, they stacked to the side.

Once I grew steady on my crutches, I went outside to ask about the stones under the guise of offering tea. Thanks to Fergus' near-weekly interference, I now had enough cups to cater for a small army. They were setting the stones aside because they were still good, the builders told me. They just needed to be put back in the right place, with the right support.

Once I was able to, I started going with Rowan to one of his group meetings. Fergus calls them Angerholics Anonymous. Everyone sits in a circle and talks about what makes them angry, when they last lost it, how they're learning to listen to and express their anger in more 'productive' ways. To my surprise there were a couple of other women there. One of them shared how she once took a shit on her manager's chair. We're supposed to share stories for accountability, but I think she shared that one for clout. I meet up with her for coffee every other week.

I also started attending online anger management sessions in earnest. I talk about my dad, and what happened at the office, and the ringing I hear in my head. It's actually alright.

Every now and then I find new alerts on my phone.

GO SEE PEOPLE.

TAKE A WALK.

EAT A VEGETABLE.

I don't know how Fergus keeps sneaking these things on, but I don't mind.

When I was able to, I walked back into Carlinsrest. All of the 'improvements' had disappeared, and it was back to looking as it always had. Maggie from the café gave me a wave when she saw me and helped me to a seat at the window, the same one I'd had that first day. The bunting and the flowers had disappeared overnight, she told me. Round about the time when 1a's roof fell in. I realised that she didn't smile at me with her mouth like she did for customers, but she raised her eyebrows like how she did with her waiting staff and regulars. A weary kind of '*Can you believe this?*' at the world in general. I raised my eyebrows back at her and nodded. She patted my shoulder and got me a macaroni pie. I hadn't been in the mood for one, but I was happy enough just to be treated as a regular, so I didn't say anything.

I took a bite.

It wasn't gourmet. No critic would be writing home about it. But it was warm and cheesy and delicious. Every bite a comfort, like a light being lit in the pit of my soul.

I let out an involuntary, "hmmmm."

I looked back at the counter and Maggie nodded.

See. Best macaroni pie in the area.

After I was done, I came across the group of teens again back at the monument. The main boy stood up when he saw me and barked in my direction. The others around him laughed.

I barked back.

And then it was me and the teens barking at each other across the street, until the red-faced man, Dave, came out of the pub on main street.

"Leave it off," he said. "You know that one's not right."

It was said in the same tone as, *Don't kick that panel, it's loose.*

Sometime later, I caught the boy sitting sullenly outside The Curtyard. I'd heard from Fergus that Dave, his dad, was often in there longer than he should be and the boy would have to come and collect money to buy his tea. The boy saw me looking and crossed his arms and looked at the wall nonchalantly. I wasn't heading into the pub that night, so I didn't need to pass by. But I felt… different for the kid.

I howled for him. Long and sombre.

He blinked at me. Frowned. Looked away. Looked at me again. Then stood up and howled, too.

We howled together until someone inside the pub yelled for someone to see to their dog. I walked off just as his dad appeared to give him some cash.

Now we just howl whenever we see each other. I'm not sure if it counts as an understanding, but it's something.

As my legs got better, I started working a few different jobs around town. I've taken some cleaning shifts at The Curtyard. I help out at the hardware and supplies store. Fergus's collection of cacti and succulents have grown. I got him an aloe vera for his birthday. I told him he can use the gel in it as a topical skin treatment, but he didn't care. He just likes its shape. Eventually Rowan let me set up social media pages for the store. I give updates on the store's channels about stock levels, new products and changes to opening times, but that's about it. I write the posts as myself, even sign my name at the bottom so folks know. I offered to show Rowan how to do all this himself, but he was happy for me to take it on. For his birthday, I built him a basic website with a map, opening times and a description of what we sold. I don't know if it's improved sales yet, but it feels tidy and I like that.

On weekends, I help Rowan at the forestry. The quiet up there has yet to get old. It's my favourite place in the world.

I only spoke to Roger once after everything that happened. I'd looked for him and Callie-Ann, wanting to let them know I'd survived my journey into the dark, but I hadn't been able to find them. Until one day in late autumn, on my way into Carlinsrest, I saw him standing in the middle of Bodach's Brig, plucking acorns out of a plastic bag and throwing them into the river. Keen not to miss him, I rushed over. Then I noticed he was alone. No sleeping wife in her wheelchair. No dog.

"Is she ok?" I blurted out as I got closer to him. "Callie-Ann. Is she alright?"

He blinked up at me for a moment then asked, "Who?"

"Your wife."

"Oh!" He rapped his knuckles against his head. "She's fine. Just at her labours. Always busy this time of year." He dumped the rest of the acorns over the side of the bridge. "And you! You've returned from Neverland in one piece. The pirates didn't give you too much trouble, did they?"

I shook my head. "No. Not too much."

"And you're still who you say you are?" He leaned close, his gaze flicking between my eyes as if looking for something. A flurry of leaves passed by on the cold wind that came down from the north. His eyebrows raised.

"Oh, I see," he said. "You've decided to share. How lucky. Dolly never got that option."

It made about as much sense as anything Roger said, so I just nodded and smiled.

"Very good of you to fix it without dying, too! Village has had enough to deal with, what with all that flower nonsense."

"Wait, I have to know. What was with all the flowers anyway?"

He shrugged "Don't ask me. It's your shadow."

Then he strode past me and out into the countryside.

A few days later, I spied them, Roger and Callie-Ann, on my drive into the village—windscreen now mercifully fixed. They were up on the hills that hung over the river, peaks now wreathed in a heavy mist. Callie-Ann was up out of her chair and trudging slowly but steadily toward the crest of the hill, beating the ground with her curious walking stick. Roger followed behind, his wiry hair looking even more like antlers, his clothes tattered and flapping like a bushel of leaves.

After New Years Eve at The Curtyard, I crashed at Rowan and Fergus' place and in my post-party lightly-buzzed state, I decided to finally check in on my old agency. I'd been avoiding it, as if the sight of the company logo alone might trigger me back to my old ways. But lying there on Rowan's old sofa, looking up at the dark outlines of Fergus' cacti guarding the window sill... I don't know. I felt ready. I looked the agency up online and was surprised to find the office had relocated. For some crazy reason I'd forgotten that things other than myself could change. I'd assumed the agency would still be in the same building, in the same part of town. That that era of my life would be there forever, ready and waiting to drag me back. But it was gone. I considered looking up the new location but decided against it. That wasn't for me. Not anymore.

Instead, I looked through past photos. The old office didn't look like how I remembered it. The people not as unfriendly. The last picture in that office was a group shot with everyone huddled around the director, all big grins from some client win. The director had a new haircut and her fingernails were painted teal. All eight of them.

I searched her smiling face for signs of trauma. Resiliency. Bitterness. Vengeful rage. For the life of me, I couldn't tell what she was thinking. I don't think I ever really could. In the blue light of my phone, in the quiet of the new year, I thought again about Rowan's words up in the hills.

A splinter of glass. A timebomb.

But a timebomb with a mind of her own. A will of her own.

My fault. And now, out of my control.

I put my phone away and went to sleep.

Back at Sgàthan Sìth, 1a got a new foundation. New beams pencilled in the skeleton of the house. The design stayed true to the original, just with improved wiring, plumbing and insulation. It leant against 1b for support as the bricks went back up. Soon my home had its twin again.

And then everything seemed to sit for a while, poised and ready, for another period of waiting.

The next summer, a car pulled up to the rebuilt house. I was sat on the lawn, stretching my recovering tendons when it arrived. A woman got out of the car, hair travel-worn, eyes squinting. She looked at her phone and frowned back at the house. She caught sight of me, surprised to see me there.

"Hi there. Everything alright?" I asked.

"Yes," she said. "Sorry, hello. Is this Sgàthan Sìth?"

"This is 1b Sgàthan Sìth." I pointed to my half. "That is 1a Sgàthan Sìth." I gestured to the other half of the house.

She looked down at her phone again. I watched her mouth '1a' and slump.

"Oh," she said, "I didn't realise that it was—"

"A semi-detached?"

Look, we're already finishing each other's sentences.

She laughed nervously, then went back to the car, face falling the moment she turned away from me.

She could have at least looked pleased to see us, that old voice whispered in my head. *We were nice and everything. No one was nice to us when we arrived. Maybe she hates us.*

Eh, I said to my shadow. *Give her time. She doesn't know us yet.*

And if she doesn't want to?

I rubbed where the dotted scars made a line along my arm.

Then, that's okay, too.

You're sure?

Positive. I'm still here, aren't I?

I thought about holding my shadow in the basement, the rising sun bringing light into that dark place.

After all, you're worth sticking around for.

END

ACKNOWLEDGEMENTS

A FIRST DRAFT takes a hermitage. Taking that draft and turning it into a book takes a village. I have been blessed with a village full of good, talented, and extremely patient people.

Thank you to Gavin Inglis, Jane McKie, Josh Holton, Louise Boyd, Ali Maloney, and S K Farell of Writers Bloc for the good crit (and sorry for inflicting early Tamsin on you). Thank you to Stuart McHardy for your short course on the Geomythography of Scotland—it was vital in the creation of Carlinsrest. Thank you to Eilidh MacLennan for helping me with the Gaelic name for the cottage(s)—any errors are my own.

Thank you to all the wonderful writers of the 2026 debut discord group for the camaraderie, collabs and Canva support. Thank you to the Edinburgh SFF writers' group for the much-needed industry advice and for insisting that yes, I did in fact need a literary agent. Speaking of which, thank you to my excellent literary agent Dorian Maffei for proving them right. Thank you to my Film/TV agent Kim Yau for seeing doors where all I see are walls. Thank you to my editor Amanda Raybould for believing in the book. I couldn't have asked for a better champion. Thank you to Chiara Mestieri for more excellent editorial support. Thank you to cover artist Katie Klimowicz for taking a pink sheep and making it one of the creepiest things I've ever seen. Thank you to Jess Gofton and Natalie Charlesworth for your marketing and PR sorcery. I still can't quite believe you got the cover reveal in People Magazine! Thank you to Owen Johnson for the important unseen work of sales—you make it so the rest of us can eat. Thank you to Charlotte Bond for the copy editing and the very kind comments (ok ok, maybe Tamsin can eat something as well). Thank you to Dagna Dłubak for production and turning this fever dream into an actual gd book. Thank you to Donna Scott for proofreading and making sure the last pass didn't rely on my eyes alone.

Thank you to everyone in the Pub? chat group for making sure I touch grass once in a while. Thank you again to Abigail Pelik for quite literally keeping me sane. Thank you to Helene Cloete and Marit Hartveit for listening to my book rants during Gaming Sundays. Thank you to the Grist and Peet families for all your cheerleading (and for letting me use your house for filming).

As always, thank you to Dale Peet. I'm writing this in the bleary-eyed days of early January. I spent years dreaming of what I might say here, but after months of edits, copyedits and now the proofread in my inbox I find all my words have vanished. Which is rather inconvenient because I'm desperately looking for the right words to describe how much your love and support has meant to me. You are my first reader, my sounding board, the first place I turn to hash out any problem, the devil on my shoulder egging me on, the gleeful witness of all my most hidden thoughts, and my best friend. I'm not sure what I did to deserve you. Team PeetGrist forever x

And thank you to you, the reader. May your shadow always be faithfully by your side.

ABOUT THE AUTHOR

RHIANNON GRIST IS an award-winning Welsh writer of weird, speculative and dark fiction. Her novella, *The Queen of the High Fields* (Luna Press), won the 2023 British Fantasy Award for Best Novella. *Home Sick* is her debut novel. She lives in Edinburgh with her partner and far too many plants.

FIND US ONLINE!

www.rebellionpublishing.com

 /solarisbooks

 /solarisbks

 /solarisbooks

 /solarisbooks.bsky.social

SIGN UP TO OUR NEWSLETTER!

rebellionpublishing.com/newsletter

YOUR REVIEWS MATTER!

Enjoy this book? Got something to say?

Leave a review on Amazon, GoodReads or with your favourite bookseller and let the world know!